"If you think I'm going to keep your secret, Do̶̶̶̶̶̶̶̶̶̶̶̶ther think com

"If you don't͟ ͟ ͟ ͟ ͟ ͟ ͟ ͟ ͟ut will be in dange

D0372562

"Let me guess. You want me to trust you about that, too."

"Yes."

Jordynn met his gaze with a challenging glare. "Is that your plan, then? Return from the dead, save my life, then just assume I'll fall into place?"

"My plan is to get you out of here before it's too late."

Donovan slid one of his hands to her back and found her wrist, intent on just taking the phone. But at the contact, a responding heat slid to his palm. It flowed through his forearm and out, searing his heart and drawing full attention to how close together they stood. Just inches apart, in fact.

Donovan's fingers were *on* the phone, its cool exterior a sharp contrast to the warmth everywhere else. But he couldn't actually make himself take it. He couldn't even move. A decade apart, and still Jordynn's touch set him on fire.

* * *

If you're on Twitter, tell us what you think of Harlequin Romantic Suspense! #harlequinromsuspense

Dear Reader,

When I first came up with the idea for *Last Chance Hero*, I was actually envisioning a short story with a horror vibe. I pictured a woman coming home alone to find signs of an intrusion—little things that only *she* would know that signaled her house has been disturbed. I had the whole scenario mapped out in my head. I pictured her walking up her driveway, an ominous feeling building in her chest. The lighting would have to be perfect—dim and spooky, with just a hint of color from the moon above. And as with most scary tales, the heroine realizes a second too late that she should've trusted her instincts.

The imaginary opening played out in my head again and again, never feeling quite right until I realized my heroine wasn't alone in the fight for her life. A damaged hero was waiting on the sidelines, prepared to come to her aid the moment she needed it.

The hero, of course, became Donovan Grady, damaged and needing redemption. The heroine grew into Jordynn Flannigan. And from the moment Donovan jumped in, I knew that instead of finding a ghost around the corner, Jordynn would find something far more nerve-racking—a second chance at first love.

As always, I hope my story keeps you on the edge of your seat, makes your heart race a little faster and leaves you with a smile on your face.

Melinda

LAST CHANCE
HERO

Melinda Di Lorenzo

H HARLEQUIN®ROMANTIC SUSPENSE

Recycling programs
for this product may
not exist in your area.

ISBN-13: 978-0-373-40204-5

Last Chance Hero

Printed in U.S.A.

www.Harlequin.com

Amazon bestselling author **Melinda Di Lorenzo** writes in her spare time—at soccer practices, when she should be doing laundry and in place of sleep. She lives on the beautiful west coast of British Columbia, Canada, with her handsome husband and her noisy kids. When she's not writing, she can be found curled up with (someone else's) good book.

For all those who believe everyone deserves
a second chance.

Prologue

From his spot on the hotel balcony, Corey "the Nose" Waller watched as the guy in the ball cap smiled at the courier, who handed over a slim envelope. He'd had Ball Cap under close surveillance for a week now, and the man's unflappable politeness was making the Nose itch. Tipping coffee servers. Holding the door open for old men. Chasing after some young mother when her baby lost his shoe in a puddle and the woman didn't notice.

"Do-gooder," the Nose muttered, pulling the binoculars away from his face for a disgusted second.

Over twelve months of solid tracking, and he could scarcely believe *this* was the man who'd fooled his employers for the past decade. Someone who had—just this morning—returned a damned hundred-dollar bill to a guy who walked away from an ATM without it. But the Nose had earned his nickname well; his bloodhound abilities were rarely wrong. Everything had led him here. All he needed now was proof.

He lifted the binoculars back up. The courier was laughing at something Ball Cap had said. He gave the other man a friendly slap on the shoulder. The Nose rolled his eyes. Two minutes in and they were best friends. Awful. A whole other minute of chatting went by before the courier finally turned to go. Ball Cap, though, continued to stand in the street, holding the envelope up to the light.

"C'mon," the Nose urged. "Open it up where I can see you do it."

He said it partly because it would be easier to report the proof that way. But mostly, he just plain *wanted* to ruin Ball Cap's day. Inject a little misery into all that kindness.

The Nose waited patiently, counting up. He only made it as far as twenty-seven before he got his wish. The other man slipped his thumb to the seal and forced the envelope open. He reached in, pulled out the thin sheet inside, then lifted his eyes. And even though the Nose knew he was too far away to be seen, he could feel Ball Cap searching him out. He made himself ignore the feeling, and continued to watch.

The other man was clearly affected by what he'd seen. Trying not to panic, maybe. His eyes flicked up and down the street. Seeing nothing, he shifted from foot to foot, tapping the envelope and its contents on his knee.

The Nose smiled to himself. *That's right. Twitch, you big suck. Go back inside and hide some more. Make your getaway plan.*

Satisfied that his search had come to an end, he started to lower the binoculars. Then stopped. Ball Cap had started to move, but he didn't turn to go back into his apartment. Instead, he took off down the street at a dead run.

"Crap."

The Nose dug into his pocket in search of his phone. He hit speed dial one. A deep, already angry voice answered on the second ring.

"What?"

The Nose didn't bother to hide his concern. "I think we're gonna have a problem. He's on the run."

"Oh, hell."

"Yeah. You want me to go after him?"

There was a pause. "No. He knows we've got him now. He'll stay hidden and he's too good at it."

"What, then?"

Another pause. "Just a sec."

The Nose tapped his thigh impatiently as the phone became muffled. What the hell could be more important than this? A few moments later, he got the answer.

A new voice—more refined and calmer than the first—came on the line. "Mr. Waller?"

Puzzled to hear his own name, he answered carefully. "Yeah?"

"Corey 'the Nose' Waller?"

"Yeah." He was impatient now. "Who's this?"

"The man calling the shots."

The Nose swallowed, suddenly very nervous. "Uh…"

"You've done a fine job finding the target."

"Thank you."

"Now I need you to do something else for us. For *me*."

The Nose cleared his throat. "Okay."

"Go after the girl."

"Me? I'm not much of a—"

"You are now. How far away are you?"

"Few hours by car."

"Good. You should have more than enough time."

The Nose tried again to protest. "I really don't—"

"You're fast and efficient and she won't be expecting you. Make it scary. I want her terrified."

"Not...dead?"

A cool laugh came from the other end. "No. I want *him*. I can use him. And if we have *her*, he'll come straight to us."

Chapter 1

As the bus wheezed around the second-to-last corner before her stop in her hometown of Ellisberg, Oregon, Jordynn Flannigan's phone buzzed to life in her pocket. She yanked it out and stared down at the flashing screen.

New Message from: Sasha.

She checked the time.

4:17 a.m.

Jordynn swiped her finger across the screen, wondering what her best friend could possibly want at this time of the morning. If it could even be called morning yet. Outside, the streetlights still glowed, and just a minute or so earlier, she'd seen a flash of the nearly full moon, as well. You up? Sasha had texted.

I am. But I have a good excuse. What about you?

Don't ask. Incident with a crayon up the nose. My fave four-year-old was sleep coloring or something. Thought I'd check in. You okay?

Jordynn's fingers were quick to reply. She smiled as she pictured her friend's son.

Sounds like a typical night in your house. And I'm fine.

The response came almost instantaneously.

You sure? Uncle Reed said you refused to let him give you a ride home earlier. Sane people avoid the bus.

She smiled again. Sasha's uncle Reed, who had been her friend's guardian since they were teens, also owned the private care facility where Jordynn worked. He often went above and beyond in the role. In fact, with her own parents gone—her dad before she was born and her mom just two years earlier—everyone in Sasha's family kind of filled the void. Her two kids were like a niece and nephew, her husband like the brother Jordynn never had, and her uncle definitely saw himself as a surrogate parent. Sasha took it as meddling, but Jordynn didn't mind the support.

Tell Reed I'm fine. I just worked a few extra hours tonight.

Uh-uh. No way. I'm not going to be the one to break his heart by telling you you're trying hard to exhaust yourself.

At that, Jordynn laughed. It was true that Reed coddled her a little at work, but she could hardly feel any resentment. And in spite of his preferential treatment, she never took advantage.

It's nice that he cares. Too bad none of his sweetness got passed down to you.

If you could see me, you'd know I'm rolling my eyes. Hard.

If it makes you feel any better, I've got the rest of the weekend off.

I'd kill for a weekend off. But...you know...kids.

There was the briefest pause, then another text came through.

You sure you're okay?

Jordynn tapped the side of the phone for a second, thinking about what to say. She knew why her friend was asking. The date had glared at her all day from the tearaway calendar on the nurses' station at work.

After a moment, though, she sighed and wrote,

Totally fine. Really. I'm just going to go home, go to bed, and not get up for at least ten hours.

There was a delay in Sasha's reply, and she wondered if her friend was thinking about calling her out for her brush-off. But when the answer finally came, it was a five-word acceptance instead of a demand for her true feelings.

All right. Good night, BFF.

Jordynn tucked her phone back into her pocket as the bus lumbered to a halt.

Truthfully, she'd spent her shift alternating between being short-tempered and ready to tear up at any given moment. But she'd promised herself she'd get through it. And she had. She'd gone the full twenty-four hours without actually crying, and without letting the ache in her chest overwhelm her.

She supposed that was probably why she felt so tense now. The lack of emotional release, coupled with the utter exhaustion brought on by three hours of overtime tacked on to an already twelve-hour shift—almost all of it on her feet—was definitely a recipe for a bad state of mind. She was so much more than ready for her own split-level house. For her hideous, bunny-eared slippers and her cushy, oversize robe. She doubted she'd ever been so glad for a week to be over.

Still, she couldn't quite shake a strange sense of worry at the thought of walking the two and a half blocks from the stop to her two-bedroom rancher.

Don't let it win, she ordered silently.

She refused to give in to the melancholy and let herself think about the past. To wallow in the things she couldn't change. Not even today, on the tenth anniversary of the day her life had become forever altered.

But as she pushed open the hydraulic doors and stepped into the chilly predawn air, her unease grew stronger. She pulled her thin coat a little tighter across her chest and glanced around quickly. The streets were empty, as was to be expected at this time of night. The neighborhood wouldn't wake for an hour or more, and for now, the houses sat still, dark and quiet. Nothing unusual. Nothing to make her fingers shake the way they were.

Jordynn increased her pace anyway. And as her feet

hit the ground, the bad feeling increased with a vengeance. It was compounded by the fact that the ring—the one she kept on a long chain around her neck—felt suddenly heavy. And the way it pressed into her sternum under her scrubs made the pressure in her chest that much more stifling. Cooler than her skin and far more unyielding, too. And when a single streetlight directly above her head flickered off, bathing her in momentary darkness, she almost turned to ran back and try to flag down the bus again.

You'll feel better when you get home, she told herself.

But oddly, the closer she got to her house, the worse she felt. By the time she'd crossed the first two blocks, her heart had started to race with worry. And when she hit the end of her own block and put her driveway in view, her feet didn't want to move another step. With a dry mouth, she pushed one shoe forward. Then the other. She made it to the very edge of the stone steps that led from the lawn to her front patio. And the next few steps wouldn't come. Because Jordynn spotted a true reason to be concerned.

The light on her porch—the one she always left on—was gone. Not turned off. Not burned out. Gone completely. The bulb and the vintage case that gave it the unmistakable orange hue were both missing.

Her eyes flicked around in a vain search for a logical explanation. She found nothing. Not even shattered glass on the ground.

It wasn't an accident.

As the realization hit her, Jordynn took a step back, fumbling to reach for the phone in her jacket. Her hand didn't even get as far as her pocket before her back hit something solid.

Not something. Someone.

It took her a second too long to figure it out. Quicker than she could even get out a whimper, a hand slammed over her mouth. A rough, distinctly masculine palm.

She fought to get away, twisting, and dropping her purse and all its contents as she tried to throw an elbow into his stomach. The man bent away easily, and his hand stayed in place. She made another attempt to free herself, this time driving her foot backward. It was a futile move. Her shoe tumbled to the ground, and her sock slid uselessly off his pants. And suddenly, she was pressed against him, her arms pinned to her sides.

"Move again, and die," warned a gruff voice. "Scream, and die. In fact, do anything I don't like…and die."

But the three-part warning wasn't even necessary. Because when he eased away, the cold tip of a blade digging into the small of her back provided motivation enough. She held very still, praying that all he wanted was her money. Her silent hope went unmet.

The rough hand came down, and a heartbeat later, a cloth took its place. Her assailant shoved the fabric between her teeth, then back farther. Jordynn wanted to gag, and fought the urge. She didn't dare make a sound. But as he forced her hands behind her back and lashed them together with a plastic tie, she couldn't stop the tears from forming in her eyes and spilling over to her cheeks.

Will it make him mad? she wondered. *Is crying something he doesn't like?*

A few seconds later, it didn't matter anyway. Her attacker slipped a hood over her head, covering up the evidence of her near-silent sobs. Then he spun her around and gave her a little shove, and Jordynn realized *why* he'd covered her face. He was going to take her somewhere, and she wouldn't stand a chance of knowing a thing about how they got there.

"Walk," the man growled.

Jordynn tried to obey him, but with the tears coming even harder, and the choking sensation growing worse, disorientation reigned. When she lifted her foot, it caught on one of the pathway stones. She stumbled, just enough to send her to her knees.

Above her, the man holding the knife snarled.

A chance. This is a chance.

But it wasn't. The moment she managed to get to her knees, thick fingers landed on top of the hood. He gripped it together with her hair and dragged her back. She hollered against the gag in her mouth. Muffled. Pointless.

I'm going to die. I moved and I screamed and he didn't like it and—

The wild thoughts cut off as a snarl reached her ears. She was sure it hadn't come from the man who held her, because he went still, then released her abruptly. Jordynn fell sideways, slamming to the grass and knocking off the hood, giving her a clear view of the strange scene unfolding in front of her. First, a flash of movement caught her eye. Then, from up the walkway—and she could almost swear the figure had come from *inside* her house—a distinctly human form flew toward her and her assailant. It flew straight into the man holding her, and he let out a yell as he was knocked sideways.

And now there were two men in her yard instead of one. The first was on the ground. He was short and whip-thin, his furious face angular and almost birdlike. The second was on one knee, and he was just the opposite—a bear of a man, with a square, beard-dusted jaw. He wore a ball cap pulled low, and under its edges, Jordynn could just see a curl of sandy hair. As he pushed to his feet, his muscles strained against his fitted T-shirt.

When the first intruder stood, the second one lifted

his face up under the cap, and Jordynn thought there
was something familiar in his gaze. And strangely, the
flash of familiarity actually sent a pleasant tingle up her
spine. After a second of staring at her, he dipped his hat
down, obscuring his features. And for some reason, that
just made her want to see more of him. It surprised her to
realize it. Checking out men was low down on her to-do
list. Nevertheless, there was no denying his appeal. The
strength in his tense jaw. The fullness of his lips. The
raw power in his physique. Even in the very dim light,
she could see how attractive he was.

And in spite of the fact that Jordynn didn't know who
he was, and even though she knew she ought to be more
than a little frightened about what he was doing outside
her home in the first place, the all-over tingle became an
unexpected—and unwanted—buzz.

She swallowed nervously.

Then he lifted his head again, the baseball hat tipping
back to expose his face. He took a small step forward,
and Jordynn's breath caught in her throat. She knew why
he seemed familiar. And why she felt such a strong, sin-
gular attraction to him.

The man standing in front of her looked enough like
the man she loved—the man she'd lost a decade ago,
today—that they could've been brothers. He was bigger.
Way bigger. Older, too. And there was something darker
and more guarded in the way he held himself than she'd
ever seen from the man who'd given her the ring that she
wore around her neck.

But the eyes...

Jordynn swallowed again, swaying a little on her feet.
That warm, mesmerizing hazel that picked up the glow
of the moon and reflected it back... She'd never seen the
shade on anyone else.

But it can't be him.

Her mind had to be playing the cruelest of tricks on her. Because the man Jordynn loved had died ten years earlier.

Jordynn Jean Flannigan.

For a minute that lasted a lifetime, Donovan Grady couldn't do more than stare into her eyes, watching the heart-wrenching fear play through them. His guilt held him as fast as his awe.

His plan had just been to check on her from afar. To assure himself she was alive and well, but not to give her a chance to recognize him. For some reason, he hadn't really thought about what would happen if she did. If his suspicions became fruitful—as they had—forcing him to get close and giving him no choice but to interact.

Maybe you just wanted so badly to be wrong that you didn't consider the consequences.

Now that it had happened, the sight of her in the moonlight floored him. It sent thoughts of caution to the very back of his mind.

He waited for her to whisper his name. Or cry it out in confusion. Instead, she stood very still. Too still. Not showing a single emotion.

Maybe she doesn't know you.

The idea cut into him.

Of course, he knew he looked a lot different than he had ten years ago. Two inches taller. Eighty pounds heavier. Hell, he hadn't been more than nineteen when his world had changed forever. Barely a man. It wasn't just the sudden, belated growth spurt, either. A decade away—a decade of pretending to be someone else—had changed him. Inside and out.

Still. He would've been able to pick *her* out of a crowd

of a thousand. A crowd of a million. He'd held her face in his mind every night for the past decade. That didn't mean she'd done the same. He hadn't even *wanted* her to hang on to his memory.

He tore his eyes away from hers, but only succeeded in moving his gaze to the rest of her face.

Ten years had turned her from the pretty eighteen-year-old girl he remembered to a ravishing twenty-eight-year-old woman. Still naturally beautiful, still clean-scrubbed and makeup free. Still perfect. It left him tongue-tied, every part of him frozen. Except his pulse, which raced through his body with long-buried desire. From his spot just a few feet away, he just stood and appreciated the sight of her. The fiery cascade of her red, red hair and the subtle curves of her athletic build. Her sky blue eyes, and the curve of her lips—that he knew to be as soft and warm and tempting as silk—working furiously against a piece of cloth that had been jammed into her mouth.

A dirty rag. Hell.

She didn't deserve to have it stuck between her teeth like that.

Donovan finally took a step toward her, determined to help her pull it out.

Before he could get any closer, Jordynn's assailant smashed against his hip and dragged him back to reality. This wasn't a romance, waiting to be rekindled. This was a life-or-death situation.

As Donovan stumbled, he didn't have time to curse his own distractibility. He spun to the side, shook the other man off, then dropped to a low crouch and prepared for a second lunge. He didn't have to wait long. With a wordless growl, the attacker came at him again. Donovan feinted to the left, the slammed out his right arm, knocking the smaller man to the ground. He gave the man no time to recover. He leaped forward to pin him to the ground, a knee in his chest and a forearm under his throat.

"Give it up," he growled.

Under his elbow, the guy let out a choking laugh. In under a second, Donovan understood why. A sharp pain pierced his side.

A knife. Dammit.

He tried to no avail to get his arms around to dislodge it. The burn of the blade only increased as it dug in farther, and Donovan would have no choice but to let go if he wanted to pull it free. He couldn't do that fast enough, either. A knee came up and slammed into him just shy of his groin. With a pain-filled grunt, he shifted out of reach. It was enough to give the assailant another temporary advantage. The smaller man dug his feet into the ground and slid up. Then he delivered a vicious kick to his chest, winding Donovan.

As he heaved in a breath, he finally did take a minute to curse himself. Stupid, to go in overconfident. Even stupider to assume the man was unarmed. Lucky, though, that it was something other than a gun.

Take what luck you can get, he told himself grimly.

He finally righted himself and reached around to yank out the blade. The wound was superficial, but it would still need attention. He knew he'd have to deal with it later. The other man had already started toward Jordynn once again, and she appeared to be fixed to the spot. Frozen in fear, maybe.

No way. No way in hell.

He tossed the knife to the ground, and as it landed with a dull thud, he wasted no time. He dived at Jordynn's attacker's legs. Together, they slammed to the grass, sending dirt flying.

"No more chances," Donovan said as he came up to his knees.

He drew back his fist and smacked it into the other guy's jaw as hard as he could. The blow sent the man sliding backward up the grass, where he groaned once, then stayed there, unmoving.

Donovan leaned down.

Thoroughly unconscious. As expected.

He turned back toward Jordynn.

She was gone.

Unreasonable panic washed through him.

His eyes flew around the outside yard in an arc, searching. No movement caught his eye. No flash of red hair. Nothing.

She had no idea of the danger she was in. That the man who'd attacked her was probably the least of her worries. The tip of the damned iceberg. If she'd taken off, she wouldn't stand a chance in hell of staying safe.

He spun back toward the house, and on the second sweep, he found her. She'd made it to the front porch, where she'd crouched down behind a bush. The gag had fallen from her mouth, but her hands were still bound, and she was eyeing him nervously.

Thank God.

But Donovan's relief was short-lived.

Before he could say a word, Jordynn's jaw dropped open, and a high-pitched scream filled the dawn air.

He sprang forward, intent on stopping the noise. Seeing little other choice, he yanked the discarded rag from the ground, then knelt down beside her and shoved it back toward her mouth. Her teeth gnashed down hard against his skin.

Pain shot through his hand, but the pang of guilt at his own invasive action was worse. This was the woman he'd promised his heart to a decade ago. Just thinking about hurting her made his gut twist. Actually doing it was like a knife with a jagged edge, slamming into his rib cage.

Forcefully, Donovan pushed both the guilt and the physical pain to the back of his mind. He had to make her stop. To make her listen.

So tell her what happened.

But he couldn't make himself do it. Not yet. Not like this.

As she continued to yell, punctuated now by gasping breaths, he held fast to the cloth, then gripped her head and worked the fabric between her lips. He got it all the way in, and held it there until she stopped struggling. Without letting go, he leaned back just enough to give her some space, but not so far that she could make an escape attempt. She sat still, her eyes squeezed tightly closed, her chest rising and falling with her rapid breaths. Donovan relaxed his grip a little, inhaling deeply. It was a mistake. Her sweet scent filled his nose—she wore the same delicately floral perfume he remembered so well. The light aroma that sometimes seemed to linger in the air when he woke from a pleasant dream.

Startled by his strong reaction, Donovan lost his grip on her completely. She jerked away, then sent a vicious kick at his knee   forceful enough to knock him to the side—then scrambled in the other direction, hitting the patio with a muffled cry.

Bloody hell.

Donovan shot up. Three long strides brought him to her side. With a grunt, he leaned down, grabbed her elbows and dragged her to her feet. She tried to yank herself away yet again. Donovan held firm.

"I'm trying to *help* you," he said, his voice soft and even. "I'm not going to hurt you, and I want to take that gag out and untie your hands. But first, you need to promise me you aren't going to scream. Can you do that?"

She kept her eyes shut. Like maybe she could will the sight of him away. After a second, though, she nodded once.

Gently, Donovan reached out to tug the cloth from her mouth. He felt her tense as he did it, and he couldn't blame her. The situation was surreal for him, too, and he wasn't the one being visited by someone he thought to be dead.

Wordlessly, he moved behind her, his fingers seeking her wrists. Even though he'd touched her twice over the past few minutes, this time it was different. Maybe because of the intention behind it. Donovan held the zip tie between his thumb and forefinger, squeezing it repeatedly to make it weak. He could feel the thrum of Jordynn's pulse underneath his attention, and even though he knew it had to be the result of her nerves, it sent heat through his own veins. With gritted teeth, he continued to work until he was satisfied that he'd compromised the plastic enough to break it. Then he lifted his leg and slapped her wrists against his knee. The cord snapped with almost no resistance, and Donovan stepped away.

"You okay?" he asked.

She drew in an audible breath. "You're not him."

"Jordynn." He turned her around to face him.

She shook her head, and continued to hold her eyes closed. "Please don't be real."

"Jordynn—"

"Stop saying my name."

Her voice held a tiny bit of rebellion, and part of Donovan was glad to see she was as strong-willed as ever.

A bigger part of him was worried that the longer they stayed on her lawn with an unconscious man at their feet, the longer they'd risk being caught. The longer *he'd* risk being caught. He sure as hell hadn't come all this way to let that happen.

"We can't stay here," he said.

"Were you in my house?"

Donovan frowned at the seemingly unrelated reply. "Yes, but—"

"How did you get in?"

"The key you keep inside the garden gnome."

"When's my birthday?"

He smiled. "December 20. But you celebrate it on June 20 so no one tries to double up your birthday and Christmas gifts."

At last, she lifted her lids. Her too-blue eyes went wide. She stared at him for three long heartbeats. Then her baby blues rolled back in her head. She slumped to the side, and Donovan caught her. With a sigh that was one part pleasure, one part resignation and one part worry, he lifted her gently with both arms, snagged her discarded shoe from the grass and started up the walkway.

And he had to admit, holding her close made him feel like no time had passed at all.

Chapter 2

At first, Jordynn thought she was dreaming.

After all, that's where she always saw him. Where her subconscious reigned, and the decades-old heartbreak couldn't quite be buried.

She inhaled deeply, trying to orient herself. Instead, she got a whiff of something sharply sweet, and recognized it right away as coming from the not-so-secret stash of brandy her mom had always kept in the cabinet beside the TV. Immediately, her eyes flew open. And that distinct, familiar gaze met hers.

Donovan Grady's hazel eyes.

The ones she'd seen just before all the blood rushed to her head and she fainted.

And Jordynn didn't just *think* she was dreaming. She *knew* it.

But if you're dreaming...then how come you saw his eyes before you passed out?

Panic hit her. She attempted to sit up, but only made it as far as an elbow before her head swam again. She squeezed her eyes shut, and a warm hand—Donovan's hand—slipped to the back of her neck and eased her down again. His touch lingered. She let it. She wanted so badly for it to be real. Tears pricked at her lids.

"Look at me." Donovan's voice.

Her heart thundered in her chest. And she refused to obey. She wouldn't look. She wouldn't open her eyes and find him there. She wouldn't see his ghost. If she stayed still for long enough, the dream would fade and so would the sadness.

"C'mon," he said.

"No," she whispered hoarsely.

"I need to make sure you're okay."

"I can't."

"You have to. Please."

In spite of her desire to keep them shut, his pleading tone made her open them. Though her vision blurred, she still had a decent view of the big man in front of her. He sat beside her on a chair, his knees brushing the edge of the couch where she was lying down. He held the brandy decanter in his hands, the crystal cap off.

Relief flooded through Jordynn. She wasn't dreaming. But clearly, her mind had mixed up past and present. Taking the scent of her mother's favorite poison and mixing it with the unusual presence of a man in her house, and sending her back ten years. Because Donovan was a skinny kid in too-baggy pants. He had an easy smile and no rough edges. This man was huge, and he wore fitted jeans and a white T-shirt, stained with dirt and what looked like blood.

"Jordynn?"

She blinked, and the dulled edges of him came into

focus. He'd taken off his hat and his sandy hair sat matted to his head in a tangle she knew well. A mess she'd run her hands through a thousand times. She blinked a second time. He didn't disappear. His hazel eyes—framed by thick, familiar lashes—were tinged with concern, their corners crinkled up. She'd stared into them enough times to be able to pinpoint each fleck. To know what they looked like sad, happy, scared…all of it.

Impossible.

She squished backward onto the overstuffed arm of the couch as an enormous, terrified lump filled her throat.

"Dono." His name was barely more than a choked sob.

"Yes."

"You're dead."

"I can explain, honey. But I'll need more time than we've got right this second."

Jordynn blinked, watching his mouth work as he continued to talk, but not hearing a word. He could explain? How? She'd attended his funeral. Comforted his grieving father. Lost herself in a year-long despair she never thought she'd crawl out of. She'd blamed herself for what happened. Blamed himself for his *death.* No explanation could erase that, or the accompanying dark moments. The pain and loss were too great.

But somehow that didn't stop her from wanting to reach out. From having an incredible need to run her fingers along that stubble on his face. To touch him, just to make sure—really sure—he was there.

Oh, God.

She tightened her hands into fists, steadying herself to stop from actually following through on the desire.

His hand landed on her shoulder, and when she flinched, he drew it away again quickly, hurt touching his eyes before he covered it again in an impassive mask.

"Hey. Did you hear me?" he asked gently.

She shook her head. "No."

"I said it's not safe for us to stay here much longer."

"Safe?"

"*Not* safe," he corrected.

"So…what?" She blinked again. "You want me to go somewhere else?"

"I need *us* to go somewhere else."

"I can't go anywhere with you, Dono." This time, saying his name hurt.

"If you come with me, I can give you at least a bit of an explanation," he told her again.

"You already said that."

"I know."

"I'm not—" She paused, took a breath, tried again. "I won't leave this—" *God, why can't I just complete a sentence? Why does it all seem so inadequate?* "No. Not with— No."

He leaned back, looking frustrated. And something else, too. Maybe a bit disappointed. Or even surprised. Had he thought that after ten years away, she'd jump into his arms? Be so relieved he was alive she'd forget the rest?

Are you relieved?

She bit her lip and told herself it was an awful thing to wonder. And she wasn't even going to answer the silent, self-directed question.

He leaned forward again, his face tense now. "I wouldn't ask you to do this if I saw another way. I wouldn't even have…"

Even though he trailed off, Jordynn heard what came next. If he'd seen another way, he wouldn't have come back at all. And it took away a tiny bit of her guilt, making it a little easier to focus on the here and now rather than the past. Easier to find the words and string them together.

"I can't even begin to guess what happened to you," she said. "Or why you would let everyone who loved you think you were dead. But you have to know that you can't expect to walk in here and tell me I'm not safe and think I'll just go with you."

Donovan lifted his hand to tug on his ear. A heart-wrenching gesture—a habit that meant he was truly worried—that Jordynn had all but forgotten about it. It made her wonder what else she'd forgotten about. How many memories had faded away with the years? How many of them had she deliberately buried? It hurt to think about it. Like a freshly closed wound threatening to open all over again.

This was just too hard.

"I can't do this," she whispered.

"You have to, honey. Trust me when I say this wasn't a random attack."

"Trust you?" The concept seemed utterly foreign.

"Just in this. Please." There was a note of desperation in his voice. "That man over there? He has some friends waiting for him, and I have no idea how long it's gonna be before they show up."

Her blood went cold. "Over where?"

He nodded his head toward a space behind him, and Jordynn forced her eyes away from his face. On the other side of the room, bound to one of her mother's antique dining chairs with some kind of wire, sat the birdlike man from outside. Somehow, she'd almost put him out of her mind. Now the sight of him made her stomach roil, both because of his attack and because of his appearance. The man's head hung to one side, a mottled bruise already fanning out along his jaw. He'd been gagged. Far more efficiently than Jordynn herself had been, she noted. A strip of sheeting had been wound around his mouth—multiple times—and knotted securely behind one ear.

Jordynn swallowed. "Did you do that?"

Donovan nodded shortly. "Yes."

"Is he…?"

"He's alive."

"So…you're just going to leave him there?"

"I couldn't exactly leave him in the front yard."

"Who is he?"

"The less you know, the better."

She met his gaze, noting the resignation there.

Resignation, she thought. *But no regret.*

Not for the man tied up, anyway. It made her heart ache even more than it already did. The Donovan she knew was protective, but loving. A little hotheaded and maybe even impetuous, but always compassionate and kind. Reverent of life. Maybe that had all changed when he'd feigned the end of his own. Which was what he must've done, she surmised.

"He would've killed you, Jordynn," he stated then, far too matter-of-factly.

She suppressed a shiver, because now she wasn't wondering what she'd forgotten—she was wondering what she'd missed. What parts of him had been irrevocably altered, and how he'd become this larger, darker version of himself.

Abruptly, like he couldn't take her scrutiny, he stood and began to pace the room.

"You should pack a bag," he said. "Clothes. Toothbrush. That kinda stuff. Enough for a few days, maybe longer. We can always figure out exactly what needs to be done when we get where we're going."

"I have a simpler solution."

Donovan paused, tugged his ear again and shook his head. "No."

"You don't know what I was going to say."

"The police aren't an option."

She ignored the way it felt so *normal* to have him practically read her thoughts. "But your dad—"

"Was the chief when he died, I know. But he thought I was dead, just like you did. All his friends on the force think it. And it needs to stay that way."

"And if I say no?" She asked the question so softly that he didn't seem to hear it.

"Have you got a car? Or access to one? I had to leave mine behind."

Jordynn cleared her throat and repeated her question, this time more firmly. "What if I refuse to go with you?"

His brows knit together. "I'll make you come with me, Jordynn, if I have to."

A spark of anger flickered. "You'll make me come with you? Just like you made me believe you were gone?"

"I'll do whatever I have to, to protect you."

The spark flamed, and Jordynn pushed herself to a sitting position, ignoring the accompanying light-headedness. She wasn't just mad—she was furious.

She opened her mouth, poised to tell him what he could do with his protection, but her phone buzzed from the coffee table, momentarily distracting her.

"Do *not* answer that," Dono warned.

"Just try and stop me."

They dived for the phone at the same time. And even though Jordynn was still woozy, she was determined. She went low, sliding under the edge of the table instead of over it. Dono, on the other hand, smashed straight into the wood, his big body landing on it hard. The wood creaked, then shuddered. Jordynn gasped. She guessed what was about to happen with only a second to spare, and she dug her feet into the area rug and dragged herself out the way, just as the table collapsed.

The still-ringing phone flew sideways, then skidded from the carpet to the laminate, its LifeProof case making a rubbery thump as it came to a halt.

Jordynn's eyes moved back to Dono. He groaned, then rolled to his back. Jordynn took advantage of his stunned state of mind. She crawled over the floor, snapped up the cell phone, then lifted it to look at the caller ID.

Boss-Man Reed.

Thank God.

"Hello," she gasped into the phone.

But Donovan had recovered. His hand closed over top of hers, his wide fingers snapping the hang-up button before she could stop him.

"Hey!"

"I told you not to answer that." His voice was dark. "Who was it?"

Jordynn stared up at him. He sounded worried. But something else, too. Jealous, maybe? He had no right to either feeling. For some reason, that didn't stop her from stumbling to answer quickly.

"It was just my boss."

"It's the middle of the night," Dono reminded her. "Does your boss always call you then?"

Warmth crept up her cheeks. "No. It's not like…*that*. He's like family. He probably knows I worked late and wants to make sure I'm okay."

He stared at her like he was assessing the truth of her statement. Then her phone rang again, and his intense gaze moved to the screen instead.

"Reed?" He frowned. "Sasha's uncle?"

"Yes. He's my boss."

Dono tapped then phone on his thigh, then held it out. "Tell him you're fine."

Jordynn snatched the slim device away irritably and hit the answer button. "Sorry, Reed."

Her boss's familiar, gentle voice came through immediately. "Jo. Everything okay? Heard you pulled a double?"

Briefly, she considered telling him the truth. Or at least a portion of it. But if Dono was telling even the partial truth... She wouldn't risk her boss's life.

"Yes to both," she said. "I'm home now, though. Hoping to get some extra sleep tonight."

"Exactly what I needed to hear."

Jordynn let out a silent breath. "Bye, Reed."

"Night, sweetie."

She clicked the phone off, then turned toward Dono, steeling herself. But it was impossible to prepare for the force of those hazel eyes. They made her ache.

"Thank you," he said. "Now we should go."

She inhaled. "You don't get to do this. You were *dead*, Dono. And now you're just a stranger."

"I can't just run out of here. No matter how badly you might want me to."

"You did it once before."

"That was different."

"How?"

His eyes filled with pain, and he turned away. Like he wanted to hide it, but couldn't. Or like he couldn't find an answer she'd want to hear.

Well, damn him. And damn his pain, too.

Jordynn stood up. And started to move. Quickly.

Donovan realized about a second too late what her intention was.

Crap.

Before he could blink, she was three quarters of the way across the sunken living room, the slim white phone still in her hands.

Double crap.

And by the time he actually reacted to what was happening, she had already reached the stairs that led up to the second floor.

"Jordynn!"

She ignored him and darted up the stairs.

He snarled a curse, then dashed after her. He got to the top step just as she reached the last door at the end of the hall. She shot him a triumphant look as she slammed it, then clicked the lock.

Crap on toast.

"Jordynn!" he yelled a second time.

He shook the handle. Nothing. He shook harder. It didn't budge. On the other side, he could hear the sound of furniture moving around. He had no problem picturing what she was doing. The big white dresser would be too big to move. The nightstand, though, wouldn't be a problem. Maybe she'd position the desk chair under the knob. Or take the narrow bookcase from inside her closet and drag it over to cover the whole hinge-side of the door. In minutes, she'd be barricaded in. She'd dial 911. Or maybe the direct line to his dad's old office. They'd both be exposed. Both be at risk.

Donovan stepped back, ran a hand over his hair, gave his ear a solid tug and stared at the closed door. Then smiled.

Hurriedly, he slipped into the den. He tiptoed over the floor, then eased open the closet door. He pushed his way through the spare coats, then ran his hand over the far wall until his fingers found the metal latch hidden there. He lifted it, letting himself into the cheater bathroom it shared with her bedroom. He slipped past the tub and toilet, then through the door on the other side. He stopped at the foot of her bed, watching as she did just as he'd pictured, and reinforced the door with the wood chair. When she'd set it firmly under the knob to her satisfaction, she stood back and gave her handiwork a nod.

Donovan stepped closer, near enough to touch her, and spoke in a low voice. "It looks good. But I still see a bit of a problem with the security of it, don't you?"

She spun, then jumped back, knocking over the chair and smacking into the door. "How did you get in here?"

"C'mon, Jordynn. The layout of the house hasn't changed. I came in through the bathroom."

Her eyes flicked over his shoulder to the closet. "Oh."

"Yeah."

"And…now what?"

"Nothing. As long as you give me the phone."

He saw her hand tighten on the device. Then she slipped it behind her back.

He raised an eyebrow. "Really?"

A surprising blush—delicate and lacy—crept up her face. "Did you think I'd just hand it over?"

"Well. I don't remember you being particularly unreasonable." He closed the gap between them in three easy steps.

"A lot can happen in ten years."

He ignored the sting brought on by the comment. "The phone. Please."

"No."

"Giving it to me before the guy downstairs wakes up would be ideal."

"Calling the *police* before he wakes up would be even better," she retorted.

With a sigh, he reached around her to take it. She

moved to sidestep the grab, but Donovan was quicker. He slammed his arms up to the wall, blocking her in.

"The phone," he said again.

"The police."

"Not happening."

"If you think I'm going to keep your secret, you've got another think coming."

"If you don't keep it, everyone I've ever cared about—everyone you *currently* care about—will be in danger."

"Let me guess. You want me to trust you about that, too."

"Yes."

She lifted her face and met his gaze with a challenging glare. "Is that your plan, then? Return from the dead, save my life, then just assume I'll fall into place?"

"My plan is to get you out of here before it's too late."

"Too late for what, specifically?"

"Too late for us to get away from the guys who know now that I'm not dead. Who know you're the only reason I'd expose myself. Jordynn. Give me the damned phone." Donovan slid one of his hands to her back and found her wrist, intent on just taking the phone. But at the contact, a responding zap of heat slid to his palm. It flowed through his forearm and up again, settling in his chest. It expanded out, searing his heart and drawing full attention to how close together they stood. Just inches apart, in fact.

Donovan's fingers were *on* the phone, its cool exterior a sharp contrast to the warmth everywhere else. But he couldn't actually make himself take it. He couldn't even move. A decade apart, and still her touch set him on fire.

He could tell she wasn't immune to him, either. Her chest rose and fell a little quicker, and she sucked in the side of her mouth. Each a telltale sign Donovan knew well.

"How's it working out for you?" she whispered.

He swallowed, unable to remember what they'd been talking about. "How's what working out for me?"

"That plan of yours."

"I've spent the last ten years without you, honey," he said thickly. "Things have been hell for that long. So from here, things are looking pretty damned good."

"What about it seems good? I'm not exactly cooperating with what you want to accomplish."

He didn't answer. Didn't bite on the wicked line she was trying to feed him. She'd always been excellent at baiting him into an argument. Trounced him every time. So he just stared down at her face, and the longer he looked, the more every detail of it seemed important.

Her wide eyes, pupils expanded enough that they nearly blocked out the blue.

The blush, which had expanded even more, covering her cheeks and throat completely.

Her lips. Firm, and just the tiniest bit damp.

The tiny scar on her left eyebrow, new since the last time he saw her.

The last thing prompted Donovan to move. He lifted his other hand from the wall and reached out to touch the small indent. He ran his fingers over the mark, disliking it intensely. Not because it marred the dark red curve of her brow, but because he hadn't been there to witness whatever caused it. Hadn't been there to stop it.

"What happened here?" he asked.

"Why?" she breathed. "Does it bother you?"

"Only knowing that it probably hurt you."

"It did."

"Badly?"

"At first. But all wounds heal eventually."

Donovan flinched. He knew without asking that her comment was really a dig. A metaphor.

But maybe it's an opening, too.

"*Do* they all heal?" he asked.

He dragged his finger from the scar to her cheek, almost—but not quite—cupping it. He hated himself for wanting her to say yes—for wanting her to be willing to overlook the heartbreak he'd caused.

She didn't resist the intimate touch as she answered. "If they don't kill you. Definitely. The human body is resilient. But wounds leave scars, too. Like that one up there."

"A reminder?" he asked.

"Or a warning to be more careful the next time."

"Jordynn…"

His thumb slipped to her mouth. For a second, her eyes closed and her lips dropped open. Then she inhaled and leaned back, out of reach.

"Do you really want to know how I got the scar?" she asked.

"Yes."

"I went on a date."

Donovan was sure she'd said it to deliberately deflect the rising temperature between them. Or maybe just to hurt him. He wished he didn't understand why she did it. The awareness acted like a bucket of icy water, dousing the desire that raged through him. Still. He had to pretend he didn't care—because really, it wasn't his *right* to care—as she met his eyes, clearly looking for a reaction.

He fought an urge to just slip his fingers between hers and pry the phone from her grip, thereby ending the conversation completely. Instead, he inhaled, then let the breath out carefully.

"A date?"

"Yes. The first one after you'd— After you were gone. You remember my friend Sasha?"

"Yeah, of course."

"Almost a year had gone by, and she thought it was time for me to start moving on. So she set me up with a friend of her cousin's. The guy was just here on a visit. Short-term commitment, Sasha told me. No pressure, because he'd be gone in a week."

Donovan pictured it. Pushy, logical Sasha, presenting a date as a reasonable argument. Jordynn unable to find a loophole to get her out of going.

"So you agreed," he said softly.

"I did. He took me bowling. Then out for dinner. He was nice. Good-looking, too. And I was trying hard not to have fun. Searching for a reason not to like him. I couldn't find one. At the end of the date, I realized I was being silly about the whole thing. There *was* no reason not to enjoy myself. So I decided to take a leap and have a good time. I let myself relax and laugh and eat a stupid dessert. When it was over, I was actually a bit sad. And relieved when—while we were sitting at the end of my driveway, in his car—he asked me out again. I said yes. And he kissed me, Dono. And it was fine. No fireworks or insanity like with you. But fine." She paused to shrug. "Until a big black truck took a wrong turn and rear-ended us. Totaled the guy's car. Smashed my head into the dashboard and split it open."

A furious range of emotions tumbled through Donovan. Jealousy and self-loathing. Fierce regret and protectiveness. He reached up to stroke the scar again, but she shook her head, stopping him from succeeding.

"The worse part," she said, "wasn't that I took it as a sign that I wasn't *supposed* to be having a good time, even though that's what my mind had already concluded.

Or that I was being punished for enjoying the date, even though I thought I was. It was knowing, at that moment, that I'd never be whole again. That some part of me would always tie everything back to the fact that you were dead."

Donovan's chest squeezed, so tight it hurt.

I'm sorry for the way I left you, he thought. *Sorry for everything.*

He opened his mouth, then closed it, unable to find something adequate to say. Nothing would seem like enough.

Jordynn spoke first anyway. "We're too late."

Donovan hissed in a breath that made his lungs burn. He started to answer, then realized her statement wasn't actually directed *at* him. Instead, her attention was focused *behind* him.

He swiveled to follow her gaze. The bedroom window had lit up with the distinct yellow glow of a vehicle's headlights. Then they winked out, and the muted sound of one car door slamming, then another, carried up from outside.

Donovan turned back to Jordynn. "All right, honey. No more time for arguing."

Phone forgotten, he slid his hands to her shoulders and pulled her away from the wall, then moved to pull back the furniture she'd stacked there. But before he could even come close to lifting the nightstand, an angry yell from below announced the intruders had already made their way into the house.

Chapter 3

Donovan froze, mad at himself. *Should've been more insistent. More forceful. Gotten her out of here and given ourselves time. A fighting chance. If she gets hurt because you couldn't keep your heart and hands in check—*

"Dono?"

At the sound of Jordynn's voice—colored by clear desperation and completely lacking animosity now—his eyes flicked up. Her gaze was on him, scared but expectant. Needing him.

Hell.

"What are we going to do?" she asked.

Donovan made himself move, made himself look around the room in search of a solution. In search of a viable plan. He was pleased when he found one immediately.

He stepped away from the barricaded door, and moved to unlock the wide window at the back of the room. With a grunt at the effort, he slid the stiff pane sideways, then knocked out the screen.

"They'll never believe we went out that way," Jordynn said with a frown. "It's a fifteen-foot drop."

"I don't want them to believe it," Donovan replied. "I want them to check it out, then assume it's a diversion tactic and start searching."

The line between her eyebrows deepened. "You want them to look for our hiding place?"

"Yep." He nodded toward the door. "And we're going to leave that stuff there and wait for them to come to us, too."

Her eyes pinched with worry. "What?"

"We don't stand a chance of getting past them. Any second, they're going finish searching down there. Then they'll come up, the only way they can. Which is also the only way down. We really can't beat them."

"But…we can't just let them win."

"We won't. We're going out the way *I* came in. Through the bathroom, into the closet, then out through the den."

"The den is right beside the bedroom," she pointed out.

"I know. But the den door is wide open, and they won't do more than glance inside. They'll assume we're behind the door they *can't* get into and they'll be so distracted with trying to break through it that they won't notice as we slip out the other one. With any luck, anyway."

"Luck?"

Donovan nodded. "Best we can hope for."

"And if they aren't distracted enough?"

He met her eyes. "Then you run like hell."

"And what do you do?"

He moved away. Something told him that if he admitted he'd be more than happy to sacrifice himself on her behalf, she wouldn't be thrilled. Maybe she'd even be upset by it.

"Donovan?" She said his full name—the way she always had when she really wanted an answer.

He didn't respond right away, and Jordynn's hand landed on his elbow. The touch was electric. A renewed buzz of need and a compulsion to answer her question honestly hit him.

You never could say no to her, could you?

He turned to face her again, his mouth open. But the thump of boots on the stairs saved him from having to admit he'd gladly let them take him if it meant she'd go free.

"Time to go," he said instead.

As they moved across the bedroom, the doorknob rattled. Jordynn jumped, and Donovan slipped his hand to hers wordlessly and offered a reassuring squeeze. He expected her to pull away. She didn't. Instead, she clung tightly to his fingers and let him take the lead. He pulled her to the bathroom, where he slid the curtain shut—not more than another ten-second decoy, probably, but anything might help—and turned out the light before lifting the latch to the sliding door on the other side of the room.

From outside the bedroom, the rattle of the knob had been switched out for a bang on the door itself, and an accompanying order to open it before they broke it down.

Jordynn inched closer to Donovan. He knew it was just because she was scared, but that didn't stop it from feeling good to have her so near.

"It's all right," he murmured as they pushed into the den closet.

He hoped he sounded more confident than he felt. The scant fifteen feet between them and whoever was on the other side of that door could've been multiplied by a hundred—a thousand, maybe—and it wouldn't have been far enough away.

Donovan closed the door gently behind them, then paused to look down at her in the dark. "You doing okay?"

"No."

He couldn't help but let out a low chuckle at her honesty. "Fair enough. Let me rephrase the question. Are you ready to give this escape attempt our best shot?"

She stared back up at him, silent and still.

"Jordynn?" he prompted.

"You laughed," she replied softly.

"Sorry."

"No. Don't be sorry. Not about that. I just— I never thought I'd hear your laugh again, that's all."

He touched her cheek, wishing he could take the time to talk to her about it. To explain, at least a little bit. She leaned into the caress for a second, then pulled away, and Donovan wondered if she would even let him try.

No time to find out now, he reminded himself.

"You ready?" he asked.

She nodded, and they slid to the wall beside the door silently, where Donovan paused to lift a finger to his lips. He stepped to the opening and leaned out.

Down the hall, a large, black-clad man slammed his foot into the door in quick succession. *Thump.* Pause. *Thump.* Pause. A second man stood beside the first, arms crossed as he waited for the bigger man to put his strength to good use.

Donovan slipped back inside, and as he did, there was a final thump, then a shattering *cr-r-rack* followed by a triumphant yell from the intruders.

"Now," he said to Jordynn. "Quickly. Quietly. And don't look back."

He took her hand again and pulled her out into the hall. Donovan made himself follow his own order to ignore the commotion coming from the bedroom and to not check behind them. He didn't even breathe until they'd made it halfway down the stairs.

He heard Jordynn let out a loud exhale, too. It was a shaky sound, and it reminded him that if he was scared, she must be downright terrified. He was the one who'd spent the past decade on the run. She'd simply carried on with her life there in Ellisberg, Oregon. Middle of the night runaways weren't par for the course for her.

"Almost there, honey," he said.

When they reached the bottom step, he pulled her to the wall, careful to keep out of view of the space where they'd tied up her assailant. He didn't know how close to consciousness the other man was, and he didn't want to find out, either. He eyed the hall skeptically. It would take them right past the living room and the man inside.

"Guess the front door's out of the question." Donovan kept his voice low.

"Do you want to go through the laundry room and into the garage?" she whispered back. "Mom's old car is out there. We can try it, but I'm honestly not even sure it runs."

"Garage door'll be too noisy and car'll be too easy to track."

"What then?"

"Still got that little deck off the kitchen?"

"Deck?"

"The platform that hangs under the window."

"You mean the one for the flower boxes?"

"Yeah," he said. "You think it'll hold our weight?"

"No."

"Do you see another option?"

"It's five feet from the window to the ground. If it breaks…"

"I'll go out first. If it does break, it'll give me a chance to use the stuntman moves I've been working on. And I'll catch you when you follow."

"How chivalrous."

In spite of the stress-filled moments ticking by, Donovan smiled at her sarcastic mutter. "Always."

For a second, her mouth turned up, too—just a tiny bit—and he had to rein in a compulsion to lean down and kiss those curved edges. He clenched his jaw to stop from actually doing it, and contented himself giving her hand another squeeze.

"Time's running out," Donovan said.

As if to emphasize his words, a crash came from above. An angry bellow followed it, and Jordynn flinched.

"Okay," she breathed. "But if this doesn't work, and we live, you're paying for the repair."

Donovan let out a low laugh, then tugged her down the hall and around the corner to the raised kitchen. He let her hand go—only because it would've been impossible to do what had to be done otherwise—and reached over the double sink to push open the window. When he'd swung it as wide as it would go, he turned to Jordynn once more.

"Forgive me for this, okay?" he said.

"For what?"

He bent down and placed a soft kiss on her lips. Heat rushed through him, fast and hard. Five seconds of pure bliss, ten years in the making. Even though he would've liked the moment to last forever, he didn't let himself linger. He didn't want to give her a chance to reject the gesture. Or to make him regret it.

So Donovan pulled away quickly. He mounted the counter, then pushed his legs through the window and tested the platform with his boots.

Solid enough, he thought, and spun around to ease himself down.

"I should be on the ground in a second or two," he said. "You can climb up and—"

The rest of the words died in his throat as he lifted his eyes and his gaze landed on Jordynn. And the man standing behind her with a gun pressed to her head.

"If either of you move an inch, you're both dead."

The gravelly voice, full of smug disdain, came from far too close to Jordynn's ear. And something about it made her want to do the opposite of what it commanded. Like staying still and obeying could possibly be more frightening than the death threat itself.

She wanted desperately to turn and run as fast and far away as she could. She actually had to force her feet to stay planted. Warm metal dug into the back of her neck, and the man's hand pressed to the small of her back.

Run! urged her brain.

Jordynn fought the urge. She stared straight at Dono, using his face to keep her rooted to the spot. She concentrated on his lips, and the memory of how they'd felt pressed into her just a minute ago. How the kiss had sent of jolt of longing through her, reminding her how much she'd missed him for the past ten years and making her hope it wouldn't be the last time she got to experience it. And it worked. Though she couldn't quite stop her body from shaking, she *was* able to keep from bolting.

For several frantic heartbeats, Dono held her gaze with his own before he pulled his hazel eyes up to the man who held her and gave a small nod of recognition.

When he spoke, his voice was calm. "Ivan. My favorite right-hand man."

"You remember me. I'm flattered."

"Hard to forget the man who ate Sunday dinner at my dad's table, then beat me soundly and left me for dead. Cracked my jaw, broke my arm and made my head ache for a month, thank you very much."

Jordynn cringed at the mental image that formed to go along with Dono's words, and the man behind her jabbed the gun into her a little harder. She steadied herself, but her mind was working at hyper-speed to make sense of the other part of what he'd said.

Sunday dinner?

Who was this man to Dono? *Ivan.* Should that name mean something to her, too? She'd spent enough time at the Grady house as a youth. But she didn't think she'd ever heard the name, nor seen the man before. What exactly had gone on ten years earlier? Would she find out, or would she simply die wondering? Unwanted tears formed in her eyes, and in spite of the way she fought to keep them in, they quickly made their way down her cheeks.

Dono's attention flicked her way for a moment, following the path of tears down her face, and his lips fixed into an angry line before he drew in a breath and spoke again. "Your boss clearly holds me in some pretty high esteem if he sent you."

"You fooled him into believing you were dead, and somehow eluded him for a whole decade," replied Ivan. "Guess that warrants some special attention."

"Guess it does." Dono smiled a smile that didn't touch his eyes, then shrugged. "Well, that, or he's pissed that you couldn't do the job right the first time."

Behind Jordynn, the man let out a small snarl. "If I'd wanted to kill you all those years ago, you would've been dead. That was simply a suggestion of how things *should* go, depending how you want to look at it."

Dono glanced at Jordynn, a flicker of worry crossing his face before he spoke evenly to Ivan. "Tell you what. Let *her* go, I'll come with you, and I won't even fight you on it. I've actually always wanted to meet the man."

The other man smiled, too, but even more coldly. "Not to sound cliché, but the first time you meet him will also be the last. And, Mr. Grady, if you didn't want Ms. Flannigan to have to face the consequences, you should never have come back and you should never have brought her into it. I'm afraid I can't let her walk away. My boss has plans for her, too."

The statement gave Jordynn a chill, but Dono stayed outwardly cool and collected.

"I didn't bring her into this," he corrected. "One of your 'coworkers' was already here when I arrived."

"That's almost true. But not quite." The gray-haired man tossed a look at Jordynn. "I'm guessing she doesn't know."

"Know what?" The question slipped out before Jordynn could stop it.

"It doesn't matter," Dono said.

But Ivan's smile had grown. And darkened.

"It's a technicality, I guess," he said. "But this isn't your boyfriend's first return to Ellisberg."

Again, Jordynn couldn't help but reply. "What do you mean?"

"That's how we found out he was alive." Ivan's voice was smug. "Showed up for a funeral."

Jordynn's eyes sought Dono. "When?"

"Jordynn…" He trailed off, but Ivan answered for him anyway.

"Two years ago," the other man stated.

Her mother's funeral.

Jordynn's head spun. He'd been there. Close enough to

see. Maybe to touch. She swallowed. How could he have come back like that, and not spoken to her?

"Accidentally got caught on camera," Ivan added. "Weird thing. A local crew was doing a news story that day."

"I remember," Jordynn whispered. "A special on the history of the cemetery. They had to stop filming before we could start the service."

"But not before someone managed to catch Mr. Grady in action. Dark coat, hood pulled up. But the angle was just right, and my boss was sure it was you."

A sob built up in Jordynn's throat, and Dono reached for her. But Ivan waved the gun menacingly, blocking him from getting any closer. And she was actually glad. She wasn't sure what would happen if he touched her right that second.

She wanted to sit down. To process it. She wobbled. And neither man seemed to notice.

"Like Mr. Grady said, though. It doesn't matter anyway. Not now." The man shrugged. "And my boss wants a word with *both* of you."

"A word?" Dono repeated doubtfully. "You and I both know he's not interested in a chat."

"To be honest, what we know doesn't matter, either," the gunman said. "Only matters that we do what we're told. And just in case you were thinking about jumping and running, I'll give you another fair warning. There are two guys out there in a car on the street. Armed and dangerous, as they say. Not the subtle type, either."

"Two thugs outside. Two upstairs. Our friend tied to the chair in the living room. And you. Six men to bring us in," Dono said. "Either that's overkill, or we really are special."

"A decade-long headache can make a man do crazy things. Step back inside. Slowly."

"You sure about that? 'Cause I'll be even more of a headache once you actually get ahold of me."

"Quit trying to delay the inevitable."

"I'm just making sure this is the way you want to go."

"Be awful to have to shoot you in front of your girl."

"You won't shoot me here."

Ivan sighed and moved the gun to Dono's chest. "You a hundred percent certain of that?"

Jordynn's heart constricted. She tried to take a breath, and couldn't. She couldn't handle the thought of seeing what would happen if Dono didn't obey the other man's order. She hadn't even wrapped her head around the fact that he was there. Or that he'd been there before.

Focus on the present, she told herself. *In spite of it all, you don't want to lose him all over again so quickly, do you?*

"Listen to him," she burst out. "Please."

He met her eyes, and she saw more than a hint of worry there. And she knew he *had* just been stalling. Trying to come up with some way of getting them out of the situation. And she could read him well enough to know he hadn't succeeded.

"Inside," the man behind her barked, clearly running out of patience.

Without taking his gaze off her, Dono put both hands on the bottom of the window frame, ready to pull himself back in. Jordynn's eyes couldn't help but stray to his fingers. She recalled just how they'd felt clasped with hers a few minutes ago. Rough. Strong. A bit dangerous. She'd thought it was a good combination, considering their situation. Lord knew Jordynn was none of those things on her own. Now, though, their reassuring solidity seemed like a bad thing. Because they'd only help in pulling him back into danger.

But a moment later, their strength became irrelevant. It was no match for gravity.

As Dono pushed himself up, a snap echoed from beneath his feet. A flash of surprise crossed his face. Then his body tipped sideways, and he lost his grip on the window. His cheek hit the frame with a sickening crack, and he slid out of view.

For several seconds, Jordynn stood still. And so did the man behind her. Then they both moved at once, but in opposite directions. The gunman surged forward, hollering for some help, clearly intent on seeing where Dono had fallen to. But Jordynn didn't need to check on him. She *knew* where he would've landed, and knew, too, what his options for escape would be. He might've hurt himself, but five feet wasn't far enough to make her worry about broken bones. Not too much, anyway. What did concern her was getting to him before the two armed and dangerous men who were somewhere out there. That... and what they might do to him if he'd knocked himself unconscious. Or worse, if he was disoriented and wandered into their sights.

And what are you going to do stop them?

She shoved down the voice in her head. *Not* trying to help Dono wasn't an option. So while her captor peered out the window, she spun on her heel and darted in the opposite direction. She leaped down the stairs and flew into the hall, then moved to open the door. But as she stepped back to fling it open, she slammed straight into a body. And it was most definitely not Dono's.

Chapter 4

Jordynn tried to pull away, but it was too late. The big man on her doorstep was stronger. Faster. And clearly more experienced at capturing people than she was at escaping from them.

She barely reached the doorstep before his arms were around her, spinning her hard and shoving her against the exterior wall of the house. Jordynn's chest scraped along the wood siding making her cry out. Her yelp earned her a sweaty hand over her mouth, and a heartbeat later, she was being turned again and lifted.

At the end of the driveway, she could see Tom, her neighbor, heading for his car.

Please, please!

Jordynn inhaled through her nose and tried to scream. But it was no use. The man's palm was pressed too firmly to her lips, his grip on her chest too tight. All that came out was a wheeze. In seconds, he'd pulled her through the door, shut it again, then dragged her to the living room. There, he set her down, then shoved her roughly enough that she landed on the rug. Bits of the shattered coffee table dug into her body. She forced herself to ignore the pain.

Breathing shallowly, Jordynn crawled to the sofa and gripped its edge. She looked up, but didn't dare stand. Especially not when she spied Ivan, pacing the room in front of the man Dono had tied to the chair. His face was dark and dangerous, and he didn't bother to stop moving to glance at her as he addressed the man who'd tossed her in.

"Rope her up," he ordered. "Pull some of that stuff off the Nose to do it."

The Nose?

But Jordynn didn't have time to consider the oddity of the nickname. Or to worry that it sounded just a little too pseudo-gangster for her liking. Because the big, rough man had begun to unwind the wire from the unconscious one. And she knew where it was going to wind up next. Her feet itched to outrun the inevitable.

"Now what?" the big man asked as he finished his task.

"I'd like to shoot them both and be done with it," Ivan muttered.

"The boss—"

"I know what the boss wants."

Jordynn kept her eyes down, pretending not to follow the exchange. Pretending it didn't scare the living hell out of her.

Ivan sighed. "We wait, Denny. Hank will take those two gun-happy guards outside, and he'll help them circle the block until they find Grady."

"He's gone? Thought he fell out a damned window."

"He did. Then he got up and ran off."

The bigger man—Denny—moved toward her, the wire in his hands. Jordynn cowered back. And wished she could help it. But he either didn't notice or didn't care. He just grabbed her hands, held them together and wrapped the wire around her wrists. Tight enough to hurt. Far tighter than necessary. When he had her secured to his satisfaction, he lifted her from the ground and tossed her unceremoniously onto the couch.

"So Grady got away. Again," he said. "And you really think he's gonna stick around?"

Ivan's eyes skimmed over Jordynn, then he went back to pacing. "He came this far. He won't leave her. Trust me."

Jordynn finally managed to find her voice. "Donovan let me think he was dead."

Both men turned her way. Denny with his eyes narrowed, and Ivan with his expression impassive.

"What makes you think he'll even bother to come back?" she added.

Ivan shrugged. "Checking up on you was his sole reason for coming back to Ellisberg. All we had to do was drop a hint that you might be in trouble, and he sure as hell came running."

A hint?

Jordynn squeezed her jaw tightly for a second to keep from asking what he meant. To keep from revealing that she hadn't the slightest clue about what was really going on.

"But now he knows I'm safe," she said instead. "So he's not going to just come back and endanger himself."

"He knows you're stuck here with me and Denny and Hank and the Nose. And our guns," Ivan corrected. "Should be more than enough to motivate him."

Jordynn shook her head. "No. He already knows you're not going to kill me. You told him your boss wanted to chat."

Ivan tapped his gun on his thigh, then cocked his head to the side thoughtfully. Jordynn's heart skipped a nervous beat at the expression on his face, and she had a funny feeling her plan to divert their attention away from chasing down Donovan had gone wrong.

He smiled, confirming her suspicion. "You're right. He probably does know you're not in immediate danger. Denny?"

"Yeah?"

"You still a pretty good shot?"

"Nine out of ten."

"Good. Tie Ms. Flannigan's feet together, and gag her, too." Ivan dug into his pocket and dragged out a set of keys. "My car's in the alley behind the house. Take her out there, drop her in the trunk, then start the engine and walk back up to the house. You can wait by that big tree in the yard for Grady. He won't be able to resist the opportunity. When he gets close…shoot him in the knee— maybe *both* knees—then toss him in the backseat."

Jordynn fought a gasp and made a last-ditch effort to save herself from being used as bait. "What if he's not close enough to see?"

"He is." Ivan sounded utterly sure.

She might've argued a little more, but Denny was on her again, his hands working fast to stuff a piece of balled up cloth into her mouth. When he was done with that, he used another piece of wire to secure it in place, then bound her ankles. In under two minutes, he had her strung up and lifted onto his shoulder.

As he carried her from her living room to the door, Jordynn couldn't decide what she wanted more—for Dono to be where they assumed he was so he could save her, or if she hoped he'd run for real. She valued her own life. But she couldn't stand the thought of being directly responsible for Dono's death. She'd experienced enough guilt over being sure she could've done something to prevent his fake one.

I can't go through that again.

A blast of air hit her as Denny opened the door, and when Jordynn saw that the sun was up almost completely now, a new hope came to mind. More people would be awake. Her neighbor—Tom—he was the earliest riser on the block. But others would be stirring soon, if not now. Making their breakfast, going to work.

Someone will see us and call the police. Someone has to.

But the hope fizzled quickly. Denny kept pressed close to the house and out of view of the street, and the large hedges that lined the yard provided plenty of cover. He slid smoothly along the edge of the building, moving like Jordynn's weight was nothing. As he snapped open the back gate and moved swiftly down the driveway toward the alley, she wished she were confident enough to drive her bound hands into his kidney and fight like crazy to get away. But she wasn't convinced she was strong enough to hurt the big man, let alone do enough damage that he'd be forced to drop her. And even if she could do it, she somehow doubted she'd be able to get away faster than he could recover.

Still.

She couldn't let herself just be taken without a fight, no matter how futile it seemed.

She lifted her arms, then slammed them into his back. Denny didn't even grunt.

Jordynn made a second attempt. He just spun her

around, bent down and dumped her to the ground. She let out a cry—or at least tried to—as her whole body smacked against the gravel. She fought the tears that wanted so desperately to come. She rolled to her back and refused to let them out, staring up at the tree cover above her.

Before that second, she'd always loved the evergreen that grew between the backyards. But right then, they served no purpose but to block her from view of anyone who might be inclined to call 911. And the sight of them above her just made her want to cry even more.

It intensified when Denny spoke. "This plan'll work even if you're unconscious. If you don't want me to make that happen…nod."

Jordynn forced her head up and down, and the big man reached down to pick her up again. Her despair grew even worse when he folded her into the sedan's trunk, then slammed the lid shut, pitching her into near-complete darkness. Then the car hummed to life, and Jordynn remembered Denny's plan to leave it running with her still inside, and those tears threatened again.

She needed something to pull her out of it. But her mind was as dark as the trunk.

So you're just going to do what? Give up? Rely on Dono, who really might not *be coming?*

Then—somehow—she found her much-needed motivation.

Donovan.

Or more specifically, the idea that once again, she might never see him. Might never hear his laugh.

His laugh.

God, how she'd always loved the sound it. The way it felt on a pillow next to her head. How it boomed when he really let it go. It was something she never thought she'd hear again. And truthfully, her memory hadn't done it justice. The bass-y noise warmed Jordynn, tugging at her heart far more than she wanted it to. She wanted to smile and cry at the same time. And wanted to hear it again.

It was enough to remind her that she had no interest in being bait.

She heaved sideways and eyed the taillights. Quickly, she decided that even if she could kick them hard enough to break through the double layer of plastic, it would do no good. And it would alert Denny to the fact that she wasn't simply letting him use her the way he wanted to.

Jordynn rolled to her back, toyed with the idea of slamming her feet into the lid, then dismissed that, too. The noise might bring help. But more likely it would just bring Denny.

Frustrated, Jordynn exhaled and tilted her head to the other side. Through the cushion backs, she could see a sliver of light. And with that…a sliver of hope.

She inched closer, then reached her bound hands out and ran them along the edge of the seats, right where they met the trunk. She squeezed her fingers into the opening and felt around for a latch. The metal hinges scraped across the backs of her wrists, but Jordynn didn't stop. She pushed farther in, and in moments, she found a stiff piece of plastic. When she closed her fingers on it, it sprung up with surprising ease. And as she nudged the seat with her shoulder, it folded forward. For a second, Jordynn was surprised into stillness.

Her brain caught up first.

You did it! Now go, go, go, it urged.

And her body was quick to listen.

She wriggled over the flattened seat, careful to keep low and out of sight. It wasn't exactly easy to be subtle with both her ankles and her wrists tied together. When her hips got stuck in the narrow opening, it took every bit of core strength she had to pull herself through. Her lungs burned with the exertion, and she was as sweaty as she got running her mile-a-day workout. But her hard work paid off. In under three minutes, she made it through to the back. Another thirty seconds—and a fight with the center console—put her in the driver's seat. The keys jangled in the ignition. Waiting.

What now?

A glance out the window told her she didn't have long to decide.

Dono's familiar form had appeared at the end of the alleyway. And Denny was already slithering along the fence toward him.

The woman he loved, in easy reach.

The woman he loved, trapped in the trunk of a car.

No one in sight and the car in question running for too many minutes.

Logically, Donovan knew it was a trap.

But logic has nothing to do with it, he thought. *And besides that...I've waited long enough.*

He slowly stalked toward the sedan, his eyes on the prize, but stopped short when a flash of red in the front seat caught his attention. He stared for a long second. There it was again.

"Holy hell," he murmured. "She got out."

Impressed and encouraged, he took another step forward. It was that one extra stride that saved him as a silenced bullet flew through the air. Instead of hitting him, it dug itself deep into the ground near his foot.

His eyes flew up in surprise.

There.

A man in the shadows and a flash of silver. And the click of a gun cocking.

Donovan dived, and this time the shot went wide, lodging in the fence beside him.

He threw himself forward, aiming his full body weight at the shooter, who clearly wasn't expecting an attack. The other man edged away clumsily, and a fist came flying toward Donovan's gut. The punch was a wild one, though, and it just grazed his T-shirt.

Donovan stumbled, sending up a cloud of dust from the gravel beneath his feet. Even though he recovered quickly, the gray dirt was already in his eyes and mouth, blinding him and making him cough. A second punch came quickly, and the blur of movement was Donovan's only warning. And this time, he wasn't quite fast enough. Thick knuckles landed on his shoulder. He spun to the side, then dodged as the attacker jumped forward again. He scrambled backward, cursing as he dug the dust from his eyes. He cleared it just in time to see that the other man was headed toward him once again—and he was surprisingly quick for a big man. He flew at Donovan, fists coming in rapid succession. The action forced Donovan to take on a defensive stance, blocking blow after blow with his elbows and forearms.

Finally, desperate to change the exhausting rhythm, he dropped his arms and let the big man land a hit to his chest. The move had the desired effect. His assailant was surprised into letting the pattern drop, and the extra heartbeat of time was all Donovan needed to gain some control.

He stepped back, then lifted his foot in a sharp jab. His boot landed on the other man's shin and sent him down to one knee. Donovan followed the initial kick with a second one, this time to the stomach. He started to issue a third, but the man beneath him reached up a meaty fist, gripped his ankle, then twisted it and brought him to the ground.

Donovan landed with a grunt, then rolled out of the way as the other man pushed to his feet and stalked toward him. As he moved, the sound of tires on gravel filled his ears.

He lifted his head and saw the sedan inching down the alley.

Jordynn.

Relief filled him as he realized she'd decided to get the car going and stood an excellent chance of escape.

As the car sped up, he turned his attention back to saving his own rear end. Though the other man had paused for a second to observe the car's movement, too, he'd already turned his attention back to Donovan.

"Looks like your girlfriend's leaving without you," he said with a smirk.

"Suits me just fine."

His attacker lunged. Donovan sidestepped. He crouched and readied his fists.

The vehicle had passed them now, and was almost at the end of the alley.

Thank God.

But then it came to a full stop.

What the hell?

The car kicked into Reverse and tore backward instead. It came in wildly, picking up speed, its back end bumping and turning with the acceleration.

"Guess she changed her mind," the other man said, then lunged again, seeking to take advantage of Donovan's temporary stillness.

It was a mistake. At the exact moment that he moved, the car's random path took on a purpose. It angled toward the big man. Then kept going, straight and steady. It slammed into him, knocking him aside with a thud.

Donovan stared at the man's crumpled form for a moment, then brought his gaze up. From the driver's seat Jordynn stared back at him, her face a mask of pale, pale shock. Like she couldn't believe what she'd just done. Then she blinked, and her mouth moved.

Get in, she was saying.

It only took him a second to comply. He darted to the other side of the car, flipped open the door and jumped in.

"Thank you," he said.

Jordynn licked her lips nervously. "Did I kill him?"

"No, honey."

"You're sure?"

"He was twitching just fine."

"Okay." She turned her attention out the front windshield.

"We should go," Donovan said gently. "Before the rest of them figure out what's going on."

"I know."

She didn't move, and he tried again. "If you want me to drive—"

"I'm fine."

"Are you sure?"

"Yes."

"Jordynn…"

She exhaled. "Let's just…not talk right this second."

She took her bound hands and slipped the car from Reverse into Drive, then placed them on top of the steering wheel.

He obeyed her need for silence, but Donovan could only stare at her delicate wrists for a moment before taking action. He fumbled through the untidy stack of objects in the center console until he found a box cutter. He promptly snapped it up and flicked it to the narrow wire that held Jordynn. She didn't quite flinch as his fingers dug between her wrists and worked in a sawing motion to set her free.

"Thank you," she said softly.

Donovan issued a short nod, then leaned away again as she guided the car to the end of the alley, this time slowly, then into the street. He fought the urge to ask again if she was all right.

Dumb question. No matter what she says about being fine, it doesn't make it true.

She was tied up. Had just found out her long-dead boyfriend was actually alive. Had been held at gunpoint, and had her life turned upside down. So *far* from fine it wasn't even funny. All because of him.

So he let her drive in silence, not asking where she was headed, not telling her where he thought they should go. Instead, he stared out the window, watching the streets pass by. From what he could see, the town hadn't changed much. Not in this area, anyway. The same grocery store on the same corner. The same elementary school across from the same high school.

Donovan had a hard time believing that at one point in his life, he'd never been farther than the town limits. Even harder to wrap his head around the idea that he'd never wanted to.

Of course, it had never been Ellisberg itself that'd held him.

His eyes slid back to Jordynn.

Twelve years old.

That was his age when he first realized he'd fallen in love with her. He'd wooed her patiently through their teen years, waiting for her to clue in that it was a forever kind of deal. The easy stuff came first. Movies and stolen kisses and handholding. Then there'd been the complicated stuff. Lovemaking and naming babies they hadn't had. And the serious stuff. Saving the money from his paper route, then from pumping gas at the local station, until he finally had enough to pay for the promise ring he gave her on her sixteenth birthday.

Donovan had never cared when people called them crazy, or said they were too young. He'd known what he'd wanted and that it would never change.

"Until it did."

He didn't realize he'd spoken aloud until she answered him. "What?"

"Nothing, honey," he said quickly. "Just thinking aloud."

She glanced his way, then back out the front again, then spoke in a shaky voice. "Did you really come back for my mom's funeral?"

He closed his eyes for a second before answering. "I needed to know that you were okay."

"Didn't you know already that I *wasn't*? That I hadn't been for eight years already?" The quaver had become a slightly angry one.

"I hoped you'd be healing," he told her. "But I just..."

"What?"

"I kept thinking about when your mom was first diagnosed, and how you told me losing her would break you. I had to come."

She inhaled a breath that somehow echoed through the car. "And what would've happened if you'd found me and I wasn't dealing with it well?"

He stared out the windshield, then shook his head. "I honestly don't know."

She went silent for a moment, then said, "If I ask you something else, will you be honest about that, too?"

"I can try."

She sighed, said a near-silent, "I guess that will have to do," then she swallowed.

"These men who are after you—after *us*, I guess—is it because you did something wrong?"

He felt himself hesitate, bogged down by years of guilt. A decade of questioning every move he'd made since that night. And on the night itself. Wondering so often if his moral code had let him down. If it had been skewed by emotion. Hell. He'd woken up countless nights in a cold sweat, haunted by the decision he'd been forced to make all that time ago.

Had he done something wrong? Maybe. Probably more than one thing.

But not the way she means, he told himself.

And he sure as hell wouldn't go back and change any of it.

"Dono?"

Her concern-tinged voice drew him back to the present. Jordynn's safety had been—and remained—the most important thing to him. He loosened his balled-up hands and placed them flat on his thighs.

"Nothing is black-and-white," he said gruffly. "But the reason they're after me has nothing to do with anything I did."

"Not something you *did*?"

"Nothing *I* did," he said, changing the emphasis just enough to change the meaning, too.

She wasn't buying it. "Either way, I don't think you really answered my question."

He winced. She'd never been anything but smart and intuitive. It made her excellent at reading him. One of the reasons Donovan loved her, and one of the reasons he hadn't been able to stay.

"Did you do something wrong?" Jordynn asked again.

He couldn't quite make the word *no* come out. At his silence, hurt flashed across her face.

"Do you know *why* I was okay, after my mom died?" she said.

Donovan didn't want to hear the answer; he was sure he knew already. "Honey."

"It was because the worst thing had already happened," she told him. "Because *you* were dead, and there was nothing left to break."

Guilt—white-hot and furious—stabbed at Donovan. Forcefully, he reminded himself that he'd done what he's done for her sake. For her safety and her life.

"Honey—" he said again.

But she cut him off with a cool glare. "Don't. Please."

He nodded and turned to stare out the windshield instead, watching the bright horizon. He didn't realize until that moment that they'd left the old neighborhood behind—the winding, house-thick streets weren't even visible anymore, which meant they'd crested the top of the natural basin that held the familiar residential area. It also meant they weren't headed in the right direction. Donovan's eyes flicked to the side and found the nearing mountain—full of hiking trails and bubbling streams and not a single place to hide a stolen sedan—and his nerves tightened ever further. They needed the highway. The city and its anonymity. Not the wilderness.

"We need to turn around," he said. "At the very least make our way to Salem."

Jordynn didn't look at him, and she didn't acknowledge the urgency in his voice. "Do you know where we are?"

Donovan lifted his ball cap and ran his fingers over his mess of hair, then tugged his ear. "Yeah. Not where we should be."

"Look again."

Frustrated by the hint of stubbornness in her suggestion, but knowing from experience that arguing with her would do no good anyway, he gave the exterior scenery another glance.

Narrowing road.

Increased tree cover.

A few birds overhead.

No way out!

He shoved down the internal shout and made himself focus. To see whatever it was Jordynn wanted him to see.

And there it was. A sign that proclaimed You Are Now Approaching Greyside Mountain Park. And just beyond that—flashing between the thick foliage—a familiar gray structure that made Donovan's stomach plummet to his knees.

Chapter 5

Jordynn heard Dono's sharp inhale as she eased the car to the shoulder of the road, then turned and took the nearly invisible turnoff that dipped down beside the bridge. Her own breath rushed through her in a noisy *whoosh*, and her pulse was thrumming in the tips of her fingers and toes, too. She stared out the windshield and reminded herself that she'd driven to this spot on purpose. Never mind that she hadn't been able to make herself come here even once since the memorial plaque went up. Some compulsion made her need to see it now. To show it to Donovan.

She let her eyes slide over the bridge.

No one in his or her right mind would call it a romantic piece of architecture. Dull reinforced concrete. It even blocked any view of the sparkling water below. It screamed utilitarian. Safety. All things practical and unpretty. But Jordynn knew better.

On the other side of all that solidity had sat a secret. A narrow ledge, lined with a wrought iron railing. And that railing was set into what was left of a much older bridge, built long before the road had been widened to accommodate the increasing tourist traffic coming through to explore the trails. And the remnants of *that* bridge were utterly synonymous with romance, at least in Jordynn's mind.

They'd found it as teenagers when, in search of a little excitement, they'd climbed past the warning sign that forbade them from entering.

She closed her eyes, remembering it.

Of course, it had started out as Dono's idea. Because he'd been *that* kind of boy. Always wanting to push the limits, always looking for another way to rebel. Projecting a tough exterior. Jordynn knew, even then, that it was a natural result of losing his mother at such an early age and being left to be raised by his strict, by-the-book policeman dad. But she'd actually liked that about him, because even though she'd had a similar upbringing— deceased father whom she'd never known, and a mother who would've preferred to keep her close—Jordynn had gone the other way. Cautious and predictable. A temper she kept under lock and key.

And once he'd dragged her over the concrete structure to the second, hidden one beneath, Jordynn had embraced it full force. Not just because the two of them had spent hours there, fingers entwined, legs dangling dangerously over the edge. And also not just because they'd spent those hours talking about life and dreams, the past and the future. But because it had given her the chance to get to know the softer, more vulnerable side of Dono. A glimpse of the man he would become. The rose on top of the thorns. Fierce, yes. But gentle, too.

So for Jordynn, the ugly structure held every warm memory.

It marked their first kiss. The first time Donovan told her he loved her. The place they'd come to celebrate her sixteenth birthday, when he gave her the promise ring, assuring her he'd be able to afford a real engagement ring sometime soon.

It was the place she'd discovered that she didn't want to live without him.

And it was the exact spot she'd lost him.

Just hours after a rare argument, Dono's car—the rickety old hatchback he'd fixed up and lovingly nicknamed "the Beast"—had barreled past that warning sign, plummeted to the rocks and rapids below, then shattered. The local news crews had been in awe of the way the metal crumpled and split, of how the river carried so many pieces so far so fast.

Like Humpty Dumpty, one astute reporter had claimed.

In fact, five years after the accident, a hiker had found the crank handle for one of the Beast's windows more than fifty miles south at the Ten Falls Canyon.

A crash no one could've survived, was the consensus.

And though they'd combed the wild creek and the rivers it fed into, though they were eventually forced to declare him dead officially, they'd never recovered Dono's body, making all of it seem much more surreal. Of course, now Jordynn knew why.

A breeze ruffled her hair then, and when she opened her eyes in response, she realized Dono had somehow snuck out without her noticing. The car door hung open, and he stood beside the bridge, his eyes on the words of his own memorial.

With the intention of joining him, Jordynn swung the door open and lifted her legs, but as she moved, she was reminded that her feet were still bound together. So she settled for studying his face from a few yards away instead.

What's he thinking?

She couldn't imagine. She had a half a dozen conflicting emotions running through her own body. She felt so many things. Relief. Confusion. Anger. And something that bordered on love. She closed her eyes again, fighting it all.

Because it wasn't fair for him to turn up on her doorstep like this after so many years of buried heartache. Jordynn doubted that she'd ever be able to reconcile the tumble of feelings, even if she got an explanation from him. Which seemed less and less likely as the seconds ticked by.

She lifted her lids and examined the curl of Dono's lip and the twitch of his brow as he lifted his fingers to run them over the plaque.

"Who had this made?" he said over his shoulder.

"Your dad."

"With just my birthday?"

"He said there was no way to be sure what day you'd actually died on."

Donovan dropped his hand, then turned her way. "What about you?"

"What are you really asking me, Dono? If I secretly believed you were alive? If I was holding out hope?"

He had the decency to look taken aback. "That's not what I meant."

"Good. Because I really thought you were dead. I mean really, truly."

"Honey—"

Her temper flared. "Don't *honey* me."

"Jordynn." He said her name firmly, and it was almost worse.

"I *knew* you were dead," she told him. "Because if you weren't, you would've come back for me. You would've crawled out of the river with a hundred broken bones. And you didn't. So you couldn't possibly have been alive."

Jordynn pulled her hands from the steering wheel and—momentarily forgetting yet again that her feet were still bound—tried to stand. And before she could compensate, she lost her footing and tumbled roughly to the ground.

The sting of stone against flesh made Jordynn cry out, and a heartbeat later, warm hands landed on her elbows and pulled her back to her feet. Dono steadied her, then propped her against the car and met her eyes. For a second, she wondered why he didn't undo her right away. But then she knew. He had other things on his mind.

As that hazel gaze of his searched her face, a surge of electricity flew from his palms, zapped through Jordynn's arms, then up to her chest. The sensation—maybe with a little help from the location, too—sent the past ten years spiraling away. And suddenly, it was just the two of them. No bad guys after them for God knew what reason, no phony death and no devastation. Nothing but his hands on her like they used to be every day. His mouth inches away from hers, the way she still dreamed of far more often than she cared to admit. And the heat between them, building just as it always had.

That fire had been palpable for as long as Jordynn had known her feeling went beyond friendship. Or maybe that was *how* she knew. It was really hard to say which came first. Either way, the burn hadn't diminished at all.

Dono's hands moved. One up to the back of her neck and the other down to her waist.

Their pose was intimate now. Probably too intimate for how much time had passed with no contact between them. But as quickly as the thought came to Jordynn's mind, it slipped away again. The tips of Dono's fingers dug into her hair and into the small of her back, sending tendrils of desire from each point.

Jordynn's breath caught, and she trembled—not with fear or worry, but with want.

His mouth was just an inch away from hers. So close that she could feel its heat, anticipate its familiar soft but firm feel. The brief and gentle kiss that he'd given her at her house nowhere near satisfied the desire running through her now.

Her lids sunk down, and she tipped her face up eagerly.

God, I missed him. Missed this.

But as she leaned forward, tingling with anticipation, her feet caught on the ground and she nearly fell all over again. Dono grabbed her and pushed her back to an upright position.

"You all right?"

"Yes." Her reply came out a little breathy, and she cleared her throat and forced a distinctly unnatural laugh and tried again. "I forgot I was tied up. For the second time."

His face darkened, and he dropped down to his knees, his hands working swiftly and furiously to free her ankles.

Jordynn took a steadying breath, and reality came rushing back. She'd been about to kiss him. This man, who'd once been the boy she'd thought she'd marry. Who was now a stranger with an unknown past and a dangerous present and a questionable future. And not just in the surprised, unguarded way she'd kissed him back earlier, but with real fervor.

She shivered and shook her head. *What was I thinking?*

But she knew the answer. She *hadn't* been thinking. Just acting on a remembered passion. One she needed to forget if she had any chance of coming out of this—whatever *this* was—unscathed.

At her feet, Dono finished his work, then stood. "Better?"

"Yes. Thanks."

He took a little step toward her, then seemed to realize the spell had been broken, and moved back, putting a foot between them.

"We should go," he said.

"Why?"

He frowned. "We need to be somewhere crowded. With cover."

He reached out like he was going to take her hand, and Jordynn slid out of touching distance, her back squeaking against the car.

Subtle.

She steeled herself against the slight droop of Dono's mouth. She couldn't afford to care about his feelings. Not right now.

"I didn't mean why do we need to go," she said. "I meant why should I go with you? Or trust you? You let me think you were dead, Dono. And since the second you walked back into my life—which I have to point out was only a little over an hour ago—I've been threatened with a gun, tossed into the back of a car, and I committed grand theft auto. You haven't offered me even a bit of an explanation."

"Hon—Jordynn—"

"Tell me something. Anything. Please."

"I didn't leave because I wanted to."

The simple statement hit Jordynn straight in the gut, and her resolve to feel no sympathy started to crumble.

Donovan sensed an opening. Jordynn was staring at him with that half hopeful, half guarded look she'd always had on her face before she'd finally figured out that she could really trust him. Not wanting to risk letting go of the potential opportunity, Donovan grabbed her hand. All he needed was a crack to slip through, and he'd jump on a second chance faster than she could blink.

"Come with me," he said. "Just as far as our bridge."

Her gaze clouded. "It's gone."

"Gone?"

"They pulled it out, salvaged what they could and mounted it in front of City Hall."

"That's..." He lifted a hand to his ear, unsure which word was the right one.

"Hard," Jordynn filled in. "And sad."

"I'm sorry." As soon as the words were out of his mouth, he sighed. "I keep saying that. I know it doesn't even graze the surface of what I put you through."

"Sometimes, I drive by it on purpose, just to look at it. Sometimes, I avoid Main Street for a whole month, just so I *don't* have to look at it." She shrugged. "I was glad, though, that the developers decided to keep it."

Her last sentence made his throat go dry. "Who pulled it out, Jordynn?"

"Fryer Developments, I think they're called?"

"Fryer?" It wasn't the name he was expecting to hear.

She nodded. "They've got a big sign down there, mapping out the details of their project."

"Show me."

"What? Why? No. Never mind. You won't tell me anyway."

She sounded less annoyed than resigned, but that didn't stop yet another stab of guilt from hitting Donovan as she started up the hill beside the bridge. He stared after her, wondering if he'd ever get a chance to make her understand. Her life was everything to him. Even if his decade-old actions seemed to say otherwise.

"You coming?" she called, and he blinked, realizing she'd already disappeared above the gray concrete.

"Jordynn?" he called, striding over the rocky ground.

Her voice carried back. "Up here."

He caught up to her at the crest of the natural hill. She stood in front of a large sign, which advertised the future home of Greyside Estates, a mountain community. And she'd been right—the company building the elite-looking houses was Fryer Developments.

Donovan gave his ear a tug. He couldn't decide if he was relieved, or just puzzled. He stared down at the tree-tops below, discomfort hanging over him. It wasn't just the woods themselves, though they certainly held their own dark place in his mind. A place his didn't want to revisit.

Seems inevitable now, doesn't it?

A light touch on his arm brought his attention back to Jordynn.

"What's the matter?" she asked.

He glanced down at her concerned face, then rolled his shoulders, trying to ease some of the tension. "I don't know yet. Something about this isn't right."

"The development? I don't like the idea of houses up here, either." She shrugged. "But I guess it's just progress."

His eyes strayed back to the sign. Twelve homes nestled into the mountainside. Access to the city below, steps away from the river and the hiking trails. It seemed idyllic. So why did it fill him with such a terrible sense of foreboding?

"Has Fryer developed here before?" he wanted to know.

Jordynn shook her head. "I don't think so. Usually it's the Haven Corporation buying everything up. They're the ones who built all the new communities and redeveloped the old part of downtown. I think they even redid the block where I work."

"Right," Donovan muttered, his unease growing.

Haven.

The name made his guts churn.

"I think we should get off the mountain."

The vehemence of the statement startled even Donovan himself, and it made Jordynn's eyes widen, too. Shaking his head, he grabbed her hand and moved quickly down the hill. When they reached the car, he lifted his face toward the road, half expecting to see Ivan turn the corner. It remained quiet and empty.

"Dono?"

"Yeah, honey?"

She didn't brush off the endearment this time. "What's going on?"

He opened his mouth to respond, but before he could speak, the distant screech of tires on pavement carried through the quiet morning air and cut him off.

Jordynn met his eyes, a silent wave of understanding flowing between them.

Someone was coming up the mountain at breakneck speed. Someone who didn't know the curve at the bottom well enough to have braked ahead of time. Or...someone who was in so much of a hurry that he didn't care.

As Donovan grabbed Jordynn's hand and forced her gently to the other side of the sedan, he wasn't sure if the sound of the approaching car was the metaphorical "saved by the bell" or if it was a missed opportunity he'd never get back. He couldn't tell her the full truth without endangering her even more. He couldn't divulge the details of the hell he'd spent on the run, or of the emotional hell he'd barely been able to climb out of. Not unless he wanted to go spiraling back.

But she deserves something. As he swung open the passenger-side door and eased her into the seat, he met her scared gaze and corrected himself. *No. She deserves* everything.

Which was the nobler reason he'd left her behind. Even if he'd been able to take her with him and manage to keep her alive, there was no way he could've given her a life that came close to normal. Frustrated by the renewed feeling of helplessness, he slammed the door, then strode purposefully to the other side and climbed in.

"Buckle up," he ordered gruffly.

She didn't move. "It might not even be them."

"Not a chance I'm willing to take."

"How would they even have found us?"

"GPS in the car? Intuition? Doesn't matter. The result is the same."

She still didn't reach for her seat belt. "If it *is* them, we aren't going to be able to just drive past them unnoticed."

"We can try."

She shook her head. "You know we'd fail. Think about it. The road is too narrow to go past each other without slowing down. They'll see us before we get close, and all they'll have to do to make us stop is turn their car and block the road. We'll just trap ourselves."

He opened his mouth, then closed it. She was right.

He'd spent enough time on the side of this mountain to know it was a no-win situation.

Dammit.

What they hell were they supposed to do? There was nowhere to go but straight into the mountains, and the sedan was hardly the vehicle for cutting through the trees.

"The old tunnel," Jordynn said softly, answering his unspoken question.

"What about it?"

"We could park the car there, go through and use the hiking path to get down the mountain on foot."

He shook his head. "Too dangerous."

"More dangerous than getting caught?"

Donovan honestly wasn't sure. Ten years ago, he would've called the graffiti-covered tunnel hazardous. In fact, he was sure that even calling it a tunnel was an exaggeration. To be accurate, it was a partially dug project. A big hole in the hillside. Dynamite blasts had rendered the whole thing unstable, and the builders had abandoned it shortly after its beginnings, in favor of the bridge.

"C'mon," Jordynn urged, sounding impatient now. "What other option do we have? It's the perfect solution. We can go through the workers' exit at the back, head toward the upper parking lot, then see if we can get to one of the ATVs in the rescue station. And it has the added bonus of being a place only locals know about."

"That doesn't rule these guys out," he admitted.

"What do you mean?"

"Nothing. Just—" He stopped, rubbed his forehead, then tried again. "Trust me. These guys have enough local connections that they'll know about the tunnel."

Jordynn's brows knit together. "They're local? They didn't follow you from…wherever you came back from?"

"It's complicated, honey."

She looked unimpressed by the banal dismissal. "No kidding."

Donovan sighed, and his eyes slid past her to the overgrown bushes, seeking the path that led to the sign that announced the proposed development. His jaw clenched.

That damned sign...

No. He didn't have time to think about it right now. They'd already waited too long to make a decision.

"Dono?"

"Fine." His agreement was grim. "The tunnel."

At the very least, it would give them a head start.

He put the car into Reverse, then angled it to face the narrow, barely there path that led to the hollowed-out mountainside. The sedan bumped along unsteadily over the uneven terrain, protesting heavily at the abuse. Beside him, Jordynn gripped the sides of her seat and pressed her lips together.

Tough and stubborn as ever, Donovan thought.

He wished he could smile about it, but the tunnel was in view now, and it looked even worse than he remembered. A pile of crumbled stones blocked the entrance, and several wild-looking bushes had grown down from above, nearly masking the entrance.

Evidence of Mother Nature's attempt at reclamation.

Donovan slowed the car to a crawl, but Jordynn's soft hand landed on his forearm.

"We have to keep going," she said.

He sped up again, ignoring the unpleasant screech that came from below as rocks and sticks scraped the underside. He pushed down the pedal, forcing the tires to spin over the final crest, then lifted his foot and let the sedan coast to a stop inside the tunnel. The vine-like plants closed behind them, and they were immediately cloaked in darkness, and when Donovan cut the engine, the only sound was their synched inhales and exhales. Jordynn still held his arm, and he was keenly aware of the skin-to-skin heat. And loath to break it.

No choice.

He eased himself away and spoke at a near whisper. "Ready?"

"In a relative way. Yes."

"All right. Let's do this, then. Before the tunnel decides to collapse."

He eased open the door, wincing at the way it groaned loudly in the dark. Jordynn's exit was far less cautious. She swung the passenger side wide, then hopped out and scurried through the tunnel, disappearing into the blackness.

"You coming?" she called, her voice already sounding farther away than Donovan liked.

He squinted. "Yeah. Trying to. Where are you?"

"Look up."

He could just barely see her silhouette. She'd already stepped onto the steep path that would lead them to the other end of the unfinished tunnel. Then out and—hopefully—to safety. Donovan pushed himself to his feet and moved toward her. The going was slower than he liked, and he bumped his toes several times before he finally reached her side.

"Sorry," he said. "I seem to have left my night vision goggles elsewhere."

"Don't worry. I'll guide us. My sense of direction was always better than yours anyway."

"You think so?"

"I know so."

Then—unexpectedly—her hand snaked out to grasp his. Donovan fought an urge to use the contact to pull her closer, and made himself let her pull him along in the dark instead. For several minutes, they walked along wordlessly, her steps as sure as his were uncertain. She slowed once to guide him around a deep dip in the ground.

Finally, he broke the silence. "You really do remember the way."

"I remember a lot of things."

The statement seemed to have an edge to it—or maybe he just heard it that way—and it made Donovan want to spit out a long, stumbling apology. Before he could even start, though, she was already speaking again, her toner lighter.

"I'm not really surprised *you* don't remember the way through," she said.

"Why's that?"

"Because you were always afraid of the dark."

"Me? Afraid of the dark?"

There was a smile in her reply. "As I recall it, there was an incident. You. Me. A so-called demon."

"Ha, ha. That was one little misunderstanding. And in my defense, the dog was enormous. And evil."

"It was a Pomeranian."

"It bit me."

"I think it was trying to lick your face."

"Cut me some slack. I was eight."

"You were twelve."

Donovan grinned. "Either way. It was a long time ago."

"It was *all* a long time ago, now."

The edge was back, this time for sure, and Donovan's smile slipped. He knew a hard conversation was coming, and he wondered if it would be easier to have it now. Here, in the dark, where he didn't have to see the hurt on her face.

Coward.

He shoved down the self-directed insult. Apt or not, it wasn't constructive.

"Do you remember what I did when I thought that dog was a demon?" he asked. "When he came flying out that gate in the pitch black, snarling and slobbering, and dived straight at you?"

"You jumped in front of him."

"I jumped between him and you," Donovan corrected.

"Yes." The one-word acknowledgment was a wistful sigh.

"I didn't know it was a Pomeranian, honey." He shrugged even though he was sure she couldn't see it. "I'm not saying I really believed it was a demon, but the important thing is the intention behind it."

"To save me?"

"To *keep* you safe. To make sure you stayed out of the line of fire no matter what. It's the same reason I had to leave."

"The same reason you'd rather have me believe you were *dead*?"

He could hear the anguish, disbelief and anger in her voice, and he couldn't help but react defensively. "Yeah, Jordynn. That's the exact reason."

"Forgive me if I think that sounds insane."

She yanked her hand away and sped up. Donovan started to call her back, a yet again inadequate apology on his lip, then stopped as he realized he could see her again. At least a little. A thin beam of light illuminated the path just in front of the spot where she'd stopped.

They'd reached the other side of the tunnel—the part that had never been finished, and now simply sat in ruin.

"We've got a problem," Jordynn told him.

He inched closer, trying to see what she saw. The only

thing in view was a pile of rocks. Jordynn nodded her head toward them.

"That's it," she said.

"That's what?"

She shot him an exasperated look. "The problem. Those rocks used to be the part of the path that led out."

Donovan exhaled and stared up. "Damn."

He eyed the way back, opened his mouth to ask if she wanted to turn around, but slammed it shut again quickly. From the other end of the tunnel, the echo of angry voices carried through, loud and clear.

Chapter 6

For a panicked moment, Jordynn was sure they'd run out of luck.

If we even had any to begin with.

But in the minuscule amount of light, she could see that Dono had a familiar, stubborn look on his face. That same one he got every time he was backed into a corner. And sure enough, after he glanced around, then up, then around again, he offered her a short nod, then grabbed her hand and pulled her toward the rocks.

"I'm going to give you a boost," he said into her ear, his words hushed. "I can get you to the top of these rocks, then climb up behind you. You should be able to pull yourself onto what's left of the landing, then through the opening. If not, I'll give you another boost."

"What if *you* need a boost? I won't be strong enough to pull you up," she whispered back.

"I'm taller. I think I can manage from the top of the rocks."

"You *think* you can?"

"Jordynn."

He said her name like a warning. And she didn't like it.

"You can't just sacrifice yourself every time things aren't going smoothly!"

Dono leaned back, dark amusement playing across his features. "I can. So long as we're being hounded by a group of men who'd like to see us dead."

"That's the *only* thing that's been happening."

"Exactly."

Jordynn narrowed her eyes, but before she could form a retort, Dono bent down, grabbed her by the legs and lifted her into the air. She just barely managed to stifle a yelp.

"I want you to put your knee on my shoulder," he said, "then grab the most stable thing you can see and pull yourself up."

Jordynn bit back a comment about not seeing anything that looked even remotely stable and instead did as she was told. She didn't relish the idea of plummeting to a stony death, but it was far better than option B—getting caught by the men at the other end of the tunnel, who were now shouting about going back to find a flashlight. With her heart somehow simultaneously thundering in her chest and sticking to every inch of her throat, she reached out and grabbed ahold of some rock. And thankfully, the rock held.

"Good," Dono said. "Now stand on me."

"Stand *on* you?"

"Quickly."

She lifted her foot and placed it gingerly on his shoulder. Then, cringing a little, she pushed her weight down. He didn't even register the impact. But Jordynn couldn't take the time to be impressed. She just inhaled and clambered up the rocks.

She could feel Dono behind her, his hands occasionally bumping her as they climbed, his voice carrying up the odd encouragement. The going was short, but it was a strenuous, uphill climb, too. And by the time she reached the ledge near the exit, she wasn't aware of anything but the all-over burn of exertion and the wheezing in her lungs. When Jordynn pulled herself up to the narrow bit of flat dirt, she was practically seeing stars, and as Donovan's thick hands appeared near her feet, she could barely push back far enough to make room for him.

"Still alive?" he groaned as his body landed beside hers with a dull thud.

"So far," she breathed back.

"Was that the hard bit?"

"You tell me."

"I'd hate to say yes and make a liar of myself." He let out a chuckle. "Ready for the next bit?"

"No."

"Let's do it anyway."

"Ugh."

Donovan pushed to a crouch, rested there for a moment, his breaths hard and fast, then stood and offered her his hand. Jordynn took it, grateful for its steadiness. Without it, she probably would've just collapsed all over again. And once she was up, she saw that the source of limited light—their escape route—was only a few feet away. Which was good, because the voices in the tunnel were back, and she had no interest in finding out whether or not they'd managed to get themselves a flashlight.

Spurred by the renewed desire to get away, Jordynn moved forward. Then stopped. The opening was there, just around the small bend at the end of the ledge. But the formerly person-size exit was covered with stringy roots. She reached out with her free hand, and one little push told Jordynn it wasn't going to be pleasant to make their way through.

"No time to think it over," Dono said.

He pulled her into a protective embrace and held her close as he shoved through the root system, shielding her from the resulting spray of dirt. And in spite of the woody protest snapping against their forceful exit, he didn't stop moving until they were fully through the mess. Once on the other side, he finally released her. But he didn't stop moving. As Jordynn coughed and spat out bits of sappy, sticky dust, Dono grabbed every loose branch in sight and piled them in front of the opening. When he was done with that, he rolled an improbably large stone—almost a boulder—to cover his handiwork. Jordynn's eyes widened. But even then, he wasn't quite done. He kept going, pulling up several more biggish rocks and depositing them on top of the first one. Up and up, until the pile completely blocked the exit. And finally, with sweat rolling off his brow, he wiped his hands on his jeans and turned back to Jordynn.

Wordlessly, he grabbed her hand again and pulled her along once more.

They trekked out of the small clearing, up the overgrown trail and through woods until they hit the main path. Years ago, they'd hiked the area with relentless thoroughness. It, like the reinforced bridge, had become a place they'd thought of as their own. They knew it all. The best spots for camping, and the areas the seasonal tourists avoided. They'd been through storms and snow and heat waves on those trails. Jordynn thought it was safe to say that they'd learned every inch of the groomed routes. And memorized the not-so-well-maintained ones, too.

And as they moved, it appeared that not much had changed.

Which is why—maybe—when their quick pace soon brought them to a familiar lookout point, high on the hillside, Jordynn felt compelled to pull away. Because in spite of the appearance that it was otherwise, it wasn't true. Everything *had* changed.

Dono didn't seem to notice the downturn of her mind. "Need a second?"

Slowly, Jordynn shook her head. "Not a second."

He offered her a small, crooked smile. "A full minute?"

"Not that, either."

His smiled wavered. "What, then?"

"An explanation."

Now the smile was nonexistent. "Now's not the time, honey."

She fixed him with her own flat stare. "Because it won't ever be the time? Or because you know that if you wait another few seconds, something will interrupt us again? Or is it just that you're waiting until it's too late for there to *be* any time?"

"I already told you—"

"I know. You're just trying to protect me. Like always. But shouldn't that be up to me?"

"You want to choose whether or not I get to protect you?" Dono shook his head. "Sorry, Jordynn. I'm not willing to take the chance that you'll make the wrong decision."

She threw her hands up. "It's not your choice!"

"Right now, it is. Let's get moving."

"No."

"No?"

"Not until you tell me what's going on."

He shot her a disbelieving look. "Or what? You'll stay here and wait for them to dig their way through?"

She met his eyes and held her ground. "I don't know *you* any better than I know *them*, Dono. Ten years. That's long enough that anything could've happened. You could be married. Be a parent. Or be a criminal."

"I'm not any of those things."

"Maybe *I* am, then."

"Are you?"

"No! But that's not my point. It's only that you or I *could* be. That much time has passed. And even though my heart tells me going with you is the safest option, there's a little voice in my head that's telling me to slow down. It's ordering me to ask you questions and to demand answers before I even think about—" She cut herself off.

And he noticed. "About what?"

About admitting that I never stopped loving you, she thought.

But she refused to say it.

"About trusting you," she replied instead.

Hurt clouded Dono's eyes, but when he spoke, his voice was even. "Trust me or don't. Either way, you have no idea who we're dealing with."

"That's my whole point. I *don't* know who we're dealing with. Or why. And I want to trust you. I really want to. So give me something—anything—to tell me that I can."

"I can't do that."

"Please, Dono."

"I just can't."

Tears formed in her eyes, and try as she might, she couldn't stop them for the life of her. "Maybe the last ten years have been easier for you than they have for me, I don't know. But I can't handle this cluelessness any longer."

"You think this has been easy for me?"

"I said easi*er*."

"Hell, Jordynn—"

"You knew I was alive. You could have looked me up anytime you wanted. I thought you were dead. That made part of me die, too. So say whatever you want about how hard it was for you to go   there's no way it was harder than being here alone."

His face clouded, and he spun away and took a few steps closer to the path that would lead them down the mountain. And for a second, Jordynn thought he was simply going to leave her there. That he was just going to walk away. And be gone. Again.

Devastation washed over her. She wasn't sure she could survive going through the loss a second time. She started to call out to him. To admit defeat. But then he stopped and turned back, and her words dried up at the expression on his face. Yes, the hurt was still there. But resolution and determination had joined it And something else. A raw, dangerous emotion she couldn't name.

"Leaving was the hardest damned thing I've ever done, but I'd do it all over again. Because I have to protect you," he said roughly. "And I will, whether you like it or not."

And before she even had time to gasp, he was striding toward her. He closed the gap between them in a heartbeat, and he dragged her body flush against his. Jordynn couldn't resist the embrace. Couldn't pull away as he slammed his mouth into hers. And as nerves and adrenaline and relief mixed together, making her pulse race, she realized she didn't even want to. She needed the release. Needed the reassuring closeness. Needed what she'd been missing for the past ten years. *Him.*

Donovan parted Jordynn's lips with his tongue and claimed her mouth. *Re*claimed it. Because it had been his once, a decade earlier.

Mine.

He'd used the word to describe her all those years ago. Almost as often as he'd used the word *hers* to describe himself.

It had been so right. So fulfilling. A slowly built relationship, founded on that elusive trust she was asking for now.

God, I missed this.

He didn't realize he'd spoken the words aloud until she answered.

"Me, too, Dono."

He dragged his hands down to her waist, then lowered them to grip her hips. In a fluid motion—one he'd never quite been able to make as a younger man—he lifted her from the ground. Jordynn's legs came up to cling tightly to him as he carried her across the small clearing and pressed her to the wide trunk of one of the surrounding trees. Donovan kissed her harder. He drove his hips forward with matching fervor, making her cry out against his mouth.

For a second, he pulled back—just to reassure himself that he hadn't hurt her. Her eyes opened, though, and all he saw there was heat. Eagerness. A need that thoroughly matched his own.

She'd surrendered, her body giving in to his completely.

Good.

But as quickly as the self-satisfied thought came, Donovan realized it *wasn't* good. It wasn't what he wanted at all. He had no desire to kiss her into submission. What he craved was that partnership they'd formed, ten years earlier. That promise of a future.

The future you walked away from.

He drew in a ragged breath and forced himself to release her to the ground.

"Ask me something," he commanded.

Her eyes flew open again, and this time they were filled with confusion. "What?"

"Something specific. Before I change my mind about answering."

For a second, she stared up at him, the only sound her quick inhales and exhales. Then she frowned.

"That sign back there…" she said. "Why did it bother you?"

"The sign?"

Jordynn nodded. "The one by the bridge. When you saw it, you looked…worried."

"That's what you want to know?"

"We're being chased," Jordynn said. "Hunted. But your face was *green* back there when you were looking at the sign. So, yeah. I guess it *is* what I want to know."

It wasn't the question he'd been expecting, and maybe it wasn't even the one she'd intended to ask, but she was right. The sign *had* worried him.

And the reminder of its existence was like a splash of cold water. Donovan pulled away from Jordynn, his mind back on their current situation.

"What do you know about the proposed development?" he asked.

She shrugged. "The proposal came through a few years ago, when Fryer Development bought the little stretch of land by the bridge."

"They never followed through on it?"

"No."

"Why not?"

"Because they couldn't." She looked at the ground.

"Why not?" Donovan said again.

"You father wouldn't let them. He never released the site from police investigation."

"He never released the— God. They declared me dead."

"I know. But…"

"Closure," he filled in.

"Or the lack of it."

Donovan moved away from the trees to position himself in front of the wooden barrier at the edge of the lookout point. He stared out across the expanse of forest and hills, regretting the hell he'd put his father through as much as he regretted what he'd done to Jordynn.

So much hurt in the wake of my attempt to do just the opposite.

He exhaled and asked, "And now that my dad's gone?"

"Fryer Development petitioned to have the land released," she replied. "It took a while. Environmental impact studies and stuff. But it's got the go-ahead now. They want to start developing it next month."

Donovan swallowed. He was sure that developing the side of the mountain would literally unearth things that needed to stay buried.

"We should get going," he said.

"Does this mean you aren't going to answer my question about the sign?" she replied, seemingly immune to the urgency in Donovan's voice.

He shook his head. "It just means that I have to talk while we walk."

She cast a doubtful look his way, then bent down to do up her shoelace. Not that he could blame her. He'd been anything but forthcoming. Anything but worth believing. He opened his mouth to say as much, but as she stood, a thin gold chain slipped out from underneath her shirt, and the delicate ring hanging from it made his heart squeeze.

She followed his gaze, then tucked it in, and turned and moved toward the path that would lead them down to the parking lot.

Donovan stared after her for a second, then scrambled to catch up. "You kept it."

Her reply was soft. "Did you think I'd let it go?"

"I hoped you would." He shook his head, then corrected the lie. "I *wished* I could hope you would."

"I didn't."

"Do you remember the night I gave it to you?"

"Yes. You told me it was more than a promise ring. That it *was* a promise."

He recalled the sentimental, heartfelt claim well, and all the emotion that went along with it. "And the time capsule, two years later? Do you remember that, too?"

"How could I forget? We were supposed to open it in ten years. But you lost it before we could get around to burying it."

"Do you remember *how* I lost it?"

She flicked a puzzled frown in his direction. "Not really. I remember we had a fight about it, after."

Donovan almost laughed. He'd worked so hard to make sure she didn't know what had happened that night, but somehow knowing he'd succeeded felt like a letdown.

"The fight started before I lost the time capsule," he corrected.

Her frown deepened. "It did?"

Donovan nodded. "I saw a light out in the woods. You didn't see it, and you thought I was making it up to keep you out later."

Her face finally cleared. "And you insisted on going anyway, and I tried to walk home."

Regret hit him hard. How many times had he thought *if only...*? If only he'd listened to her, and simply gone home. If only he hadn't been so insistent about proving that he was right.

By now, they'd be married. Maybe—probably—have a couple of kids. She might've finished college like she'd wanted to, and he would've had more than "hiding out" and "running away" on his own resume.

"I wish I'd been a little less stubborn," he said now, his voice hoarse with emotion.

Jordynn's warm palm landed on his arm, then slid to his fingers, which she squeezed reassuringly. "I always admired your persistence."

He shook off the flattery, but held on to her hand. "Not about that, you shouldn't. If I'd been just a little less pig-headed, I wouldn't have seen what I did see that night. I would've just laughed it off and driven you home."

"I don't understand. You caught up with me, didn't you? I'd barely made it a mile down the road before you pulled up. And you told me you were wrong and sorry and—"

"I lied."

She tried to pull her hand away then, but he refused to let go.

"I lied," he said again. "Because the alternative was too hard to explain. I was scared as hell, and I didn't want to say something that would scare you, too. And by the time we got to the bottom of the hill, I'd decided telling you would just make things worse."

She stopped struggling. "Why, Dono? What did you see?"

He made himself say the words. "A man being murdered, honey, and carried off into the woods."

"You…" She trailed off, her face pale.

"I went into the woods, and I walked in the direction I thought I'd seen the light. And I found it. *Them.* Three men and a flashlight, out by the bog. I was so damned pleased with myself that I didn't notice what was happening until it was too late. One of them had a gun, and another was on his knees. The third one had the light. It was quick. A flash and a surprisingly small bang, and it was over. I think I yelled. Or maybe I just inhaled a little too loudly, who knows?" Donovan shrugged. "Doesn't matter which. The end result was that the man with the flashlight pointed it at me, just long enough to blind me. I never saw his face. But the other two… I could identify a victim. I could identify his killer. And I knew that wasn't good."

"What about telling your dad?"

"That's where it got even worse. It was the middle of the night, so I waited, even though I shouldn't have. But I was nineteen years old and I didn't know any better. I took you home to make sure you were safe, then went home myself, and went to bed. I didn't think I'd even be able to sleep. But I did. For almost sixteen hours. When I woke up, the sun was up, it was a gorgeous day and everything seemed so…normal. I was half convinced I'd imagined it all. Or maybe I just wished I had, and that was close enough. I stayed in my bed, thinking about it. Wondering if had been a dream. A nightmare. One so vivid I could recall the blank look on the dead man's face, and the cold expression of the man who shot him."

"I'm so sorry." Jordynn's statement was heartfelt, and her hand tightened on his even more.

"I think I'm the one who's supposed to be apologizing." Donovan managed a small smile. "Quit stealing my thunder."

She didn't smile back. "If I'd known what you were going through, I would've helped you."

"I wish you'd been able to." He let out a breath, recalling the next sequence of events. "Seeing the murder was terrifying. But finding the man who committed it sitting at the kitchen table with my father was far worse."

Chapter 7

For several minutes after the chilling statement, Donovan went silent. And Jordynn let him stay that way, not pressuring him to say anything further. Her own chest was burning, and not from the exertion of hiking. Her whole body hurt with sympathy for him. And understanding was creeping in, too. In spite of whatever she felt about losing him and everything that went along with discovering it had been a lie, Jordynn was having a harder and harder time finding fault with his decision to leave.

The burden he must've been under...

She could see it now, highlighted by the tightness of his jaw and the frown etched into his brow. It made her want to cry. To pull him close and reassure him. To just tell him things could go back to the way they'd left them, ten years ago.

Jordynn drew in a big pull of the mountain air, but the question that came out as she exhaled wasn't the one in her head. "What did you do, all this time?"

He glanced her way. "In what way?"

She lifted her shoulders, then dropped them. "I don't know. For work?"

"At first, anything I could do for cash. Washed dishes. Some construction stuff."

"Nothing in accounting?"

She remembered that had been his dream. She'd always teased him about it, unable to grasp why he loved numbers enough that he wanted to spend his life looking at them. Literature and history and science she loved. But math made her shudder.

He smiled. "Kind of. Eventually. For five years, I more or less wandered around, sticking to the bigger cities and avoiding Oregon altogether. I didn't want to come within five hundred miles of Ellisberg. But I kept wandering closer and closer, and finally settled in a town a few hours away. I met a guy in a pool hall—I was doing a bit of custodial work there—who said I looked like someone who needed a fresh start. Usually a comment like that meant it was time for me to move on, but he must've caught me at a low moment, because I challenged him to find me one. And he did. Carlos Hernandez was his name."

Jordynn listened intently as he went on, explaining how the stranger in the pool hall turned out to the one person who really could help him get on his feet. He hooked Dono up with a solid new identity. He helped him find a decent place to live. Not that the man was exactly an angel. His connections were shady at best, and the things he was involved in were illegal. But Dono told her that it was easy for him to turn a blind eye, because what the man did with those connections was nothing but good. His benefactor had dedicated his life to helping people—women and children, mostly—escape from domestic violence. He got them new names and new homes and whole new lives. And his day job—the one he put on paper—was no less noble. He ran a boxing club for underprivileged youth.

"Isn't that a bit backward?" Jordynn asked. "Funding antiviolence by using violence?"

Dono chuckled. "A bit, maybe. But most of the kids you find in the gym are in violent situations at home already. The boxing gives them a constructive outlet. And Carlos runs a hell of a tight ship. Hard to fault him for much of anything. He bought my bus ticket, no questions asked, on five minutes' notice."

Jordynn stole a sideways glance at Dono's now-relaxed face. A small part of her was almost jealous of the way that he spoke about Carlos Hernandez. And she was downright envious of the way the man had been able to help him when she hadn't even known he needed it. His genuinely affectionate smile as he finished telling the story didn't help, either.

"Of course, running a business like his is expensive," he said. "So when Carlos found out I was good with numbers, he gave me a job managing his books. I was glad to make a difference."

Abruptly, Jordynn stopped walking.

"What's wrong?" Dono asked right away, his expression still lacking the tension it had had since the second she laid eyes on him.

"Everything."

"Wh—"

She stepped forward, stood on her tiptoes and cut him off with a kiss. She made it gentle, but deliberate, too. She needed him to know she meant it, but she didn't want to get carried away in the moment. She lifted her arms and caressed the back of his neck, running her fingers over the bristly tendrils of hair there, then pulled away.

"I hate that you needed Carlos to get you a new life," she said softly. "I hate that he gave you what I couldn't."

"Jordynn…"

"I missed you, Dono. I tried so hard to let your memory go, and I never could."

He stared down at her, pain and warmth mingling in his gaze. "I'd take away the hurt if I could, honey."

Jordynn believed him. "Right now, I'd settle for getting off this mountain."

"Two more feet, then around that bend up there, and we'll be in the clear. At least for the moment."

She slipped her hand back into his, reassured by how right it felt to have him close. How good and normal. But minutes later, she was reminded that things were anything but okay. Because as they stepped into the parking lot, the first thing she saw was a bright red SUV. And the second was the man who leaned against it.

"Denny," she whispered.

From where they stood, she could see he looked far worse for wear than he had when they'd left him behind in the alley near her house. And that was saying something, considering that he'd been facedown in the gravel after just being hit by a car.

Now his cheeks were peppered with cuts. His pants were torn, and one of his boots had come undone. When he shifted, his expression became a grimace. Jordynn could see, also, that he had one arm wrapped in a sling, and the other tucked into his jacket. The pose seemed odd until she realized why he stood that way.

He must have a gun.

And like he could hear her thoughts, the beaten-down man swiveled their way. She tensed. But Dono was quick to react. Before Denny could possibly have seen them, he grabbed her elbow and dragged her out of view. He positioned them together on the other side of the huge trail map at the edge of the lot. And standing there—hiding— Jordynn realized something else, too. There was no getting around what was happening. They weren't on some sweet trip down memory lane; their lives were at stake, and until they did something about it, they'd be running, just like this.

"We need to find a way to get past him," Dono told her in a low voice. "The rescue station's on the other side of his damned truck, and we can't chance trying to get back to the path we just came off. He's definitely watching it. Maybe we can circle back and make our way around to the other path. The one that comes down over there on the other side."

"Maybe."

"Sit tight for a second while I see if there's a break in these trees up here."

But Jordynn didn't have any interest in sitting tight. Or in sneaking around. *They* were the good guys. *They* deserved to come out on top.

So as Dono stepped up to assess the terrain behind them—muttering to himself about safety and time—she decided to take matters into her own hands.

Matters…and a weapon, she thought, surveying the ground.

Immediately, she spied what she wanted. A large stick, narrow on one end and thick on the other. A perfect club. She snapped it up and slunk along the edge of the trees, her eye on Denny and her mind on his visibly weakened state.

Satisfied that they could push through the forest and get back onto the path, Donovan stepped down from the tree line. And found the spot behind the sign empty.

What the hell?

He turned back to the woods. Nothing. He took a breath and pressed himself against the map, then inched around to scan the parking lot, willing her not to be there. The only things in sight were the big thug—Denny, was it?—and his truck.

What the extra *hell?*

Donovan forced himself to stay as calm as possible. Slowly, he leaned out again. He ran his eyes over the area, taking it in, foot by careful foot.

Then a flash of movement caught his attention, and his heart rate tripled. It was Jordynn—moving quietly but steadily toward Denny with a determined look on her face.

Donovan's gut and jaw clenched simultaneously as she took another step, and he spotted what she had in her hands. A tree branch. Even factoring in the element of surprise, it would be useless against the gun undoubtedly hidden inside the thug's dirty coat. The man wouldn't be afraid to use it, either.

"What're you thinking, Jordynn?" Donovan muttered, running a hand over his hair, then tugging on his ear.

And more important…how can I stop you from doing it and likely getting yourself killed?

His eyes stayed glued to her stealthy form for a single second longer.

He could only think of one way.

With a wild yell, he leaped out into the parking lot.

Denny spun, his arm moving into his jacket as he did. Donovan knew he was going for the gun, and he readied himself to tuck and roll. But the other man didn't get any further than drawing it halfway out. Jordynn was already on him, her body twisting with the effort of lifting the branch. She swung it with surprising force, though, and it hit Denny in the back of the knees. The man's legs buckled and he landed hard, letting out a yell that was one part fury, one part pain. The gun fell from his grasp and landed on the ground a few feet out of his reach.

Donovan let out a relieved breath, but the other man wasn't ready to give up. He threw himself toward the weapon.

"Dammit!" Donovan spat.

He bolted forward to grab the gun himself, but Jordynn was still closer, and quicker again. She took a second swing, this time at the man's shoulders. Denny bellowed a string of curses as he collapsed forward. He stayed down this time, breathing heavily and groaning a little.

As Jordynn raised the club and took aim again, Donovan reached her side. He tried to grab her arm, but she yanked herself away, her grip on the wood so tight that her knuckles had gone white.

"Don't," he said.

She looked at him, her eyes a little wild. "We have to *stop* them."

"We will," Donovan assured her. "But you don't want to do it like that."

Her chest rose and fell heavily, and she shook her head, but after a moment, her hands dropped to her sides and her weapon fell.

"You good?" he asked.

"Yes."

"You promise not to pick up that stick again?"

"Yes. Well. Unless he tries to hurt you."

"Guess that'll do." Donovan turned his attention to the man on the ground, crouching down to roll him over. "Hello, Denny. Do you happen to have anything useful to share with me about your employer's intentions? Or for that matter…who's actually in charge?"

The thug groaned, opened his eyes groggily and spat out a reply. "Go to hell."

"And if I threaten you?"

"With what? No threat'll match up to what'll happen to me if I tell you a single thing."

"That's about what I thought," Donovan said evenly.

"You're both dead anyway."

"Not yet, we're not."

Denny gurgled a laugh. "Might as well start counting your minutes."

Donovan could tell the conversation wasn't going to go anywhere. He glanced at Jordynn.

"Look away, honey."

"What?"

"Look away."

"Why?"

"Please."

She inhaled, then complied, turning her body around completely. Quickly—so as not to give her a chance to look back and see what he was about to do—Donovan drew back his fist and delivered a perfectly placed punch to the side of Denny's chin. The other man didn't even make a sound. His head just lolled to one side, and the rest of him slumped to the ground.

Right away, Donovan dug through the man's pockets for the keys to the SUV. As he stood, he saw that Jordynn had turned to face him. Her gaze flicked from him to the unconscious man, then back again.

"Sorry, honey," he said right away.

She shook her head dismissively. "Don't be. But…you did the same thing with the guy—the Nose—when he attacked me at my house."

"You weren't supposed to be watching."

"I didn't have to be watching to hear it."

Donovan cringed. "Sorry. Again."

She shook her head a second time. "Seriously. Don't be. You're good at it."

He didn't take the observation as a compliment. How could he? There sure as hell wasn't anything wonderful about being "good" at sending another man into oblivion.

"Boxing with Carlos," he said, his tone as neutral as he could manage. "Picked up some techniques at his gym. Mostly the ones that could save my life. Solitary knock-out punch works well."

"It seems to," she agreed, her eyes finding Denny once more. "Are you just going to leave him there?"

"I'll drag him out of view, but yeah. Unless you want to take him with us?"

Her blue eyes widened. "What? No! I just…"

"Just what?"

"Nothing, I guess."

Donovan stepped toward her, then reached out to tuck a piece of loose hair back behind her ear and said firmly, "This is the way it has to be. His guys'll come looking for him. Trust me. They keep tabs on their hired help."

She hesitated, then nodded. "Okay."

Donovan gave her a quick kiss, opened the SUV for her to climb into, then got to business.

Unfortunately, it was harder than he expected. The big man was dead weight, and not easy to move. Donovan grunted with the exertion of trying to do it, his body protesting heartily against the effort. Worse than that, he could feel Jordynn's eyes on him as he worked. What was she thinking? Was she wondering exactly who he'd become and speculating on how he could be so callous? Or regretting her confession that she'd held so tightly to his memory all these years? He couldn't stand the idea of her believing he was anything like the man he currently had by the feet.

He gave Denny a final tug, then stepped back and surveyed his handiwork. From any farther away than two feet, his big form would be invisible.

Perfect.

He swung toward the SUV and caught sight of Jordynn's pinched expression. Even from where he stood, he could see the conflicting emotions run across her pretty face, and he understood. She'd been ready to pummel the man with a club a few minutes earlier. Now she felt guilty about leaving him behind. To her, the world was still black-and-white. Good versus bad.

But Donovan was well acquainted with the gray.

Too well acquainted, he acknowledged.

With a frustrated sigh, he made his way back to the vehicle, let himself in, then turned over the engine and guided them out of the parking lot wordlessly.

Jordynn, though, wasn't interested in silence, and just as Donovan thought, her mind was on the well-being of the man who he'd just dumped in a ditch.

"Will he be okay?" she asked.

"He'll wake up with a bad headache," Donovan replied through clenched teeth. "Just in time to find out that his friends are searching for him."

"What if they don't come? Or someone else finds him first and calls the police?"

"The former is unlikely. Reliable, loyal gunmen are hard to find. And the latter…well. That won't be our problem. He's sure as hell not going to tell anything to the cops."

"Not even if he paints himself as the victim?"

There was the little rub. "You think he could play a role convincingly?"

"We *did* hurt him."

"Self-defense. Unequivocally."

"We jumped him in a parking lot. I hit him with a tree branch."

"Jordynn…the man had a gun and would've been more than happy to use it. He stuffed you in a trunk earlier. So I don't think we'd have a problem convincing the police we were in the right."

"No. I mean. It's not that hitting him was a problem."

"What, then?"

He sensed a brief hesitation before her next question, which came out in a rush. "Have you ever killed someone, Dono?"

He had to work at not being offended. "No."

"Not by accident? Or in self-defense?"

"What the— No. I've never killed anyone. Period."

"What if I did?"

He whipped his head toward her and for a second lost his grip on the steering wheel. "What?"

She appeared unfazed by the way the car careened sideways before Donovan regained control. "What if I accidentally killed someone? Or did it in self-defense?"

"Why the hell would that happen?"

"Because we're being chased by men who want to kill *us*. And I don't want to die. I don't want you to die. So. Can you teach me?"

"Teach you what?"

"To hit like you do?"

He almost laughed—but a quick glance at her face told him she was utterly serious. "I'd rather not."

"You said it could save your life."

"And it could."

"What if my life needs to be saved?"

"You have me."

He saw the way her eyes clouded, and he knew she had to be wondering if she could truly count on him. His chest squeezed. But then she spoke, and Donovan realized that his assumption about her feelings was way off.

"It's not that I think I'm totally defenseless," she said. "But I can't be *helpful*, either."

Donovan felt his jaw twitch with a surprised laugh, and he forced it down. "You can't be...helpful?"

Seeming not to notice his amusement, she issued a single nod. "You can't be with me every second of every day."

"I can try."

"Realistically."

"I can *realistically* try."

She went silent for a long minute, staring out the windshield pensively, then finally said, "I might've killed Denny, back there. Not because I wanted to, but because I thought hitting him in the head would stop him. Who knows if he would've lived or not?"

"I wouldn't have let that happen," Donovan replied.

"That's exactly my point. *I* want to be the one to stop it from happening."

He tapped his fingers on the wheel, unable to think of a truly good reason to argue against teaching her a bit of self-defense. Aside from his own need to guard her like a porcelain doll. Which she clearly wasn't.

"All right," he said. "I'll give you a few pointers on how *not* to kill a man accidentally."

"Thank you."

Another quick look told Donovan his agreement had made her happy. As she leaned sideways and pressed her cheek to the passenger-side window, a little curve turned up lips, and her blue eyes nearly sparkled. Damn, how he liked making her smile. Liked doing anything that would elicit a bit of joy. For a second, it was almost enough to make him forget the dark reason for her pleased expression.

Then the SUV jostled him, and the gun he'd snapped up from the ground dug into his side, reminding him all too well that there was nothing enjoyable about being the reason a woman needed to learn to protect herself.

He tossed her another glance. She'd rested her head on the window and closed her eyes, but the tension in her forehead was back already.

Damn.

Donovan opened his mouth, then closed it without saying a word. He brought his attention to the road and tried desperately to find a way to make it so she'd never have to think about throwing a knockout punch ever again.

Chapter 8

The sound of water hitting glass dragged Jordynn back into consciousness.

Rain, she thought, and it made her reluctant to open her eyes.

She tucked her chin into the blanket and sighed, trying to hold on to the crazy dream she'd been so immersed in. She was with Dono. They were being chased. He was driving, and the car was full of his alluring scent, the one that made her want to— She sat bolt upright, cutting her thoughts off.

"Not a dream," she said.

And though Dono's scent definitely still filled her senses, she *also* definitely wasn't in the car anymore. She blinked, trying to clear away the sleep that crowded her brain.

She was in a bedroom she didn't recognize, bundled in a cushy duvet that was crisp enough to feel brand-new, and seated on a firm, king-size bed.

She fought to recall how she got there, but her mind refused to cooperate.

"Dono?" she called softly.

He didn't answer, and a quick survey of the room told her he definitely wasn't in it. The decor was bare-bones—a simple nightstand and a single dresser, with no sign of any personal items.

Strange.

Where was she? A friend of Dono's? She couldn't imagine that he'd held on to any in Ellisberg. So what did that mean? Breaking and entering?

Jordynn swung her legs sideways, pressing her bare feet to the cool ground.

Bare feet?

She glanced down and saw that yes, her feet had been stripped of their shoes and socks. She wriggled her toes, then stood and stretched, and realized she could still hear the slap of water on glass. But when her eyes drifted to the window, she couldn't see any evidence of rain. The sky was dim. But clear. How long had she been asleep?

"Dono?" she called again, this time a little louder.

Still no answer. So she moved across the room to flick on the light. Then paused, her hand halfway to the switch, as her eyes landed on a slightly ajar door on the other side of the room. The rainy sound was coming from inside. And then Jordynn recognized it for what it actually was.

A shower.

She abandoned the light switch in favor of the bathroom. She placed her hand on the door, and pushed, telling herself she just wanted to make sure it was him.

"Dono?" she said a third time. "Is that—"

Her words dried up in her throat. Because it *was* him. One hand lifted high, clinging to the showerhead, the other pressed sideways against the marble wall as the water beat down on his body. And he was breathlessly perfect. Hard, and wide, and marked with evidence of suffering in the form of scars. Ten years ago, Dono had been leanly muscular, his frame attractive, and not boyish, but not like...this.

Jordynn swallowed. She couldn't tear her eyes away, even though she knew she ought to.

Helpless to stop herself, she traced the line of him. Strong, solid-looking feet. Defined calves. Thighs made for running. A rock-hard rear end that led up to a well-cut back, then a set of shoulders that spanned the shower stall.

And as Jordynn stood there staring, he shut off the water, then turned slowly. Like he could feel her eyes on him. And in spite of the way her face burned with the embarrassment of being caught, she *still* couldn't stop.

His strong jaw, peppered now with day-old stubble.

His Adam's apple. Moving up. Then down.

His chest.

His pectoral muscle, his abs, his—

Jordynn drew in a sharp breath.

A red slash, just below Dono's rib cage, glared angrily up at her. He followed her gaze, lifting his hand to cover the cut for a second before he swung open the glass door and snapped up a towel from the rack.

"You okay?" he asked as he wrapped himself up.

"I'm fine," Jordynn said. "But *you're* hurt."

"It's not bad."

"It's not good. Let me look."

She pulled him from the bathroom into the bedroom, turning on the light as she moved past it, then positioned Dono beside the bed and sank down to the mattress so she was at eye level with the wound.

"When did it happen?" he asked.

"Sometime between punching the Nose and…well, punching the Nose."

Jordynn looked up sharply. "You had this the whole time?"

"*Most* of the whole time."

"Why didn't you say something?"

"I'm not sure we actually had a good moment for me to bust in with, 'Hey, honey? You remember the Nose? Yeah? Well. He poked me a little with his small knife. And no, I'm not sure whether or not that's a direct parallel for the rest of him.'"

She covered her sharp inhale under the guise of leaning in more closely. "Not funny."

"You sure about that?"

"As a matter of fact, yes, I *am* sure." She gently probed the edges of the cut with her fingers. "Does this hurt?"

His abdominal muscles tightened under her touch. "No."

"Lying about it won't help."

Dono sighed. "It stings. A bit."

She leaned closer. The edges of the cut were a little jagged, but it wasn't deep. She leaned back and let out a relieved breath.

"I think you got lucky," she said. "But even if it doesn't need stitches, it should still be disinfected. We should grab some alcohol wipes and some bandages."

"Gonna be hard-pressed to find either of those in here."

She frowned, remembering that she had no clue where "here" was. "What do you mean?"

He eased down to the bed. "Shove over."

She did, and Dono lifted his thickly muscular legs onto the bed, then laid his head back on the headboard.

The towel slid sideways, exposing a significant amount of thigh.

Jordynn fought to keep from jumping up and drawing attention to the fact that she'd even noticed, and forced her eyes to stay on his face as he explained.

"A first aid kit probably isn't on the list of the recommended decorations in a show home."

"A show home?" It explained the lack of personality, anyway.

Dono nodded. "One of the final ones in Glenn Ridge. Marble tubs and heated floors and no Band-Aids. When I commit a B and E, I do it with style."

"Seriously. You're not funny."

He grinned. "I'm a little bit funny."

She shook her head, her eyes drifting to his torso and the wound. "Would you think it was funny if the roles were reversed? If I got stabbed trying to save you?"

His smile fell away. "No."

"So stop making jokes. You're hurt, and it's because of me."

She tried to stand, but Dono sat up quickly, one of his rough hands landing on the inside of her elbow and pulling her back down. Then both his palms came up to cup her face.

"Honey, I'm not hurt because of you," he said. "I'm hurt because of what that son of a you-know-what, Ivan, did ten years ago. I'm hurt because of how I dealt with things when I was nineteen years old and too stupid to think of a better way."

"But you did those things because of *me*," Jordynn pointed out, her voice small.

"You're wrong about that, too. I did it because of *me*. I couldn't stand the thought of losing you." He ran his thumb over her cheekbone, then dropped his hands to his lap. "I put you through hell so I could know you'd keep living. And I'm so sorry for what I did to you. I'd take a thousand jabs of the Nose's knife as punishment if I could."

She could hear the fierce honesty in his words, and it scared her. "Promise me you won't."

"I won't lie to you."

She reached for his hands, grasped them both and pulled them to her heart. "I don't want you to lie. I want you to promise and mean it. You can't let yourself get hurt because you think you deserve it. You *don't* deserve it."

He stared back at her, his eyes burning with a desire to trust her words. But tinged with self-doubt, too. And suddenly she wanted to hear it all. She wanted to know what he'd experienced so she could try to understand what made him choose the path he did, even though it had clearly scarred him. *Continued* to scar him.

"Tell me," Jordynn said softly.

"Tell you?"

"The rest of the story. About what happened when you found Ivan at your dad's house."

"You don't want to hear it, honey."

"I don't want to hear it? Or you don't want to tell me?"

Then he took a breath. He nodded. And he started to talk.

"I came downstairs that afternoon, knowing my dad had worked the overnight shift the day before. He was pretty big on routine, so I expected to find him at the table with his coffee and his paper. Decaf, always. And the comics before the news," Donovan said, trying to sound lighter than he felt. "And he *was* there."

"But not alone," Jordynn filled in.

"No. And I was speechless. My dad served lunch. He

poured the other man coffee, and introduced him as Ivan Lightfoot. A rep for a real estate development company."

As he spoke, he closed his eyes. He couldn't help but acknowledge that Jordynn was right. He would rather have discussed about almost anything else. His father's death. The first hungry days he spent in the street. Even the ache he'd felt when he was sure he'd never see her again. Recalling the past aloud gave it a power he didn't want it to have. It turned him into his young, scared self. A man he'd rather not go back to being. After all, that younger version of himself was the one who'd left her behind. The one who hadn't been able to find another way out.

God, how he hated that he'd had to do it.

Jordynn squeezed his hand then, and he opened his eyes again. He reached out and dragged her close, and thankfully, she didn't pull away. Instead, she just settled comfortingly against his chest.

"Was it Fryer?" she asked. "The development company Ivan was representing?"

"No. He said he was from the Haven Corporation. The one you said built everything around here."

"Including this community we're in now," she pointed out.

"Yep. Glenn Ridge. Four Tops. That big apartment building where the ball field used to be… I'm pretty sure they wanted the mountainside, too. A project that would bring in millions—a lot of millions—and take ten years to complete."

He heard her draw in a sharp breath. "So the building started the year you left."

"That's right."

"But Haven didn't get the mountainside. Fryer won

the bid." She tipped her head to look up at him. "Is that why the sign back there bothered you?"

"Could be," he agreed, thinking about it.

Why *had* Haven let Greyside go? Who were Fryer Developments? Were they involved, or was it just a co-incidence?

Donovan shook his head to clear it, and went on. "But of course… I didn't know anything about the developments while I sat and ate with my dad and Ivan. It was surreal. Ivan gave no sign that he knew me, and my dad sure as hell had no clue what I'd seen the guy do in the woods. Dad was excited, because the Haven Corporation had picked him to show their spokesman—Ivan, who said he was their head of security—around Ellisberg. They wanted someone who'd been born and raised here to lead the so-called tour. Someone who was in a position of authority, but who was also a familiar face to the locals. He was so damned pleased about it."

Jordynn pulled away, then repositioned herself so she was facing him. "You decided not to tell him because of that?"

Donovan shook his head. "No. I mean, I knew Dad wouldn't be pleased to hear me accusing his new friend of being a killer. You know how much friction there was between us after my mom died. I never seemed to be able to please him. And it wasn't like I could just blurt it out while the guy was sitting there, stuffing his face with my favorite casserole. But you remember my dad…"

"Cop first, dad second, everything else last."

"Exactly." He offered her a small smile. "Not always my favorite priority list, but true nonetheless."

"And you knew it meant he'd want to hear the truth."

"I had to wait for Ivan to leave before I said anything, and I could barely choke down the food with Ivan there anyway, so I excused myself as quickly as I could get away with. But before I could even get through my bedroom door, someone jammed a gag into my mouth and tossed a hood over my head." He paused. "Sound familiar?"

When she nodded, he went on.

"They dragged me out of the house—right under my dad's nose—and threw me in a car, then drove me out to the woods. We went back to the exact spot where the man had been killed the night before, and they beat me with a baseball bat. Chest and stomach only. Nothing broken, and nothing anyone would notice." He touched his abdomen in remembered pain.

"No one but me," Jordynn corrected, her eyes widening with sudden understanding. "Strep throat. You said you were sick and missed ten days of work and refused to let me visit."

"I couldn't take a chance you'd see my injuries and ask questions."

"I would've lost it." She frowned. "But when you were talking to Ivan, you said he *did* break some bones. And left you for dead."

Donovan covered a cringe, wishing he hadn't let that slip. He slid his finger over her bottom lip, then dropped his hand to his lap and shrugged.

"That came later. A different part of the story," he said casually. "But right then…those two men held me there for hours, waiting for Ivan. When he finally showed up, he was calm, which scared me more than the beating did. He said the only thing stopping him from killing me right that second was his worry that it would jeopardize their development projects. Apparently, my life was worth saving…in exchange for millions of dollars in profit, of course. He told me if I breathed a word of what I'd seen, he'd make me suffer. He'd ensure that the murdered man's death was traced back to me."

Donovan closed his eyes for another moment, recalling the dead-serious look in Ivan's eyes. The coldness. The total lack of doubt.

"Dono?"

He found her hand by touch and held it tightly, lingering there, using the feel of her to steady his mind, then pulled back and opened his eyes. "I believed him, honey. Every word. And Ivan made sure I didn't forget. Over those ten days I spent recovering from the bruises, he came by four times. Brought me soup. I was afraid to eat it because I assumed it might be poisoned. I thought I was going crazy. But that was just the beginning. I went back to my regular life. Or tried to, for a few weeks anyway. I showed up at the office, and so did an unmarked car. I took you out for dinner. The car waited outside. I was so on edge."

And that still *wasn't the worst of it*, Donovan thought.

But there were things she didn't need to know about. Not then. Not ever, if he could help it.

"I tried to send you away," he reminded her, skipping over the scariest bit. "I brought you the college application."

"You said we should change our plans. I should give up the idea of working and saving money, and you'd follow me in a few months."

"It broke my heart, because you thought I was trying to get rid of you. Trying to get some space. It was the last thing I wanted." Donovan tugged his ear. "I feel like I have so many things to be sorry for, honey. I just don't even know where to start."

"You don't have to."

He sucked in a breath. It was almost worse that she was

so willing to forgive him. The idea that it would be so simple for her—that she would accept it all so easily—made him feel even guiltier.

"I owe you ten years," he said roughly. "You can't possibly just let all that time go because I said *sorry*."

"What do you want me to do, Dono? Yell and scream and tell you I hate you for making me hurt?"

"It would be better," he muttered. "Or at least make a little more sense."

She stared at him intently, then placed her hand on his cheek. "I'm so angry that it hurts. Those years you owe me… I can't get them back, and you can't undo them. But if we want to get through this, Dono, we can't sit around being mad about the past. We have to be constructive."

Her statement reminded him why he'd brought her to this spot in the first place.

"That's the reason we're here in this house, in this community," he said.

"What do you mean?"

He jumped up, strode across the room and tipped open the blinds so he could tap on the window. "Right there, Jordynn. I think the answers I need are in that little building on the hill."

Chapter 9

Jordynn's brain had to work hard to catch up with what Dono had just said, because she was too busy being distracted by the fact that he was standing at the window almost completely naked, all his rough edges on display. He seemed unconscious of his own exposure, and of the effect it was having on her.

But there was no denying the way her heart stuttered in her chest as she noted another scar, just below his left shoulder blade. How had he received it? She wanted to know. Wanted to hear every story.

It had always been like that with Dono—just when she was sure she knew him as well as she knew herself, something else would leap out and grab her. Make her need him all the more. She was pleasantly reminded of that fact as she let her eyes slide over him.

"Jordynn?" he prompted.

She blushed, then stood up and joined him at the window. She could feel the heat of his body, even though there were a few inches between them. It drew her in, and she had to force herself not to close those inches as she followed the direction his finger pointed.

Her gaze landed on a squat building at the edge of the property.

"What is it?" she asked.

"It's the only thing the Haven Corporation brought with them when they decided to start their project. A portable office. From there, the foreman can oversee the building as it unfolds. And Ivan can keep an eye on everything else."

"Don't lots of constructions sites have them?"

"Yep. But this is—literally—the only office they own," Dono said. "The Haven Corporation doesn't have a place in a big building somewhere. They don't have a publicly listed CEO, or CFO, or any corporate bank accounts. But they buy and sell billions of dollars' worth of property. So where are they keeping their records?"

Jordynn stared at the beige structure again. It looked ready to fall apart. Even from where they stood, she could see the rust, spreading out from the bolts and threatening to overtake the whole thing.

"You think they're keeping them *there*?" She couldn't keep the disbelief from her voice.

"They have to be somewhere, either in a computer or in a filing cabinet… No way does a company with that kind of buying power *not* keep tabs on its money."

Jordynn pursed her lips thoughtfully. "Couldn't they just be holding it at someone's house?"

Dono shook his head. "I've had ten years to think this over. Whose house? Who would be willing to be culpable? Not whoever is in charge, that's for sure. And they wouldn't be able to trust anyone else."

She met his sure gaze. Clearly, he *had* had time to consider every angle. And had done so thoroughly.

"So what now?" she asked.

"I'm sure there's a connection between the murder and the Haven Corporation. One that can be used to prove what I saw. I've tried, over the years, to find one. But aside from the fact that they like to tear old things down and build new things up…" He shrugged. "I've got nothing."

"And you think that if we walk into that makeshift office, we'll find something."

"Exactly. Except for the part about *we*. I'm going in alone."

"While I do what? Sit here and twiddle my thumbs? I don't think so, Dono."

He shot her a level glare. "I'm not willing to negotiate."

"Because you'd rather be a martyr?"

"I'm not going to get killed."

"Can you guarantee me that?"

"It's something I'm definitely going to avoid."

"Not good enough."

"It's the best I can do."

Jordynn lifted her chin. "Then I'm coming with you."

Dono shook his head. "You're not."

"I am."

"I'll tie you to the bed if I have to."

Her face warmed. "That's exactly what you'll have to do."

He sighed. "Be reasonable. If we break into the office together, and something goes wrong, who will come to our rescue?"

"Does that mean you're giving me the go-ahead to rescue you?"

"In the unlikely event that I need rescuing...I'll leave you the gun and you can fire from up here."

"Even if I stood a hope in hell of actually hitting something, *you* might need the gun."

He let out another sigh, louder than the first. "Can you *try* to make this easier?"

"If you wanted easy, you shouldn't have got on the bad side of some criminal mastermind."

"Hilarious." He grabbed her elbows and spun her to face the window, then positioned himself behind her and pointed again. "I'm going to climb up the back of the hill there. The only way someone could see me is if they were in this exact spot. And since you're the only one here, I think I'll be safe until that point. When I get to the side of the building, I'm going to climb that little ramp there. I'll be visible from the road, but I'll also be able to see anyone coming in before they see me. If I even *think* someone's coming, I'll make a quick exit. If not, I'll pick the lock, get in and get out. If *you* happen to see someone coming while I'm inside, twist the blinds closed, and I'll know. I'll check every thirty seconds or so to make sure you still have them open."

He'd clearly spent time thinking this plan over, as well. Which probably meant he was right, too.

That doesn't mean I have to like it.

But if they wanted to get to the bottom of what had happened, what other choice did they have? Unless...

"Ivan said his boss wanted to talk to us," she said.

Dono met her gaze. "Nothing more than a euphemism."

She didn't have to ask what it was that Ivan felt needed to be glossed over. She shivered.

"So maybe we could just run."

"Run?"

She nodded. "Like you did before. But…together."

He stared her, his hazel eyes considering. Was he picturing it, she wondered? Seeing the two of them, living together on the road. City to city. Living a nameless life. Jordynn could almost imagine it herself.

Then, without warning, he leaned down and pressed his mouth to hers. Long and deep.

Jordynn could feel an outpouring of love and hope in the kiss, and it made her burn for this to be over. To give themselves a fighting chance at going back to being *them*.

But when he pulled away, it was with another sigh. "We'd never have any peace, honey. Trust me on this one. Even when they thought I was dead, I never really stopped looking over my shoulder. It's rough and hard and every moment is a struggle. There's no settling down, no roots. I don't want that life. Not for either of us."

It was Jordynn's turn to let out a breath. "No. I guess I don't want that, either."

He gave her another soft kiss, then spoke against her lips. "I should go now. The quicker, the better."

She knew it was true, but as he released her to move toward the bathroom, she couldn't stop herself from wanting him to stay—at least for another minute or two. The need to keep him there was a physical ache.

"Wait," she said.

He paused in the center of the room and turned back to face her, too far and too close at the same time. "For?"

"The self-defense pointers," she said, her voice not quite steady.

"Now?"

She nodded. "Yes."

The corner of Dono's mouth tipped up. "Lesson one. Don't get near the enemy when he's practically naked."

"I'll try to keep that in mind."

But now that he'd drawn attention to it again, she couldn't keep her eyes from traveling the length of his body. From appreciating the raw masculinity of his form. From drinking it in and trying to sear it forever in her mind.

And her amusement dried up as she realized *why* she was desperate to keep him from leaving. The thought of letting him leave the house without her—even losing sight of him for a moment—filled her with a fear that she'd never see him again. For the second time.

"Jordynn?"

The soft, concerned way he said her name made unwanted tears form in her eyes. Self-consciously, she reached up and brushed them away, hoping he wouldn't notice. But it was too late. In spite of the way she fought to keep them in check, they spilled onto her cheeks. Immediately, Dono strode toward her, then engulfed her in a secure hug. And for several moments, Jordynn was happy to just enjoy how safe and right she felt, pressed into his arms. But it was impossible not to notice that there was more to their closeness than just a need for comfort.

His wide, bare chest was pressed to the thin material of her T-shirt, making the sensitive skin underneath tingle. His abs were rock hard against the soft slope of her own stomach. And below that...

Jordynn swallowed.

There was the towel.

Nothing *but* the towel.

Dono ran his knuckles over her back, then swept her hair to one side and placed a trail of kisses along her shoulder. Then he shifted, and the towel might as well have been air. There was no doubt about where his body's interest lay.

As his hardness pressed into her jeans, his mouth

moved up her throat to find her lips again. His hands were still going, too. Through her hair and along her throat and down her shoulders, they kneaded and stroked, bringing Jordynn's insides to life. She could feel her own need rising, increasing with each *thump-thud-thump* of her heart.

And just when she thought they wouldn't be able to turn back, Dono pulled back, and lifted her chin to look into her eyes. He let her go, and Jordynn couldn't say whether she was relieved or disappointed.

"Okay." His voice was thick, and barely controlled. "*Real* self-defense lesson number one. Strike where it's going to hurt most."

Before she could stop herself, Jordynn glanced down. "Um."

Dono chuckled. "Yes. There."

"Oh."

"If you don't want the lessons…"

"No. I do. You'll be gone. I might need to protect myself."

His face darkened—as if the fact that him being alone also meant *she* would be alone just registered. "You need to keep the gun."

"I can't even *fire* a gun."

"I can teach you."

"Accurately? In less time than you can teach me where to kick?"

He looked like he wanted to argue, but he just shook his head. "Don't just use your feet. You can also go for the throat or eyes. That'll work, too. When you're hitting, stick with an open hand. Use the base of your palm for force, or your nails if you want to add a little bite."

"Is that how you'd do it?" she countered. "By fighting like a girl?"

"That's an insult to girls everywhere." He grinned, but

his expression sobered quickly. "Seriously, though. You need to be able to pull off these moves under stress. You'll want to lash out, so you have to harness that. Martial arts or competitive fighting is a whole other ball game. They each take years of training. But a knee in the groin or an elbow in the gut is going to help you right away."

"Like this?"

Jordynn stepped toward him and did a series of moves, miming each of his suggestions. She got through the knee. Then the feigned eye scratch. And even the flat-palmed blow to the chin. But when she spun to deliver the fake elbow, her feet got tangled in a sheet at the foot of the bed. She tried to stop, but momentum got the better of her, and her arm flung backward to hit Dono smack in the gut. For real. He let out a groan, and Jordynn sputtered an apology.

"Oh, my God, I'm so—" Her words cut off as Dono grabbed her hand and spun her around. "What are you— Oh!"

He twisted again, then tossed her onto the bed, gripped her wrists and immobilized her. "Lesson two. Don't underestimate your enemy."

"Ha, ha." She struggled against his hold, but he didn't budge. "Didn't you say that you had to leave?"

"Didn't *you* say that you really wanted to learn some self-defense?"

"I don't think this counts."

"All I'm doing is demonstrating that the second you let your guard down is the second your attacker wins."

"So you think you're winning?"

He shook his head. "Definitely not. All you have to do is ask me nicely, and I'll let you go. If that's what you want."

Jordynn stared up at Dono, mesmerized. His damp

hair hung down over her face, framing his strong features. His wide shoulders stretched out around her, straining as he both held himself up and kept her in place.

And she was tongue-tied. Unable to voice a lie and say no. But also too damned scared to admit that no matter how much her brain warned her heart that it had to be cautious, her body had other ideas.

Donovan watched Jordynn's expression, half willing her to beg him to stay, half willing her to ask him to let her go. Not because he was torn about wanting her.

Hell, no.

There was nothing he was surer about. He loved her. Every move he'd made ten years earlier had been because of it. Every move since, too.

What made him hold back was something far more complicated. He needed her to reciprocate. To say it aloud. Not just to want him back, but to acknowledge it outright. The quiver of her lip and her short inhales and exhales that made her chest rise and fall a little wildly gave away her physical desire. He knew her well enough to read her signals, even after all these years. But he could see in her eyes that she had her doubts. Worries that he couldn't blame her for, concerns that were so very, very founded. How could she let the hurt go, when he couldn't do it himself?

And he wouldn't let her settle for halfway. He wouldn't let her ask him to stay there, like that, when she wasn't one hundred percent sure it's what she wanted.

He lowered himself slowly, placed a soft kiss on her lips, then pushed back up and stood. He had to admit that the flicker of disappoint that flashed across her face made him feel the tiniest bit of satisfaction. He leaned down to drag his mouth over hers once more; it was becoming a habit again, and he liked that, too.

He moved from the bedroom to the bathroom to grab his clothes, talking as he dressed.

"The quicker I go, the quicker I get back," he called. "But if you want to grab a shower, I can wait. There's a couple of sandwiches in the fridge, and a bottled water. Grabbed them from the gas station while you were out cold."

Jordynn interrupted him. "You went to the store?"

"We *have* to eat," he said as he came back into the room. "If I learned anything from being on the run, it's that you can't neglect the basic necessities, or everything else will fall apart. C'mon. I'll feed you before I leave."

"Are you stalling?" she asked.

"Definitely."

She sighed, but when he grabbed her hand, she let him lead her downstairs. He was careful to keep the conversation light as they ate. He tossed jokes her way as she took a five-minute shower—that is, until she called him a creep for standing outside the door—and then he threw himself back onto the bed and whistled a nameless tune until she was done. But the forced levity couldn't quite override the undercurrent of tension, and as he gave her instructions on which lights to leave on and which to leave off while he was gone, Jordynn grew more and more serious. By the time she led him to the door, her face was so stiff that Donovan thought it might crack.

"Hey," he said in one final attempt to make her smile. "All I'm saying is not to answer the door or tell anyone you're here alone."

Her expression only grew stonier. "I won't."

He touched her cheek. "I know you're worried. But

I'm going to get in and out so fast you'll barely have time to make the bed."

"It's not that," she said. "Well. I mean, that, too. But… what if someone recognized you?"

"What?"

"At the store where you got the food."

He shook his head. "They wouldn't have, honey."

"*I* did."

"Would you have known it was me, though, if I hadn't gotten so close?"

Her eyes ran over him, head to toe. "Maybe."

"I'm eighty pounds heavier," he pointed out. "And two inches taller."

"But you're still *you*, Dono."

He couldn't hold in a pleased smile at how sure she sounded. "To you, I am. To everyone else, I'm a stranger. Ellisberg—as a whole—thinks I'm dead. And if they happened to be remembering me at all, it would be as the kid I used to be."

"Still…"

"I wouldn't have stopped if I thought there was a risk," he told her.

"Really?"

"Of course not. I wouldn't do anything that might put you in harm's way, and I'm not trying to be a martyr here, either."

"Are you sure about that, Dono?"

She inhaled and tugged on her still-damp hair, and he reached up to stop her from yanking it out by the roots.

"Why would you even ask that, honey?"

"Because you've as much as told me two or three times that you'd sacrifice yourself if you had to."

"Not if it meant sacrificing you, too."

"That's exactly what I'm talking about," she told him

with a vehement head shake. "You think that if *you* sacrifice yourself, that it will save *me* somehow. It's not
even close to true. I know from experience that my life
without you isn't much of a life at all. It took me years
to even—" She broke off then, a crack making her voice
wobble. But when Donovan reached for her, she waved
him off. "Just...when you're out there, digging around
or whatever...do me a favor and remember that, okay?"

"I will," he said. Then he opened the door and stepped
out into the evening.

He paused on the front steps, waiting for her to slide
the lock shut behind him. With no watch, no cell phone
and no accurate clocks in the house, it was impossible to
say what time it was. He couldn't help noticing, though,
how the sky had been pitched into blackness already.
Donovan couldn't even see a star.

He flipped his gaze to the house once more, reassuring himself that it looked undisturbed from the outside,
then turned toward the little hill that held the portable
office building.

He reached the office quickly and cleared the ramp
that led to the door in two wide steps. Once there, he bent,
working the lock with a paper clip he'd found in the show
home. It only took a few seconds to click the mechanism
in just the right way, and the door swung open.

Donovan slipped in and took quick stock of the dark
interior, searching for something that stood out. A large
wooden desk, pockmarked and wobbly looking, sat in
one corner. A worn chair was tucked underneath it. The
far wall was lined with clear-fronted cabinets—made
of some kind of durable plastic, Donovan thought—and
those were full of rolled blueprints. He scanned the room
further, and his eyes landed on a wide cabinet. Nondescript. No locks.

There, he decided.

Hiding in plain sight, just like the building itself.

When he opened the top drawer, he found a thick collection of red folders, all labeled with untidy printing. Not alphabetized, not seeming to be dedicated to anything in particular. There were names of development properties and names of people. Donovan flipped through them as quickly as he dared, not wanting to overlook the one he needed. Not that he knew what it would say.

"This is why the world went digital," he muttered. "Keywords, all the way."

Of course, it was probably also the reason the Haven Corporation *hadn't* switched over to the wonderful world of technology.

He closed the first drawer and moved on to the second. And he spotted it: "Greyside Mountain."

He didn't hesitate. His gut told him that this was exactly what he wanted. With a tiny, grim smile, he snapped it up, then gave the drawer a shove to close it.

As he exited the building, the memory of the expression on Jordynn's face made him hurry. She'd been scared—impassioned, too—on his behalf. She wanted him to stay safe. If she had doubts about anything else, she definitely didn't have any about that. It buoyed his heart. It gave him hope and stirred a need to prove that he was worthy of a second chance.

Only one way to do that. Get through this. Do it right. Then spend every second of the next decade making up for the last one.

And the folder in his hands put him one step closer to being able to do it.

Fighting an unease that made her skin prickle, Jordynn held her breath and counted to sixty, waiting for Dono to reappear. Then she exhaled, inhaled again and started over. For five full minutes, she saw nothing but darkness. Nothing but stillness. Finally, on the fifth time through, she at last caught a flash and spotted his familiar form, stepping from the building and moving toward the hill. He turned and gave a small wave in her direction, then blew her a kiss.

"Quit being cute," she muttered. "Get in, then get out, like you said."

Like he'd heard her, he took a wide step, then started to walk again quickly.

Jordynn started to let out another slow breath, but froze as a yellow light appeared from somewhere behind the office building. It flickered, then disappeared. With her heart hammering in her chest, she peered out the blinds, trying not to be seen, but trying to pinpoint the source of light, too. And when she spotted it again, noting the way it bobbed up and down, she knew what it was.

A flashlight.

And whoever had it in their hands had somehow managed to bypass the main road and come in through the back. Right behind Donovan.

All they had to do was move the light across the hill and they'd see him.

With her pulse racing furiously, Jordynn reached up and flicked the blinds shut in their prearranged sign.

At least he'll have a bit of warning, she reasoned.

But seconds later, she realized she had no way of knowing whether or not Dono had even received the signal. And even if he *had* seen it...

He'll have no way to get back here unseen. Not with someone that close.

She pushed aside the panic that threatened to overtake her. She almost wished she'd kept the gun.

But you don't have it, she said to herself. *And you have to do something anyway.*

She took a breath and moved from the bedroom to the stairs, reviewing her options as she went. But truthfully, there didn't seem to *be* any options. She couldn't think of another way to attract Dono's attention without also drawing attention to herself.

At the bottom of the steps, Jordynn paused.

That was it.

She *needed* to draw attention to herself. It was the only thing that would stop whoever was out there.

For a second, she considered running out onto the front step screaming. But she realized there was a quicker, quieter solution.

She pulled her hand away from the door and lifted it to the light switch instead. With another steadying inhale, she flicked it on. The front entryway lit up. She flicked it off. Then on. Then off and on in rapid succession. When she was satisfied that the flickering *had* to have been spotted, she turned the light off a final time and peered out the frosted window beside the door.

Sure enough, the beam of the flashlight was bouncing down the hill as its bearer moved toward the house.

Jordynn let out a relieved sigh. But she didn't have time to waste. She had to get out. And get to Dono.

Moving swiftly, she abandoned the front door in search of another way out. She went through the living room and into the kitchen, where she spotted a set of sliding glass doors. A quick glance outside told her the doors led to a patio, which in turn led to a grassy backyard. In the dark, she could see a gate that led from one yard to the next.

Perfect.

Jordynn undid the latch. She slid open the door, then

stepped out into the cool air. And regretted it immediately. Because a big form slipped in from behind her,
pinned her arms to her sides and dragged her backward.

Chapter 10

Donovan wasn't expecting the violent reaction to his embrace, and he was ill prepared. A fast elbow slammed into his stomach, forcing him to let Jordynn go, and winding him badly enough that he couldn't quite form a sentence. The folder he'd procured from the office slid to the ground, and he stepped back, wheezing. Before he could recover, a palm came up and grazed the edge of his jaw. He stumbled out of the path of another wild swing. He smacked his back against the railing behind him.

Taught her too damned well, he thought, mildly amused.

But his amusement slipped away as he lifted his head and saw that she still hadn't recognized him. Her mouth dropped open.

Crap.

Donovan rushed forward, slammed a palm against her lips and prayed no one but him had heard the beginnings of her scream. He spun her around and pulled her close.

"It's me, honey," he said into her ear, careful to keep his voice calm.

She twisted and writhed, trying to get away. She got a hand loose for a second, and swiped it against his forearm.

"Jordynn." He put a little more urgency into his tone.

She finally stopped fighting and sagged against him. He dropped his hand and spun her again, this time to face him. Her eyes were wide and wild, her hair a beast of a mess.

"I didn't know it was you," she gasped.

"I hope not." He touched her face gently. "Sorry, honey."

Her gaze traveled his body. "You're…"

"Covered in mud," he filled in. "Slipped coming down the hill. Why are you even out here?"

Panic filled her eyes. "Didn't you see the signal?"

"Yeah," he replied. "But I was already out before that security guard showed up."

"The security guard?"

"Little guy with a flashlight."

"You *knew* about the guy with the flashlight?"

Donovan nodded. "Yeah. I told you I had a lot of time to think this thr— What's wrong?"

Her face had gone pale. "He's on his way to the house. I didn't know he was a security guard. And I *really* didn't know that *you* knew when I did it."

"When you did what?"

"I flicked the lights. You didn't see?"

"No. You must've done it while I was sliding around in the mud."

"Well. I did flick them. A lot. I was trying to divert his attention down here. And I think it worked."

Donovan cursed his own protective stupidity. When

he'd disclosed his plan, he'd deliberately left out the fact that there was likely a guard wandering around because he didn't want to worry her even more. It hadn't occurred to him that she'd catch sight of him.

"I'm sorry, Dono."

"It's not your fault."

She shot him an incredulous look. They didn't have time to argue, and even if they did, he wasn't going to let her blame herself.

"You didn't know," he said. "And it doesn't matter now anyway. We just need to worry about getting out of sight until he's gone."

"Out of sight?" she repeated. "No. We need to *go*. The garbage from the food is in the house and the bed is unmade and...where's the Jeep?"

Damn. "In the garage."

"So we go on foot."

Quickly, Donovan scanned their surroundings. There was a little gate between this house and the next, but using it would leave them fully exposed. Anyone coming into the yard would be able to see them. So would anyone peering out a window from inside.

The other side of the house was neighborless. Open to the street, and probably considered a perk by whoever bought the big corner lot, but it wasn't working in their favor at the moment.

Next, he eyed the high fence at the back of the house. Behind it, he could see the outline of thick brambles. Impassable, even if they could get through to it.

His eyes sought the gate once more. "Guess that way's our only option. We'll have to move fast. And stick to the edge of the fence as much as we can. If someone sees us...we'll run as fast and hard as we can. South. The Haven Corporation has a massive debris pile down past the building site. I saw it when we came past. Plenty of places to hide. If we get separated, I'll find you there. Sound good?"

Jordynn nodded. "Okay."

He grabbed the folder from them ground, then slid his free hand to hers. He started to move across the patio, then went still. An arc of light illuminated the path between the houses.

"Someone there?" called the security guard.

Donovan lifted a finger to his lips, then tugged Jordynn to the exterior wall beside the sliding glass doors.

"If you're out back, might as well make yourself known now," the guard said. "Doin' a perimeter search and got a Taser ready. And I'm not a fan of surprises."

"Back into the house," Donovan whispered. "Quickly."

They slipped inside just as the flashlight's beam hit the patio. Donovan knew it would slide up in a moment and land on the open door. He didn't pause to watch it. He pulled Jordynn along through the kitchen and into the living room. Very briefly, he contemplated finding a place to hide. A closet or the basement or the large wardrobe in the master bedroom. As fast as the thought came, though, he dismissed it. Jordynn was right—they'd left behind too much evidence of their presence.

"Front door," he said instead.

He was pretty damned sure the security guard would be calling for backup any moment, and whether the call went to the police or to Ivan and his men, he didn't want to risk becoming trapped. They'd have a better chance of escape running through the streets.

But when he twisted the handle and flung open the door, his plan backfired.

A slick, dark-colored sedan had just turned up the road and was parking at the end of the driveway. From where they stood, Donovan could see a stranger behind the wheel. And Ivan's familiar silhouette in the passenger seat.

It took Donovan less than a heartbeat to realize that even though he could see Ivan, the other man hadn't spotted them yet.

With his teeth gritted, he yanked on Jordynn's hand and propelled them to side of the house. There, he released her fingers and slammed them into the exterior wall, making sure their backs hugged the vinyl siding as tightly as possible. Then realized his mistake.

"We're stuck," Jordynn said softy, voicing his thought. "Ivan's going in the front, and if the guard comes back this way…"

Donovan sucked in a frustrated breath. "Yes."

"What are we going to do?"

"The only thing we *can* do. Wait. Hope."

The slam of a car door echoed through the night air. Feet on pavement followed, then a pause.

"Door's wide open," said a rough voice.

Then came the click of cocking gun, and Jordynn shivered beside him.

"Think it's them?" asked the voice.

Ivan's reply was disparaging. "Who the hell else would come up here at this time of night?"

"Hoodlums?"

"Shut up, Hank, and point the gun."

The footsteps stopped, and Donovan could picture them. Ivan, standing casually behind the other man, looking bored but in actuality being fully cognizant of every little sound, aware of every hair of every detail.

The security guard's voice—muffled from inside the house—lifted up to them. "What now? Who the hell is—

Oh. Mr. Lightfoot. You got here faster than I thought you would. Did any of the silent alarms go off on your end? Damnedest thing. Nothing on my end, but we definitely had a break-in."

For a minute, Donovan tuned out the exchange that followed. It seemed to be revolving around the merits of motion sensors and security cameras, and he already knew he hadn't triggered any alarms himself. He'd cut the right wires on the way into the house, and the office building had been left without security. The latter was done deliberately, Donovan thought, to fool the average criminal into thinking there was nothing of value inside. Though he had known better.

His fingers squeezed the folder.

Ivan's voice cut through his thoughts. "You find anyone in the house, Joe?"

"Nah," said the security guard. "Looks like teenagers busted in. Had a snack, made use of the, ahem, king-size bed, then left."

"They still in there?"

"Nope."

"Teenagers, you said?"

"Yeah, I'm guessing so. Weird thing was I actually came out because I thought I saw somebody up in the office."

"Oh, yeah?"

"Uh-huh. Nothin' in there worth lookin' at, though. Not even a computer or anything. But the file cabinet was open. Think something might've been taken from inside. Then I saw a light flickerin' up in the house, so I made my way down here."

"Anything in particular go missing? Something you might've seen?"

Donovan's grip on the folder tightened even more. Ivan

was speaking about the thin stack of papers. No doubt about it. Being sure of that just confirmed what he already suspected. The link between the Haven Corporation and the murder were recorded in there somewhere.

Joe laughed. "Hard to say. So many piles of stuff in there."

"So what makes you think there was a theft?" Ivan didn't sound amused.

"Well. Someone slammed the file cabinet shut, that's for sure. The latch jams and it bounces open a half inch."

There was a brief pause, then Ivan asked, "Did you call the police?"

"Just you, boss," Joe said. "Guess I'll have to do that, though, hey? Unless you don't want me to?"

"No." Another pause. "I don't want you to."

Something in Donovan's head screamed a warning that now was the time to get out. That even if it just meant moving from the side of the house to the backyard, they should do it. Whatever was coming next, he didn't want to hear. And more important…he didn't want Jordynn to hear it. Before he could grab her, though, Ivan spoke again.

"Take him around back, Hank. Then take care of him."

Joe's reply was a short laugh. "What?"

"You sure?" Hank sounded dubious.

"No more loose ends," Ivan said, his voice completely sure. "No more mistakes."

Damn, damn, damn.

Donovan closed his eyes for one second. Then he opened them and shoved the file folder toward Jordynn and met her eyes. She looked terrified, and he couldn't blame her. His own body was covered in a nervous sweat. They were stuck in the crosshairs of a very bad situation, and the only way out was to head straight into the fray.

"South," he ordered. "I'll find you. I promise."

The sound of a struggle had started already. Feet on rocks. Noisy protests, then a yell. All coming their way.

Donovan crouched. He didn't have space to build up steam, so he'd have to use his body. He bent as low as he could without losing his balance, and as the security guard was shoved into view, he used his legs like a spring. He vaulted forward and slammed hard into the big man with the gun—Hank—who let out a startled holler. They fell to the ground in a violent tumble. Thankfully, the gun flew out of Hank's hands, giving Donovan a moment of satisfaction. It was short-lived.

Ivan burst around the corner then, his shock visible even in the dark. His expression quickly turned angry, though, and he fumbled at his waist, clearly in search of his own weapon.

"Run!" Donovan shouted. "Now!"

Both Jordynn and Joe heeded his advice. They barreled past Ivan, knocking the man against the house.

Donovan didn't give him time to recover. He didn't dare let the career criminal get ahold of his gun. He kneed Hank in the groin, then dived at Ivan.

The older man sidestepped at the last second, making it just far enough that Donovan accidentally thumped into the wall. Fierce pain shot up one shoulder. With a grunt, he righted himself in time to see that Hank was moving toward the gun on the ground.

Not happening.

Disregarding Ivan for a moment, Donovan pushed away from the side of the house and threw himself toward the weapon. His hands closed on it seconds before Hank could reach it.

Donovan rolled, flicking the gun back and forth between the two men in front of him. Hank lifted his hands in surrender, but Ivan just stared at him impassively.

"You won't shoot," he stated.

"Not a safe assumption," Donovan replied as he pushed to his feet and steadied himself.

"You won't shoot to *kill*," Ivan corrected. "Not at point-blank range, not unprovoked."

"You think I'm not feeling provoked?"

"Doesn't matter. You're not a killer."

"Maybe not. But you won't get very far with a blown kneecap or a hole through your shoulder. And I'm damned sure you'd rather not have to make a visit to the hospital to have your stomach sewn up."

The older man didn't even blink. "Ten years have changed you, haven't they, Mr. Grady?"

Donovan refused to be baited. "They haven't changed *you*."

"I suppose not." Ivan let out a sigh. "You think you have the upper hand here, but I can assure you that you don't."

"Not yet, maybe. Once we get down to the police station, though, that'll change."

"That's your plan? Take me in and hope I confess?"

Ivan barked out a laugh, and Donovan shrugged. He hadn't actually thought through what would happen if he got ahold of Ivan and his men before he got ahold of the evidence that would put them away for good. Sure, he'd fantasized about throwing punches and demanding justice. But in his mind, those things had always come *after* he'd turned over irrefutable proof to the police. He'd assumed that he'd be in the clear and that Jordynn's safety would be guaranteed. That was the eventuality he'd planned for. Turning it on its head...

What other option is there, though? he wondered.

The older man was right. Donovan wouldn't kill him. He wasn't a murderer and wouldn't become one.

As if sensing Donovan's uncertainty, Ivan spoke again, this time softly. "Have you forgotten what I told you a decade ago about who'd be blamed if that body out there ever surfaced? Have you forgotten what—and *who*—is at risk?"

Donovan stiffened and steadied his weapon. "I've had a lot of time to think about that, actually. And I'm about ready to call your bluff. I had no reason to kill that man. I don't even know who he is. Not even after all these years. You can't get to me through threatening my father anymore, and no matter what they believe, the cops will make sure Jordynn is safe."

"You really believe it's that straightforward, Mr. Grady?" Ivan smiled.

"I do."

"I want to reach into my pocket so I can show you something."

"If it's the wrong end of your gun, I'll take a pass, thanks."

"I give you my word it's not a ploy."

"Your word?" Donovan scoffed. "Is that supposed to mean anything to me?"

"You do it, then," Ivan said. "I'll put my hands on my head. You can disarm me. My gun's holstered at my back. Then you can reach into my front jacket pocket and take out the phone inside."

Donovan considered the offer. Maybe it was genuine, maybe not. Either way, he couldn't risk getting close enough that the other man might gain an advantage.

"Just show me the phone," he ordered.

With exaggerated slowness, Ivan put one hand on his

head, then stuck the other into his coat. He pulled out a slim, white device, and waved it back and forth.

"You recognize this?" he asked.

It only took Donovan a second. "That's Jordynn's phone."

"And Jordynn's contacts. She only has two personal ones. Did you know that?"

It was a dig. How would Donovan, who'd been gone for ten years, have a clue who Jordynn kept on speed dial? So he stayed silent, staring at the phone.

Ivan lifted his shoulder in a one-sided shrug. "Guess not. But your girl does have a pretty good friend in here. Lots of texts and jokes. Bit of worry here about the fact that Jordynn hasn't answered her latest ones. Her name is Sasha. You know her?"

Donovan's blood ran cold. "Yes."

"Sasha's husband works out of town. But they have two kids. A boy and a girl. Sweet. At least they are when they're sleeping. Wanna see a picture?"

Gut-rot sickness washed through Donovan. "Give me the phone."

Ivan held it out. "Doesn't matter anyway. The contact info's already been transferred. Recorded. Sasha's house is being watched, and any false move you make puts them all at risk."

Donovan snapped up the device, then stepped away. "You're a real piece of work."

"Cooperate with me, Grady."

He stared into the other man's cold, gray eyes. "Cooperate with you? By doing what? Choosing between Sasha's family, or Jordynn and me?"

"I don't see how it's a choice, really. Sasha and the kids haven't done a thing. And you put the accidental nail in your own coffin a long time ago. As far as Jordynn is concerned…collateral damage."

It took every ounce of willpower Donovan had to keep from lashing out. "Tell me who signs your paychecks, Ivan, and I'll think about cooperating."

The other man actually laughed. "Do you think I got this far by being a rat?"

"I think you got this far because no one's challenged you."

"Is that what you think you're doing now?"

"Your boss's name, Ivan."

"Might as well just shoot me."

"Believe me, a large part of me would like to." Then an idea occurred to him, and he turned his attention to the big man, who knelt on the ground with his hands on his head. "Hank?"

"Yeah?"

"Is your loyalty in line with Ivan's? Or would you be willing to barter? What would it take, Hank? Money? A new identity? Both, maybe. I can arrange it," he said. "Just a name."

Hank opened his mouth. Then closed it. He shot Ivan a nervous look. Donovan was pretty sure he had the guy's attention. That, or Hank was just really worried that Ivan would *think* Donovan's suggestion appealed to him. He didn't get a chance to find out which was true.

Without warning, Ivan spun, ducking low and kicking out his foot. The older man's boot landed in Hank's side, knocking him flat. The move was quick. Agile. Completely unexpected. And in the split second it took for Donovan to react, Ivan lifted his foot a second time and slammed it into Hank's chin.

As Donovan pounced on Ivan, Hank's eyes rolled back into his head.

Dammit.

"What hell are you doing?" Donovan slammed Ivan into the rocky pathway.

"I said no more loose ends." The reply was a grunt.

A string of curses ran through Donovan's mind, but he didn't see the use in uttering them aloud, so he pressed his lips together and concentrated on securing the man beneath him.

Never underestimate your enemy, he reminded himself grimly, echoing the teasing warning he'd given to Jordynn.

He held Ivan tightly, rolled him to his back, then ripped the other man's gun from his shoulder holster. He pushed him hard against the ground, driving a knee into his back to keep him in place. Ivan bucked one more time, and the struggle sent a second phone—this one in a black case—flying out of his pocket.

"Keep. Still."

Donovan punctuated the order with an elbow to the kidney. Ivan groaned, but finally stopped moving.

Careful to keep a good grip on the other man's wrists, Donovan freed one of his own hands to snap up the phone. He tapped the plastic case, and the screen came to life.

Jackpot.

"Not password protected," he said. "Not smart."

He scrolled, one-handed, through the contacts. Nothing stood out on the first look, but Donovan was sure the man had put something of value in there. He went through a second time. Slowly.

HC.

The initials appeared unobtrusive enough, but he knew better. They could only stand for one thing. The Haven Corporation.

Donovan double tapped the listing, and though no number popped up, an address did.

"Where will this take us?" he asked.

"Not where you think it will."

"Forgive me for having a hard time believing you."

Donovan highlighted the address, then copied it and pasted it into the phone's browser. Immediately, a list of options appeared on the screen. Houses for sale and listings for those already sold. An offer to provide GPS directions. And an advertisement for Four Tops, a community of tidy homes and green lawns.

Donovan stared at the third option. *Four Tops.*

It was one of the Haven-built developments.

"Is this his address, Ivan?"

The older man said nothing, and that was enough. Donovan yanked him to his feet.

"I guess we'll pay your boss a little visit at home."

"You're going to be disappointed."

"I somehow doubt it." Donovan smiled and waved the gun toward the car. "I'll even let you drive."

"I'd really rather not."

"It wasn't a request."

He gave the older man a shove and pressed the weapon between his shoulder blades, then shot a regretful look Hank's way. He couldn't think of a way to move the man. Of course, he doubted the big thug would be eager to get back into the fray anytime soon after he woke anyway. With any luck, he'd just stumble off into oblivion, thanking his lucky stars Ivan hadn't actually killed him. God knew the man was capable of it.

Donovan let himself glance south, just once, and issued Jordynn a silent command to stay put. He wouldn't risk picking her up with Ivan in tow, but he sure as hell didn't want her wandering around unguarded, either.

Sit tight, honey, he thought, and then turned his attention back to the task at hand.

With any luck, this would all be over before Hank woke, before the sun came up the next day, and before Jordynn had a chance to do anything reckless on his behalf.

Jordynn inhaled through her nose and exhaled through her mouth, trying to more thoroughly catch her breath. She'd run south through the building site, just like Dono had said to. Not because she thought they should separate, and not because she wanted to, but because of what Dono had said to her before. One of them had to be the lookout. One of them had to be able to come to the other's rescue.

And as weird as it seemed—especially considering the way she was huddled behind a pile of discarded wood— she had a feeling it was going to be her this time around.

The security guard had gone in the opposite direction without so much as a glance backward. She imagined that he wouldn't be back anytime soon. Or maybe ever. If he was smart, he'd run fast and far. And he'd never come back.

Like Dono shouldn't have.

The thought was like being kicked in the gut. Logically, she knew it wasn't really her fault that they were being hunted. It wasn't even her fault he'd come back. The blame lay at the feet of the people who'd murdered the man up on the mountain, all those years ago. But knowing it and applying it to her heart were two very different things. If he got any more hurt than he already was, she'd never forgive herself.

She tipped her head back, fighting tears.

Please, please be okay.

Then, as if in reply to her silent prayer, the sound of tires on pavement carried through the air.

Jordynn sat up straighter again.

What did it mean? Were more men coming? Backup for Ivan? Or had Ivan captured Dono, and was now leaving with him in tow?

She couldn't stand not knowing.

She pushed to her feet and crouched behind the wood, inching up until she could see over the top. For a second, there was nothing in sight. Then a dark sedan crested the hill, and Jordynn's heart stopped.

Even from where she was positioned, she could see that one man sat in the front. And there was no mistaking the wide-shouldered form in the back.

Dono.

She took comfort in knowing that he was alive.

But for how long?

She started to stand up all the way, prepared to once again divert the attention her way, then went still. A slight parting of the clouds above had let through a sliver of moonlight, and that wax-colored light flickered off something in Dono's hand. And again, Jordynn had no doubts about what she saw. A gun.

She exhaled, this time with the deepest relief. She sank back to the ground.

Whatever was happening, Dono wasn't just safe, he was in charge.

"So what now?" she said aloud to the chilly air.

In spite of what he'd said about finding her, he couldn't possibly expect her to sit there all night. Abruptly, she remembered the folder. She lifted it from the spot where she'd tucked it away and squinted at it before flipping it open.

The information inside seemed minimal at best. A list

of properties, all held by the Haven Corporation. Dollar values attached to each. The only thing that seemed to stand out was the page of names. At first glance, Jordynn assumed that they were Haven employees. But when she lifted the paper up for a better look, she realized it was actually an account of the major players at Fryer Developments, the company who were set to build on the mountain. Maybe no one else would have thought it an odd thing to keep. Maybe *lots* of companies kept lists of their competition's employees. Headhunting purposes. Or just to keep general tabs. But Jordynn was sure that the names on that page were indicative of a greater connection between the two corporations. Possibly even one that would lead to finding out who'd been killed ten years earlier, and why.

And maybe deciphering the connection will lead me to where Dono's headed now.

Hugging the folder close to her chest, Jordynn stood up again. What she needed was access to a computer. An internet connection, so she could plug those names in and see where they led.

But where am I going to find that?

The only place she could think of that even had public internet was the library, and she somehow doubted they were open in the middle of the night. And as tempting as it was, she knew she couldn't just go home and log into her laptop.

So…a hotel?

Jordynn shook her head, dismissing the idea as quickly as it came. It was too risky a move. Ellisberg only had two hotels, and either one might have staff who'd recognize her. And of course money was an issue in that she *had* none. In fact, she couldn't even reason out a way to get back into town. Three miles on foot, in the dark, held zero appeal.

She eyed the row of show homes. There was a possibility that one of them had a computer set up. But she'd heard Joe and Ivan's discussion, and she knew that the houses were equipped with motion detectors and alarms. And whatever Dono had done to bypass the ones in the home that they'd spent the evening in, Jordynn had no similar expertise.

She stared at the dim skyline for another moment, frustrated. Then a flash caught her eye, making her go still. It was another car, moving slowly down the hill that Dono had disappeared over just a few minutes earlier. There was a chance they'd even passed each other.

Jordynn let herself watch the vehicle's descent for another few seconds before she turned to hide again. But as she turned, she realized that she recognized the car. And it wasn't a car at all. It was a forest green crossover, made distinct by the oversize antenna topper. Jordynn had gifted that elephant-shaped bobble to the owner, who's blonde ponytail could be seen even from this far away.

But what was Sasha doing out there in the middle of the night?

And then the van turned sharply, angling toward Jordynn.

Dammit.

Very briefly, she considered running. But what good would it do? Her best friend had clearly already spotted her. If she suddenly turned and bolted, it would only give rise to a hundred more questions. Maybe even prompt Sasha to call the police.

Jordynn stood still, trying to school her expression into one of nonchalance. One that said she was just out for a stroll. In the wee hours of the morning. At a construction site. That suggested that there was nothing weird about that. But any illusion of being calm and collected went by the wayside when Sasha rolled down her window, gave her a thorough once-over, then opened her mouth.

"My Lord, Jo," she said. "Are you *barefoot*?"

Jordynn looked down. Sure enough, her toes poked out from under her jeans.

"I guess I am," she said.

Her friend shook her head. "Don't get me wrong. I'm glad to see you're not dead. But what in God's name is going on?"

And Jordynn didn't know whether to laugh or cry. So she settled for both.

Chapter 11

Jordynn's tears didn't clear until Sasha had guided the van far enough from the construction site that Jordynn couldn't see it anymore. And though her friend didn't pressure her to speak, she could feel the other woman's eyes each time they glanced her way. She could sense the puzzlement and the curiosity. And she couldn't answer any questions, no matter how badly she wanted to.

At last, though, she decided she'd better say something. "How did you know I was out here?"

Sasha whipped a surprise-tinged glance her way. "That's what you're going with?"

Jordynn stifled a sigh. "You don't think it's a valid question?"

"If you're going for that best-defense-is-a-good-offense thing…then it's totally fine."

"Cut me some slack."

"I *am* cutting you some slack. I'm not freaking out and

demanding that we check you into a mental ward. Which is what my instincts tell me I should do."

In spite of herself, Jordynn smiled. "Noted."

Sasha sighed. "When I got your last text, I panicked a little. It didn't even sound like you. And then you didn't answer me…"

"Which text was that?" Jordynn asked, her voice carefully neutral.

"The one about going to bed?"

"You didn't think maybe I *did* go to bed?"

"Oh, please. As if you ever go straight to sleep after work. Besides that, when I asked if you were being deliberately obnoxious, you didn't answer. Not like you to *not* try and get the last word. So I went by your house."

Jordynn's heart thudded hard. "You did?"

"Lights were all out. Even that one you leave on when you're getting some damned *shut-eye*." Sasha laughed lightly, and Jordynn forced a smile, too.

"Then what? You just thought you'd come up and check the development site?" she asked.

"Not exactly."

"What does that mean?"

Her friend flicked a nervous look in her direction. "I checked all your sad spots."

"My what?"

"I knew today—well, yesterday, now—was the anniversary, and… I don't know. I thought maybe you'd go somewhere that reminded you of Donovan."

"Where did you look?"

"I took the kids and drove up near the trails. Then that ice cream place you used to go. Blaine and Izzy hated that part." She laughed again before quickly sobering. "I checked his old street and the park and just about any place I could remember the two of you going."

Jordynn bit her lip. Sasha had no idea how much danger she'd put herself in. And the worst part was that Jordynn couldn't even tell her. The last thing she wanted to do was make her friend vulnerable by giving her information that could be used against her. She bit her lip, realizing how closely the situation paralleled the one Dono had been in. Her chest tightened. For weeks after he'd witnessed the murder, he'd held it in. Not daring to breathe a word. But he must've wanted to. So badly. Especially if the dark feeling in Jordynn's gut was any indication.

"Jo?"

She exhaled. "Sorry. Spaced out."

"I was just saying how after I couldn't find you anywhere, I went home and talked to Uncle Reed. He told me you probably just needed some time alone. He's usually such a worrier, you know, so I felt kind of silly about stalking you. But the day went by and it got dark and… I tried to get my own bit of *shut-eye*, but there was no way in hell *that* was happening. So I started thinking about good places to bury a body."

"Sasha!"

"What? It worked, didn't it?"

"Not because I was being buried somewhere."

"I don't suppose you're going to tell me the real reason you're wandering around out here?"

"No."

"Damn you and your *shut-eye*."

Jordynn shot her friend a puzzled look. "Why do you keep saying that?"

"It's what *you* said."

"What? When?"

"In that last text before you stopped answering me. You said you were getting some shut-eye. You sounded like my grandma."

The uneven thump started up again in Jordynn's chest. "I didn't send you a text that said that."

"Um, yeah you did."

"What time?"

"Yesterday morning at about nine? Don't you remember?"

"I didn't send you a text about getting some shut-eye," she said. "The last one I sent was when I got off the bus. When I told you I was going to bed."

"So who sent me the message asking how the kids are?"

Jordynn closed her eyes, recalling how she and Dono had squabbled over the phone. How it had fallen to the ground with a thud when Ivan and his buddies broke into her house. And was left there.

The world spun, and Jordynn fought to keep herself from spinning with it.

"Speaking of the kids..." she said, working to keep her voice steady. "Where are they?"

"At home with my uncle. Sound asleep when I left," Sasha replied. "But you didn't really answer my question."

"My phone went missing this morning."

"Seriously?"

Jordynn swallowed, and reaffirmed the lie by fleshing it out. "Yeah. Must've dropped it right after the last time I texted you. But I didn't notice until a little while ago."

"Oh, creepy. Some punk texted me about my *kids*?"

"Super creepy."

"Should I call the cops?"

"No. I'm sure it's some stupid teenagers, thinking they're funny. I'll call and have the phone canceled."

"If you say so."

Sasha sounded dubious, and Jordynn wanted desperately to say something else. To offer a warning. Instead, she found herself settling for the only thing she could. Her own reassurance.

"Do you mind if we go back to your house instead of mine?" she asked. "It's been a rough night, and I could do with seeing the kids in the morning."

"Of course. They'll be glad to see you, too."

A niggling of guilt—*was checking on Sasha's family putting them in* more *danger?*—crept in, and Jordynn fought it. Ivan and his men already had her phone. They'd already made contact. If they were watching the house and watching Sasha, they already knew where she'd gone.

And it's not like I'm going to stay. I'm just going to see that they're fine, borrow their computer, then find an excuse to get out.

"Jordynn…" Her friend trailed off, hesitance clear in her voice. "Are you okay?"

"No," she admitted. "But it's not something you can fix."

There was another moment of hesitation. "Is it a Donovan thing?"

Jordynn shook her head, but she answered truthfully anyway. "Yes. And I know you're going to tell me again I should let him go. But this isn't like that, okay? And I'll explain it all as soon as I can."

"That's all I'm going to get, isn't it?"

"Sorry."

Her friend tapped her fingers on the steering wheel. "Okay. But if the kids ask you to make them raspberry pancakes in the morning, you have to do it."

"Deal."

Jordynn noted that Sasha's frown didn't fade. *But I'll take what I can get.*

She turned her attention out the window then, and was

glad that she did. Because as they turned up the street, she spotted a dark sedan. It moved slowly up the road, then stopped just a few houses away from Sasha's place. And two figures were inside—one in the front, and one in the back.

"Turn left," Jordynn urged.

"What?"

"Left. At the stop sign."

"But my house is right there."

Unable to stop herself, Jordynn grabbed the steering wheel and yanked it hard. The van careened to the side of the road, and Sasha let out a yelp before slamming on the brakes and whipping her head toward Jordynn.

"What are you *doing*, Jo?"

Jordynn decided it was time for a bit of disclosure. "There's a car up the street from your house, Sasha. Inside it are two men. One of them is very good, and one of them is very bad. I don't know why they're here, but it can't be for a cup of two a.m. tea. I don't have time to tell you anything else, but I need you to trust me on this."

She winced at how much she sounded like Dono, and delivered him a silent apology for being so hard on him.

Her friend's eyes widened, then went frantically toward her house. "The kids. And Uncle Reed."

"I know."

"We have to get them out."

"On foot," Jordynn cautioned, then—as her friend started to open her door—added, "And you might want to park the van first."

Sasha responded with a shaky laugh, but she did guide the vehicle to the side of the road before she turned to Jordynn. "What now?"

"We go in through the back door. Quickly and quietly. We get your uncle and the kids out. Then we bring them to the van, and you take them anywhere but here."

"To the house at the lake?"

"Yes. Sure."

"What about you?"

Jordynn knew she couldn't answer honestly. But she didn't have the energy to lie to her best friend, either.

"We'll make sure everyone in your house is safe first. And worry about me after."

Sasha looked like she might want to argue, but her eyes drifted up the street, and Jordynn knew she was too worried about her family to put up a fight.

As they walked silently up the back alley, Jordynn reached for Sasha's hand. She didn't have the words to comfort her friend properly. Not without telling her the truth.

This is just a small taste, she told herself. *A tiny glimpse of what Dono was feeling when he came back to save me.*

And it hurt.

They reached the edge of the yard, and she squeezed Sasha's hand once more, then released it.

"C'mon," she whispered.

She didn't know how long it would take for Dono and Ivan to get to the front door, and she didn't know for sure what their goal was—but she was a hundred percent certain that she and Sasha had to beat them to it.

Wordlessly, they stepped up the path. Jordynn gestured for her friend to unlock the door, and as soon as it was done, they slipped inside.

"I'll get Reed," Jordynn said. "You grab the kids."

She moved through the house as confidently as if it were her own, bypassing the main floor kitchen and heading straight for the office-turned-bedroom where she knew she'd find her boss sleeping. He always stayed with Sasha when her husband was on a long haul.

Jordynn paused in the doorway, taking a moment to collect herself. Reed would likely want an explanation that she couldn't give. He'd want to go to the police, like any sane person would. But he—like Sasha and Jordynn herself—would put the safety of the kids first. And they didn't have time to waste.

She rapped lightly on the door. "Reed?"

The older gentleman didn't stir. Jordynn stepped into the room.

"Reed?" she said, a little louder this time.

He sat up then, blinking in the dark. "Jordynn? Is that you?"

"Yes, it's me."

"Is everything okay?"

She nodded, then changed her mind, shook her head, and phrased her next statement as carefully as she could. "I don't want you to worry, but you and the kids need to drive out to the place at the lake."

"What?"

"It might be nothing," Jordynn replied, still cautious. "But someone took my phone, and they found Sasha in the contacts and they sent her a weird text."

Reed sat up. "What kind of weird text?"

"Just…implying that they know where you guys live. Freaked Sasha out."

She waited for him to point out that it was the middle of the night, and to ask questions about her timing. He didn't. He just frowned, then tossed back the blankets, revealing a pair of plaid pajamas that would've made Jordynn smile on any other occasion.

"Did you report it?" he asked.

"To the police?" Jordynn shook her head. "No, not yet. Like I said…"

"Could be nothing," he filled in, then sighed and ran a hand over his sparse white hair. "But could be something."

"Exactly."

"All right."

Jordynn let out a breath. But a sharp knock on the front door quickly overrode her relief at his acquiescence. And Reed was out of bed like a shot, his pajama pants swishing as he moved to the closet and swung open the door.

"What are you doing?" Jordynn asked.

"Up above," her boss said. "I've got a gun."

"You…what?"

Jordynn watched as he pulled a heavy lockbox down from the shelf and set it on the desk. He moved to the nightstand, yanked open the drawer and pulled out a key chain.

"I bought it years ago," he said as he stuck the key in and turned. "In case Sasha needed protection while Bob is on the road. Never thought she'd actually—"

"Uncle Reed?"

His hand hung suspended over the box, and Jordynn spun. Her friend stood in the door, her son on her hip, her daughter clutching her knee and a pair of shoes in her hand.

"I told them we're taking a surprise vacation." Sasha's gaze drifted to the bed. "What's that?"

Jordynn angled herself between her boss and the weapon, blocking the box from sight. She gave her boss a head shake. The last thing Sasha needed to see was the gun, and there was no way her friend would want it near the kids.

"You need to go," Jordynn said.

"We're ready," Sasha replied, then paused and frowned. "Wait. *We* do?"

"Quickly."

"You can't stay here, Jo."

Jordynn shook her head. "I won't. I'll get out as soon as I can. But can't go with you."

"Why not?"

Because I have to warn Dono that whatever upper hand he thinks he has…he doesn't really have at all.

But she couldn't say that aloud, so she settled for "It's too complicated to explain right now."

"*Complicated*? Don't you think that word might be a little inadequate?"

"Maybe," Jordynn conceded. "But it doesn't change anything."

The doorbell rang twice in quick succession, and Reed stepped toward Sasha.

"I don't know what's going on," he said, "but I do think we should listen."

A loud thump made Sasha jump, and Jordynn couldn't help but cringe.

"Go," she urged.

Sasha's face crumbled, but she gave Jordynn a quick sideways hug, then handed over the shoes. "Promise me you'll stay safe."

"I promise you I'll try." Jordynn cringed again, this time with an awareness of how much she sounded like Dono.

"Okay."

In the seconds it took for Jordynn to slip the shoes on her feet, the closest thing she had to a family was on its way out the door. And she was arming herself with a gun she didn't know how to use.

* * *

"Again," Donovan ordered roughly.

Ivan shot him a calm—but still unimpressed—look. "I can only bang so many times."

Donovan tapped the gun against his thigh emphatically. "And you haven't reached the limit yet. I told you to try again."

"This isn't going to work out in your favor."

Donovan ground his teeth together.

The man had told him on repeat that he wouldn't find what he was expecting on the other end of this address, adding a few times that he wouldn't like it, either.

And Donovan had to admit that when they'd initially pulled up to the Four Tops area and he'd spotted the rows of clean, middle-class homes, he'd questioned if they were in the right spot. After all, what kind of rich property developer lived so far below his means?

The expression on Ivan's face now, though—expectant, a little too self-assured—was enough to confirm that whatever the reason might be, the other man was hiding something.

"Do it," Donovan said.

Ivan lifted his fist yet again, then slammed it against the door and raised an eyebrow. Though the noise was thunderous, it didn't bring anyone to the door.

"I don't think anyone's home," the other man stated.

"Or they're not answering. Hit it again."

Donovan leaned sideways and eyed up the window. He could swear he saw a flash of movement inside, and he suddenly knew why the owner of the Haven Corporation would choose to live here, in one of his own houses. So he could hide in plain sight.

Not for much longer.

"Break it down," he commanded.

"That seems like the kind of thing that's going to draw attention that neither of us wants," Ivan pointed out.

"I don't care."

"How do you propose I do it, then?"

He's stalling, Donovan realized. *He saw that flash, too.*

With a growl, he shoved his weapon in his waistband, took hold of the other man's collar and lifted his foot. He aimed a solid kick at the space just below the handle. The frame heaved. Donovan took a step back, then aimed again.

Before his second kick hit the mark, though, the door opened on its own. Donovan crouched down defensively, using Ivan as a shield. The front entryway was dark and empty, and there was no sign of whoever had opened the door.

He drew in a breath, lifted his gun and yelled, "Show yourself!"

The sentence barely made it out of his mouth before he froze, stunned. Because the person who stepped in view was Jordynn, her shaking hands pointing a gun straight at him.

Chapter 12

Donovan didn't know what he'd been expecting to find inside the house, but it wasn't a familiar tumble of wild red hair, insanely blue eyes and big shiny weapon.

Clearly, neither had Ivan.

"What the *hell* is she doing here?" the other man said.

It was a good question, but there was no way Donovan was going to admit that he was just as curious. So he just released Ivan's collar and gave him another satisfying shove instead, and then issued an order to go inside.

Jordynn stepped back to make room, and Donovan pressed his weapon into Ivan's back. As he guided the other man through the hall in search of a good place to interrogate him, he was vaguely aware that the general decor didn't jive with what he'd expected. Framed pictures hung on the walls, and the house had a messy, lived-in feel. Nothing about it screamed of a reclusive millionaire trying to cover his own rear end.

Donovan forced himself not to think about it. He was sure he was right.

No time to worry about the significance of family pictures.

He pushed Ivan to the living room and pressed him to a sitting position on an overstuffed chair, then positioned himself on the coffee table across from the man.

"Where is he, Ivan?"

The older man smiled. "Where is *who*?"

"Cut the crap."

"They're gone," Jordynn interjected.

"Who is?" Donovan asked, and she swung toward him, making him wince as her gun found his chest again. "Could you *not* point that at me?"

Her hands dropped, then lifted back toward Ivan. "Sorry."

"Who's gone?" he asked again.

"I don't know where Ivan told you he was taking you, but this is Sasha's house."

For a second, Donovan thought he'd heard wrong. "Sasha?"

Jordynn nodded. "And her family."

Then it clicked. Jordynn's phone. Ivan's threat. The entry in the address book hadn't been anything but a clever decoy. Donovan's temper flared, and he shot Ivan a furious glare.

"You're a real son of a—"

"I told you it wasn't what you expected." Ivan was smug.

"You let me try to break down the damned door in a house with *kids* in it."

"I tried to warn you."

Donovan eyed the other man. *Something isn't right.*

"It doesn't matter now, anyway," Jordynn told them

both. "Sasha and her family got out. And they're not coming back until this is over."

"You think you're pretty damned smart," Ivan said. "But you don't have a clue how far in over your head you've gotten."

"Enlighten us," Donovan suggested darkly.

Instead of answering, Ivan turned his self-satisfied gaze toward Jordynn. "*You* might want to ask your boyfriend what he could've done to avoid all of this in the first place."

Renewed guilt, thick and sour, washed over Donovan. And it was the gut-wrenching feeling that slowed him down when, a moment later, the siren-free but oh-so-recognizable flash of lights—red/blue, red/blue—burst through the curtains. Some well-meaning neighbor had clearly called the police.

And though Donovan was distracted by his own remorse, Ivan's reaction, on the other hand, was quick. He leaped up from the couch, feinting toward Donovan, then diving at Jordynn instead. He overpowered her easily. Even as fast as Donovan recovered from the dupe, even as swiftly as he was able to lift his weapon, Ivan had twisted Jordynn into a parody of an embrace. A deadly one. The gun was still in her hand, but the other man had his fingers closed on top, and together, they pressed the barrel to her temple.

"Lower your gun, Mr. Grady, or your girlfriend will be committing a horrific act of self-harm," Ivan said.

Donovan swallowed. "You won't fire with the cops outside."

"Won't I?"

A half a dozen reasons for the other man to *not* shoot Jordynn right that second flew through Donovan's mind.

But all of them paled in comparison to the possibility that he might be wrong. Even a slim risk wasn't worth it.

Ivan read his face perfectly. "I want you to hand over your weapon. Slowly, of course, and butt end first. Keep your other hand up. Put it on your head, if it makes this feel more official. And remember…all you have to do is bump me the wrong way, and *bang*."

Wishing he could do just about anything else, Donovan turned the gun as instructed, then stepped toward Ivan, who—without even the hint of a misstep—took the weapon and tucked it into his waistband.

"All right," said the other man. "My guess is that we have less than a minute before those cops get to the door. And less than five before they decide if they have probable cause to enter. I want to be out the back door before either of those things happens. So step in front of me. Move quickly and move quietly. And don't trip. I'd hate for my finger to slip and spoil things for all of us."

Donovan obeyed, and the only sound as they moved from one end of the house to the other was the heart-rending whimper that escaped from Jordynn's lips.

The air outside was impossibly still. From the backyard, the flashing lights were invisible. The neighbors' homes were dark and quiet. All of it was directly at odds with the way Donovan's mind raced in search of a solution. A way to take them back to safety. He couldn't believe he'd let Ivan get the upper hand again. At least twice now, he'd underestimated the man's abilities.

Or maybe you're just overestimating your own.

As quickly as the disparaging thought came, Donovan shoved it aside. He sure as hell couldn't afford to drown in self-loathing. He might not have dug way into this mess ten years ago, but he'd chosen to come back. Chosen to bring himself back into Jordynn's life. She was counting on him to make sure they got out alive.

So do it, he silently commanded as they stepped from the patio onto the grass.

His eyes flicked around. The layout here was similar to the one from the show home in the other community. A small, square yard, fenced on either side. Only two options for escape—up one side of the house, or up the other. Which wouldn't matter anyway. Not unless luck went their way.

I need something—anything—to draw Ivan's attention away from Jordynn, Donovan thought.

The stillness, though, seemed to tell him it wasn't likely.

And then it happened. Luck favored him, just a tiny bit.

In the distance, a dog barked. Donovan saw Ivan's head lift in surprise. The other man's arm lowered, and with it, the gun. At the same second, Jordynn slipped on the patio. One knee buckled, and her body dropped. And the scant few inches between Jordynn's head and the weapon—for the scant few seconds they existed—were exactly the window Donovan needed.

He tossed an elbow to the side, slamming it straight into Ivan's stomach. As the other man bent over in pain, Donovan went for the gun. Vaguely, he noticed that Jordynn had slid sideways and hit the ground. Her eyes were open, and she looked a little stunned. He wished he had time to do something about it, but the man in his grasp commanded his full attention.

They swung back and forth, locked in a struggle as silent as the evening. One cry would draw the attention of the police and bring them around the house.

Ivan was swinging his arm wildly, trying to dislodge

Donovan's hold. Or maybe just trying to get to the trigger. Either way, Donovan wasn't going to let it happen.
He kept his hand closed tightly on Ivan's wrist.

The other man drew in a hissed breath, then aimed
his head at Donovan's chin.

Donovan leaned out of the way, and Ivan's hair barely
grazed him—but the backward movement was enough
to make him partially dislodge his hold. Silently cursing his own mistake, Donovan fought to regain his grasp
on Ivan's wrist. Instead, he knocked the weapon loose.
It skidded across the concrete, then disappeared under
the low wooden deck. Donovan followed the path with
his eyes, then moved to go after it. He stopped quickly,
though, when he realized Ivan wasn't doing the same.
The other man was reaching toward his back.

The other gun, Donovan remembered.

He pounced. Ivan stumbled out of the way, then tried
for the weapon again. Donovan reached him just as he
drew it from his waistband. For the second time, he managed to get his palm on Ivan's fingers. He squeezed. Hard.
The move kept the other man from reaching the trigger, but it earned him a knee directed for his groin, too.
Donovan spun to the side and took it in the hip instead.

He bent down and drove his shoulder into Ivan's chest.
Together, they flew across the patio and landed on the
grass. But nothing louder than a grunt came out of either of their mouths.

Donovan rolled, in charge for a moment. Then Ivan
lifted his hips, twisted and flipped him over. The other
man lifted their joined hands, then smashed them to the
ground.

Donovan bit down so hard that he tasted blood. And
for about three seconds, he thought he might lose the
battle.

C'mon, c'mon. Donovan willed the universe to toss him another favor.

It was Jordynn who came through for him. One moment he was lying on the ground, his grip on the gun weakening, his other arm flailing to gain a hold on Ivan's neck. The next, he was staring up at her pretty freckles, while she stood over him with a garden rake in her hands.

Donovan rolled to his knees and pushed himself up, both an apology and an expression of gratitude on his lips. The words died on his lips as Ivan groaned beside him. He spun just in time to see the other man pulling himself across the lawn toward the discarded gun.

No.

Donovan reacted automatically. He threw his body into Ivan's, crushing the man beneath his full weight. The career criminal collapsed underneath him. Ivan's hand, though, had already reached the mark.

Reacting instinctively, Donovan tightened his arms around the other man's waist, then pulled them both up. With a heave that strained every muscle he had, he stood, with Ivan still in his thick-fingered hold. He strode forward and smashed them together into the house.

Then his plan went awry. As they hit, Ivan's hand flew up and hit the exterior wall in just the wrong way. The gun discharged. The shot echoed through the night, and both of them froze as the bullet cracked into one of the eaves above them. And holding still turned out to be a mistake.

The thud of the shot hitting wood turned into a crack. The crack became a drawn-out creak. Then a chunk of wood fell from above and smacked against Donovan's temple hard enough to make his vision swim. He lifted a hand, trying to sort out the ringing inside from the cacophony of everything that was happening around him.

Shouts.

Thumps.

Jordynn, saying his name.

Ivan, snarling something incomprehensible, and turning *toward* the sound of boots hitting the ground.

Then a wave of dizziness hit, and Donovan found himself blocking out everything in favor of trying to simply stay on his feet.

"Dono!" Jordynn kept her voice low, but it was the fourth time she'd said it, and he had yet to straighten up and look her way.

She knew they were seconds away from getting caught. And Ivan's reminder—*remember what happens if you talk to the cops*—before his sudden and strange stride in the cops' direction made her very nervous. The fact that the cops called out Ivan's name when they spotted him…that was a whole other worry.

Jordynn reached out and put her palm on Dono's elbow. He swayed.

Damn, damn, damn.

The big chunk of debris had to have hit him harder than she thought.

"We need to *go*," she said.

She slung an arm across his waist, then lifted his hand and pulled it to her own shoulder. Though he leaned on her a little, he thankfully carried most of his own weight. But every time Jordynn glanced his way, his eyes were closed. She decided she'd have to worry about his overall well-being later. For now, she just had to get them to immediate safety.

Careful to keep close to the edge of the house, she moved to the other side of the yard. The direction opposite to the one Ivan had headed. She held Donovan close, hugging both him and the wall, and slid along the full length of the building.

"Hang on," she said when they reached the corner.

She positioned Dono against the exterior wall, prayed that he wouldn't simply collapse and leaned around the edge. She could see the police car—still only one, in spite of the shot fired. She could see also that a few neighbors had turned on their lights. Likely, they were peering outside curiously. Her gaze slid up the street to the car. At least it was far enough away that no one would be paying attention to it. But that also meant it was far enough away that it was going to require some effort to get to.

Quickly, Jordynn mapped the fastest route that would also have the most cover.

The right side of the house to the overgrown mess of hedges on the edge of the property.

The police car parked beside the driveway.

Three minivans in succession.

A flower-covered bush just past those.

And that would get them six houses up. Just two away from the vehicle.

And after that? Jordynn shoved down the question with a dismissive reply. *We'll worry about that later.*

She moved back to Dono and lifted his arm over her shoulders again. "You ready?"

He lifted his lids and gave her a sloppy nod. "Okay."

"We can do this," she said.

She was unsure if she was telling him, or if she was telling herself. And she really didn't have time to think about it. They had to hurry.

She drew in a breath, pulled Dono out of the cover of the house and directed them toward their first checkpoint. The walk seemed agonizingly slow. With each step, Jordynn expected a door to fling open and a voice to call out and give them away. But except for the continued flash of red and blue, the night remained still. She couldn't hear anything but her own increasingly labored breathing and the light tread of Donovan's boots as he shuffled over the driveway.

This is good, she told herself. *Quiet is good.*

As they reached the shrubs, she hazarded a glance toward Sasha's house. The police and Ivan remained out of sight.

Also good.

She tugged Dono along to the squad car, but didn't risk stopping there. She moved them quickly to the row of minivans, then to the flowers, where she paused again to make sure they hadn't been spotted. There was no telltale flick of anyone's blinds. No tripped motion lights.

Now, though, they'd have to cross the street. It would mean a good ten seconds of complete exposure.

No choice.

She slipped out from under Dono, threaded her fingers through his and said, "Run."

She didn't give him a chance to protest, and she didn't wait long enough to give herself a chance to think about whether or not his current condition would stop him from being able to actually keep up. She just squeezed his hand and bolted out into the street. And thankfully, his grip stayed true all the way. When they reached the nondescript sedan unscathed and unnoticed—and together—Jordynn had to fight back tears of relief. She swung open the passenger door for Dono.

"Chivalrous," he said. "But I think that was *my* job."

"We can fight about gender roles after we're far away from here."

She helped him into the car, then rushed around to

the driver's side, climbed in and reached an arm over toward him.

"The keys?" she said.

He leaned forward and put his head in his hands. "Ivan has them."

Jordynn's heart dropped. "You're kidding."

"Wish I was."

"Crap."

"Yeah." Dono's head lifted as he shrugged, then dropped back down.

Jordynn tapped the steering wheel and eyed the street nervously. From where the car sat, she could see both the police vehicle and the edge of Sasha's front yard. But she couldn't see Ivan or the cops. And even if she *had* been able to, she couldn't exactly walk up and demand the keys.

She shot another surreptitious glance Dono's way. He looked rough. Eyes closed, breathing shallow, head now pressed to the window. Chances were good that he had a mild concussion. Jordynn didn't think it was a good idea for him to be on the move, but she didn't like the idea of trying to wait out whatever Ivan was up to with the police, either. She doubted they'd be able to maintain an advantage. Especially since the cops clearly knew him well enough to issue him a friendly greeting. And no matter what the nature of the criminal's association with them really was, she was sure she and Dono should be running in the other direction.

She eyed the street once again. Could they hide somewhere close? Take a chance and go back into Sasha's house?

I hate this, she realized, knowing now why Dono was so adamant that they finish what he'd started rather than running from it.

"Screwdriver."

Dono's voice made her jump.

"What?"

"Screwdriver. If you get me one, I can break off the ignition cover and use it to get this thing started."

Hope buoyed Jordynn's heart, but only for a second. "Where am I going to get a screwdriver at three in the morning…subtly?"

"Check the trunk. If not there, maybe a neighbor's garage."

Jordynn bit her lip to keep from pointing out that she had zero experience breaking and entering. She'd try the trunk and hope for the best. And if it didn't pan out… she'd worry about it only then.

Wordlessly, she depressed the release lever for the trunk, then hopped back out of the car. She dug around quickly, hoping she looked like a woman rooting through her own trunk rather than a woman on the run, getting ready to highjack a car. But there wasn't much inside to look through anyway. A few loose pieces of paper. A flashlight and an unnerving pile of rope. But no screwdriver. Not even an emergency roadside kit.

With her nerves roaring, Jordynn reached up to shut the trunk lid. But she paused as a flash of something silvery— lodged in beside the wheel well—caught her eye. Hoping it would be a screwdriver, she reached in and grabbed it. When she pulled it out of its hiding place, though, she saw that it wasn't the much-needed tool at all. It was a pair of scissors.

"Dammit."

She moved to close the trunk. A sharp rap on the back windshield stopped her. Dono had managed to twist his body around, his long arm pushed all the way from the center console to the rear of the vehicle, and he was point-ing emphatically at the scissors.

"What?" Jordynn held up the scissors, and he nod-ded. "Seriously?"

But she wasn't going to argue. Time was ticking by far too quickly. She shut the trunk, then made her way back to the front seat, where she handed the scissors to Dono.

"Hold on to the ignition like this," he said, and pinched his fingers on the silver mechanism to show her what he meant. "Don't let it move until I say."

Obediently, Jordynn positioned her fingers in the way he'd demonstrated. Dono gave her wrist a squeeze, then took the pointed blades, opened them and jammed one blade into the narrow opening. He wiggled and pushed until a tiny click sounded.

"Turn," he said.

Doubting it would have any effect, Jordynn twisted her thumb. And the engine came to life, and stayed that way even after Dono pulled the scissors away.

"It's that easy?" she asked incredulously.

"Old car, old tricks." He smiled, then sobered and nod-ded toward the road.

A quick look in the side-view mirror afforded Jordynn a flash of navy blue. The cops were back at their own vehicle, and Ivan was nowhere to be seen.

"Better get moving," Dono said.

And Jordynn didn't have to be told twice.

Chapter 13

Donovan leaned the seat back and took the ride one breath at a time. His temple throbbed, and the urge to close his eyes was so strong that it was almost overwhelming. He knew, though, the last thing he should do was fall asleep. Watching the scenery as it passed and changed—from the tidy rows of new houses, to the older neighborhoods with their wide laws, to the sparser, spread-out properties that bordered on farmland—lulled him even further, and his eyes threatened to close a few times before he realized he needed something else to occupy him before he fell asleep.

Conversation.

But when he tossed a glance Jordynn's way, he couldn't think of the right thing to say. He had to admit he felt guilty for letting her take charge. It wasn't that he minded handing over the reins for a while—he wasn't an egomaniac and he had no issues with a woman in control.

It was the simple fact that he wanted to protect her at all costs. Head injury or no head injury. So having to rely on her instead pricked at his sense of heroism.

But a large part of him was impressed, too, at how well she'd come through and how well she was still holding up.

He eyed her again.

Her face was determined. Remarkably calm. Beautiful, as always.

Impressed was definitely *not* the right word. What he felt was far more poignant and lasting.

She caught his stare and offered him a small smile that made his heart expand even more.

"Hey there," he said.

"Hey there yourself," she said back.

"You got a destination in mind, or are you just driving as fast and far away as possible?"

She blew out a breath that made her hair ruffle. "I don't know. I was thinking of the Rio Motel."

"The Rio?"

"If you don't mind sidestepping town for just a bit."

A slight blush crept up her cheeks, and Donovan couldn't help but grin. That particular spot held more than a few hot-and-bothered memories for him. For both of them. Located in the next town over—just ten miles from Ellisberg—it was a run-down place that looked like it was one step above having rent-by-the-hour status. Ten years ago, it had been the perfect spot for them to be alone. Away from the scrutiny of his cop father. Away from her mother's long-term battle with cancer. Away from everything but each other.

"Sounds about perfect," Donovan said, failing to keep his voice neutral.

Jordynn's color deepened. "I'm just not sure how we're going to pay for it."

"Pocket change?" Donovan teased.

"Very funny."

"Seriously...if we dig through the seats..."

She sighed. "I'm pretty sure that's not going to cut it. And I'm guessing you aren't carrying around a ton of cash?"

"Sadly, no."

"And a credit card—not that mine is very helpful when it's sitting in my purse at home—would be out of the question."

"Too traceable," he agreed, then strummed his fingers on his thigh, thinking. Then he paused and said, "Carlos Hernandez."

She only looked puzzled for a second before her face cleared. "Your friend with the boxing gym?"

"Mmm-hmm. Keeping people hidden is one of his specialties. When we get to the Rio, we can give him a call. He'll set up payment under a name that can't be tied back to him or us."

"You trust him?"

"Implicitly."

"The Rio it is, then."

As she flicked on the turn signal and took the turnoff that would lead to the short bit of highway between the two towns, Donovan offered her a sly, sideways grin.

"Should we ask if room eleven is available?" he asked.

His question made Jordynn jerk the car sideways, and Donovan laughed, which earned him a sharp pain at the base of his neck and a concerned look from Jordynn.

"Your head!" she exclaimed.

Donovan shrugged it off with another smile. "Been hit harder by worse people."

"Not exactly reassuring."

"Sorry."

She was silent for a second before replying. "Me, too."

Donovan frowned, sensing she meant more than the momentary loss of control over the car. "*You're* sorry?"

"I just… I guess I wasn't thinking about how all this affected you. And I didn't make it easy for you to walk back into my life."

Donovan frowned harder, which made his brow ache. "Why would you have made it easy? There's nothing easy about what's going on."

"I know. But once I got over the fact that you weren't a ghost, I could've given you the benefit of the doubt."

"Didn't you?"

She laughed a short little laugh. "I guess you didn't notice the part where I tried to run away from you. Or the fact that I haven't accepted a single thing you've said at face value. Or how I've been questioning every move you've made since you *saved my life*. I'm sorry, Dono. I spent all of ten minutes trying to keep Sasha from figuring out what was going on while still keeping her and her family safe, and I felt terrible the whole time. As much as I wanted to tell her what we were really up against, I couldn't. I can't wrap my head around how you did it."

He reached over to squeeze her hand. "Simple. Knowing you were safe kept me going."

"But how *could* you know? You weren't here."

She sounded more tired than angry, and it magnified Donovan's guilt all the more. He stared out the windshield for a moment, searching the horizon as though it would give him an answer that didn't seem false. He tugged absently on his ear, then settled on telling her the truth—no matter how contrived it came across.

"I checked the papers, every week," he said. "No matter where I was, I made sure to look up Ellisberg online. I plugged in your name, too, whenever I looked. That's how I knew when you mom died. I saw other things, too. Like when you graduated from the community college. I went out for a celebratory drink that night. I saw everything I could. And other than that…I was damned sure I'd just *know* if something went wrong. I always did when we were together, so why would it be any different when we were apart?"

Jordynn fixed him with a stare—so long that he was surprised they didn't crash—then turned her attention back to the road as she asked, "Is that why you came back now? Because you sensed it?"

He shook his head. "Not quite."

"What, then?"

"For about two weeks I felt like someone was watching me," he told her. "I had that creepy feeling between my shoulder blades every time I went out. I kept brushing it off, telling myself it'd just been too long since I moved, and that I was being paranoid. I reminded myself about a hundred times that ten years had gone by, and that no one knew I was alive, so no one would bother looking for me. But then I got a piece of registered mail."

Donovan paused to clear his throat of the thick, oily feeling in it. All he succeeded in doing was sending it down to his stomach. He forced himself to go on.

"It was two pictures. One was a still frame of me, at the funeral. The other was something else. Blown up and full recognizable."

"Was it me?" Jordynn interjected, fear clear in her voice.

"No. A key."

"A key?"

"Our key."

Her gaze found him for a second, understanding registering on her face. For years—since she was a teenager, actually—Jordynn had kept a wide, flat key hanging on the back of the door to her room. Donovan had teased her about it all the time, asking if it was the key to her heart, or the key to her success, or if she was just being deliberately mysterious. One day, she'd finally told him to shove it, saying that the key was just a key and she only kept it because she liked the way it looked and thought maybe the box it opened would come in handy someday. But when she'd shown him the metal container, the idea of the time capsule had been born. They'd spent a year filling it with keepsakes. All ready to be buried on the night he witnessed the murder.

"When I got the photo," Donovan said, "I knew that itch I'd been feeling all week was real. I contacted Carlos, got on the next bus and here I am."

"You didn't think maybe they'd already...got me?"

"I would've come anyway. But I knew it was just a threat. And before you ask, no, not just based on a feeling. They sent me similar stuff ten years ago."

She slowed the car as they approached the exit for the roadside motel. "What do you mean?"

He waited until she'd navigated the vehicle to the parking lot before replying. The answer was one he'd rather not share. But also one he didn't think he could keep a secret anymore. Not if he wanted to truly rebuild the trust between them.

"The pictures started a few days after I healed from the first beating Ivan's men gave me," he said. "The photos were of small things. A pair of shoes. A bracelet. That key. They were *your* things, honey. And none of them would've meant a thing to anyone else. But to me... I knew the shoes were the ones that your mom gave you for graduating."

"I hated them," Jordynn said softly as she pulled into

the lot and put the car in Park. "But I couldn't tell her because I didn't want to hurt her feelings."

"You kept them in the back of your closet, still in the box," Donovan agreed. "And the bracelet...it was the one I bought from that kid who was turning garbage into art. You weren't ever able to wear it because it turned your wrist green."

"But I kept that, too."

"I know. You pinned it to the corkboard by your desk." He met her eyes. "They were threats. All of them. Little reminders that they knew who you were and what you meant to me. And even more than that, they were telling me that they could find out whatever they wanted to find out."

Jordynn shivered. "And you did...what?"

"I confronted them. I took the pictures and went straight up to the worksite Haven was at. I demanded to speak with Ivan, and I told him if he came anywhere near you, I'd kill him myself."

"I'm guessing he didn't take you seriously?"

Donovan's mouth tipped up with sardonic amusement. "I was a hundred-and-thirty-pound kid with a pre-existing chip on my shoulder because of how things were with my dad. They held all the cards and knew my weakness."

"Me."

"Yes."

"And that's when they beat you up again?"

"That night. They dragged me out of my bed. Beat the hell out of me. And I realized that no matter what I did, no matter what I said, they'd never stay out of my life. Or out of yours."

"You called me," she said. "You canceled our date for the next night, and I was mad."

"I did. And you were." He touched her cheek. "I kept telling you I loved you."

"But I hung up and when you called back…"

"You didn't answer. I took it as a sign."

Her expression became incredulous. "What kind of sign would that be?"

"One that would give me the courage to leave, when all I wanted to do was stay."

He cupped her face and leaned in for a kiss, but a demanding tap on the driver's-side window made him freeze.

With his heart in his throat, Donovan eased away from Jordynn's tempting lips and prepared himself to face whoever was on the outside of the car. Surreptitiously, he reached for the discarded scissors, tightening his fingers on their handle, but keeping the makeshift weapon low.

It's not much, he thought, *but it's better than nothing*.

He lifted his gaze up. And just about burst out laughing. On the other side of the window stood a face he knew well. One that hadn't changed a bit in ten years. Ella Rio. The dour woman who owned and ran the motel.

"You're kidding me," he said, his voice full of the genuine disbelief he felt at seeing her there.

She mouthed something, her wrinkled skin flapping with the words Donovan couldn't hear.

"I don't think she's kidding," Jordynn said. "And I think she wants me to roll down the window, too."

"I'll do her one better," Donovan replied.

He swung open his door and climbed out. He briefly considered pretending to be a complete stranger, but decided quickly that it was better to acknowledge the past in case she recognized them on her own.

"Hi, Ella," he said.

She squinted up at him. "Should I know you?"

"It's been a while, but we used to be regulars."

The old woman's eyes moved between him and Jordynn, then widened in recognition. "Romeo and Juliet?"

"The nickname seems a little ominous now," Donovan said drily. "Maybe today, we'll just be Mr. and Mrs. Smith."

Ella's eyes sought his ring finger, aiming a searing glare where the band ought to be. "Either you lost something, or things didn't turn out the way I expected it would with you two."

Jordynn—who'd climbed out and joined them—reached into her shirt and dragged out the promise ring.

"*Soon*-to-be Mr. and Mrs. Smith," she amended.

"Hmph," Ella said. "Good thing the honeymoon suite is open, then. Follow me. Before all your loitering starts bringing down the property value. And by the way, you're not coming into one of *my* rooms in those filthy clothes."

Jordynn waited with nervous anticipation as Dono borrowed the phone to call his friend Carlos and made the payment arrangements. Being at the motel was a lung-squeezing rush of buried emotion and sweet recollection. If the mountainside had been their favorite place of refuge as teens, the Rio had definitely been the equivalent for their burgeoning adulthood. With Dono's father a perpetual bear of a man, and Jordynn's mother dwindling away, they'd needed somewhere to be alone. Somewhere to explore their deepening love without the buzz of their everyday lives interfering.

Dono finished up on the phone, then pressed one of his hands into the small of her back. He held out a stack of tidily folded—but obviously mismatched—clothes in the other.

"Ella has generously offered to lend us these, and she's given us permission to get changed in her office, too," he explained, his eyes flashing with amusement, but his mouth flat. "And she offered to wash and dry our clothes, too."

"For a fee," the wizened woman added.

"For a fee," Dono repeated, and the corners of his lips twitched. "Which Carlos is happy to pay."

Jordynn fought a smile. But her amusement faded as she realized the office in question was a six-by-six square with a squat desk taking up about a quarter of the already limited space. And that Ella expected them to change together.

And the expectation makes perfect sense, Jordynn told herself as the older woman ushered them into the room. *Because we're supposed to be a hot-and-heavy couple.*

It didn't make the butterflies in her stomach calm down as Dono closed the wooden door behind them.

"We'll make it quick and relatively painless," he said as he handed her a big white T-shirt and a pair of puppy-print pajama pants. "Like ripping off a Band-Aid."

But when he leaned down to unlace first one boot, then the other, the world slowed down instead of speeding up. It got worse when he straightened up and tried to whip off his own shirt, because the sleeve snagged on a loose nail on the wall, and he had to wriggle free. And there was nothing quick or painless about the responding buzz in Jordynn's skin. Heat crept up her body slowly, making her ache all over. Yes, she'd seen him topless— *more* than topless—back in the show home, but there was something different about getting undressed in the tiny room while Ella waited on the other side of the door. Something different about the way, when he moved to and fro, trying to get himself loose, he brushed against her accidentally. The room seemed warmer with each passing second. The sound of his zipper coming down spiked it to sauna level.

Jordynn breathed in through her nose and out through her mouth, trying to stay calm. It had little effect. Because somehow, their escape plan had taken an illicit turn. She definitely could feel that same tingle of excitement she'd had each time they'd checked in, years earlier.

"Hey." Dono's amused voice just about made her jump. "Is that what we're supposed to do?"

"Um. What?"

"Close our eyes?"

Her lids flew up. She hadn't even realized she'd closed them. Dono was grinning at her, fully changed now into a pair of too-short pants and a too-snug dress shirt. He'd slipped his boots on again, but had left them unlaced. He should've looked ridiculous. Instead, he looked mouthwatering.

"Well?" he prodded.

"Yes," Jordynn replied quickly. "Actually. Please."

He laughed, dragged his eyes over her once more, then closed them and lifted his hands to cover his face. "Go for it."

As swiftly as she could manage, and careful not to expose any part of her body for long, Jordynn slipped out of her own clothes and into the borrowed ones. She kept her gaze on Dono the whole time, sure he was going to help himself to a peek. But he didn't. And instead of relief, Jordynn experienced a sharp stab of disappointment.

Shoving it down, she snagged the room key off the desk, then jangled them in Dono's direction. "Ready?"

He closed his hand over hers, stuck his finger through the key ring and used it to pull her close. Then he dropped a long, firm kiss on her mouth. And Jordynn's disappointment was immediately forgotten. Her body molded to his, buzzing once more as his hands slid over the badly fitted clothing. She deepened the kiss, now appreciative of the small space. And it was he who pulled away, sliding his hand down to pull away the key from her loose grip.

He held it between them, and said teasingly, "Room twenty-eight? We're moving up in the world."

"Honeymoon suite," she replied, her voice shaky with desire. "I'm guessing that means a coin-operated bed and free adult films."

Dono laughed his low, sexy laugh, then tugged her from the office back into the lobby. As they slid past Ella, she warned them to leave their muddy shoes at their room door, and he laughed harder, which made Jordynn laugh, too. She buried her face in his side, trying to cover it. But by the time they actually reached the room, Jordynn was shaking with mirth.

"There's…nothing…funny…about…this…situation," she gasped through her giggles.

But Dono was leaning against the stucco siding, doubled over with his own laughter. When he lifted his head, he was smiling as wide as she'd ever seen.

"You're right," he said, then laughed again. "Not a damned thing."

She wiped her eyes, fighting another uncontrollable snicker. "I missed this."

"What? The laughing at nothing together like two crazy people?"

"Exactly."

"I did, too, honey." His eyes raked over her, and her breath caught and her pulse raced.

"Should we go inside?" she asked.

"Mmm-hmm."

He put his arm around her waist, jabbed the key into the knob, then eased the door open.

And in spite of Ella's claim that this was the honeymoon suite, room twenty-eight was identical to the one where they'd spent so many evening ten years earlier. A desk, circa 1965, decorated one corner, and a plush two-person lounge chair took up another. There was no table in the room, but Jordynn was sure that if she opened the brown cupboard in the corner, she'd find a couple of rickety TV trays. Perfect for snacking away while watching something on the ancient set that weighed down a wooden stand across from the bed.

But in spite of the age of the room—and its antiquated decor—it was spotless. A hint of lemon and pine dusted the air, and the bedspread was as crisp as it was worn. There wasn't a speck of dust or a smear of dirt anywhere to be seen. Jordynn remembered, then, that Ella had always boasted about the fact that she cleaned every room herself. And it looked like she still did.

"It's kind of like coming home, isn't it?" she asked softly.

"In a *Twilight Zone* kinda way," Dono said.

Jordynn laughed. But when he flicked on the light, then closed the door and sank down onto the bed, he winced a little, reminding her of his injury.

"I should check you for a concussion," she told him.

"I think I'm okay."

She raised an eyebrow. "And I think *I'm* the expert."

"Right," he said. "Nurse Flannigan."

"Care aide, actually," she corrected. "Close your eyes and tip your head up."

He lowered his lids. "Aha. So you change diapers instead of bandages."

"As a matter of fact, I change both. Open your eyes

and look at the light above the bed." He complied, and when his pupils dilated normally, Jordynn let out a relieved breath. "Full name?"

"Mine or yours?" he teased. "Donovan Jason Grady. Jordynn Jean Flannigan."

"Good enough. Do you feel nauseous? Or dizzy at all?"

"My stomach is fine," he replied. "And my head aches, and I did feel light-headed when the chunk of house hit me, but it's not bad now."

"Good? Or just not bad?"

"Smack-dab in the middle."

Jordynn put a gentle hand on his forehead—not because it would tell her anything about his state of mind, but because it made *her* feel better. "I think you got lucky."

He reached up to thread his fingers with hers. "Yep. More than once. In this exact hotel."

Heat crept up Jordynn's cheeks. Dono might've been giving her a hard time, but his expression was serious. He dragged their intertwined hands to her face and traced the line of her blush with his knuckles. The action made the heat spread down her throat and into her chest.

She pulled away—because she wasn't entirely sure she was ready for what was coming next—and moved to start up the coffeepot on the desk.

"You might not actually be concussed," she said in a rush, "but I still think you should rest. But be careful about staying awake, too. We can look through that file and see if any of it means anything. Maybe ask Ella if the motel's upgraded to anything that looks vaguely like the internet. And if not, then—"

"Jordynn?"

She took a breath and faced him, forcing her heart to stay calm as she met his hazel gaze. "Yes?"

"How come you gave it up?"

"Gave up what?"

"The nursing. You were working so hard to save the money for college. You had all the prerequisites."

"It just didn't work out that way. When things settled after—well, just *after*, Sasha's uncle came to me and offered me the job at the care home. With pay almost as good as nursing and the fact that I could start right away—there was no way I could say no. I took the care aide program at the community college at night, and I worked during the day. Her uncle even paid for the program. He called it work training."

"Sounds like things lined up perfectly."

She heard an edge in the statement, and she bristled in spite of her effort not to. "Nothing about it was perfect. But it was the best it could be under the circumstances. I needed an excuse to stay in Ellisberg."

"Because of me?"

The edge was still there. Jordynn stepped closer and she recognized it for what it really was—poorly veiled guilt.

"No, Dono," she said carefully. "It wasn't because of you. Not just, anyway."

"Not just. That doesn't make me feel any better."

She sat beside him on the bed and took his hand. "When you were first gone…I was a mess. A walking disaster for a full year. I don't even remember anything about those months. I didn't have any direction. But I knew I didn't want to leave the place where I grew up. I would've just been running away from the hurt instead of facing it. And my mom was still sick. She needed me. Taking the job at the care home was the best thing to do."

He put his head in his hands. "I'm sorry."

"I know."

"If I could…"

"You did the right thing."

His lifted his gaze, surprise evident on his face. "What?"

She went silent. She was as startled as he was. But after a few seconds, she realized she'd been leading up to the conclusion all night and into the early hours of the morning. Maybe even since the second he started to explain. The more they ran, the greater she understood what he'd gone through. The understanding had grown and grown and now…she *knew*.

"If you hadn't gone, Ivan would've killed your dad," she said. "He would've killed *me*. And if he'd thought you were alive, he'd would've come after you, too. At least three of us would've been dead."

"That really *should* make me feel better. But it just doesn't."

Jordynn offered him a smile. "It's not as though I *like* admitting you were right."

Dono didn't smile back. His face was stony, but his eyes blazed with self-directed anger.

He can't forgive himself, Jordynn realized.

"But I can," she said softly.

A small frown clouded his features. "You can what?"

"Forgive you."

For several long seconds, his expression didn't change. Not one hair's breadth. The same disbelief stayed there, making Jordynn's heart ache.

She cleared her throat and repeated it more firmly. "I can forgive you, Dono. I *do* forgive you."

"The past—"

"Is the past. We can have ten *new* years. And a future with you is all I ever wanted."

"I want to give you that," he said fiercely.

And his face finally *did* change. It filled with surprise and relief. And blatant desire.

Chapter 14

Jordynn leaned in as Dono reached for her, actively seeking his attention.

He touched her face first, caressing its curves. Thumbs on cheekbones, fingers on brow, worshipping her skin. Then he tipped his head down and pressed his lips to hers. Firm and tender. Hot and insistent. He tugged the bottom one open, then plunged his tongue into her mouth, twining it with hers in a familiar, welcome dance.

In spite of the way their breaths quickened together, Jordynn noticed that Dono didn't hurry. He didn't push. Instead, he explored slowly, like he might never get to again.

And it might be true, she acknowledged, closing her eyes as his fingers slid to her neck. *This might be our only chance.*

Face.

Collarbone.

A light touch on one aching breast, then the other.

A kiss.

And back again.

Over and over, until Jordynn's whole being was alight with desperate want.

She freed herself long enough to reach down and lift her shirt up, then off completely, and she heard Dono's breath catch as his gaze ran over her exposed form. Heat seared each spot where his eyes landed. She shivered under the warm scrutiny.

Did she look different than she had, ten years earlier? Better? Worse? Older? Softer?

Then he spoke, his voice slow and thick with want, and his words dashed away any worry. "You are so damned beautiful. My memory didn't do you the slightest bit of justice."

He placed a finger on her cheek, trailed it down to her cleavage, then flattened his palm against the exact spot where her heart thundered hard against her rib cage.

"Every night, I dreamed of you. Of *this*. Of just touching you for one second more or holding you for one more night," he said.

And when she met his gaze, she found another source for his slow but attentive study of her body. A silent question. Or maybe an offer to go no further.

But the last the thing she wanted was to give up this opportunity.

Not trusting her voice, and not wanting to risk breaking the spell, Jordynn nodded once. Dono let out a throaty noise—one part growl, one part sigh. Then he slid a hand under her, turned her sideways and pressed her back onto the bed. He gave her another long, deep kiss before he stood and stripped down. First went the shirt, revealing his thick, well-muscled chest and his defined abs, marred only by the angry slash of his earlier wound. Next came the jeans, and with them, his snug boxer briefs.

Jordynn's breath stuck in her throat. She'd loved looking at him for as long as she could remember. Through every stage of their young lives together. And now...he was stunning. But he didn't give her much time to continue with her unabashed stare. He moved back to the bed, pushing a knee between her legs to part them, then rested himself against her, unmoving.

And in spite of the fact that he was bigger, stronger and on top, there was something vulnerable about the pose. Him, completely naked. Her, protected by her jeans and bra. But when he dropped his mouth to hers, any illusion of vulnerability flew away.

He kissed her, hard and tender.

He kissed her, slow and deep.

He kissed her like she was the one and only thing that had been on his mind for the ten years they'd spent apart.

She rose to meet his amorous attention, devouring him with equal fervor. When he at last released her lips, he didn't give her time to mourn the loss. He moved on quickly, nipping and sucking the skin along the constraining edge of her bra, then sliding the strap down to free her. He took her into his mouth—hot and oh so much of a turn-on—and Jordynn couldn't help but cry out.

He let her go again, and pushed himself down so that his face was in line with her stomach. He used his tongue to create a lazy circle of her navel, then put his teeth to her jeans button and tugged it open. He fought with her zipper for second, then gave up and yanked down the pants forcefully.

"Holy hell," he swore, his voice rough with desire.

Jordynn lifted her head and found his gaze on the pair

of simple black lace panties she'd thrown on for work. Not her usual, everyday selection, but…

"I missed a laundry day," she blurted, then blushed.

"That shouldn't be a sexy statement," Dono replied, "but I'll be damned if I've ever heard something sexier."

He dropped to the bottom edge of the bed then, and lowered his head, marking her ankles with his mouth. As he worked his way up, Jordynn gasped and flopped back onto the pillow, her embarrassment forgotten.

Dono found her calf. Then her knee. And her thigh. Then he kissed her lightly over her underwear. And back down again on the other side. He started a second pass, this time with his tongue.

"Dono." His name came out in a moan.

He paused. "Yeah, honey?"

"No, don't— Ah, don't stop."

He chuckled against her thigh, then let his mouth go to work. Up. Down. Increasing in intensity each time. Jordynn was on fire with wanting him.

"Donovan, please."

Obediently, he lifted himself back up onto the bed, somehow managing to flick her underwear off at the same time, then held himself poised over her. His face grew momentarily serious.

"I love you, Jordynn," he murmured. "Never stopped."

She opened her mouth to reciprocate, but as her lips parted, Dono thrust forward, entering her in a way that made it impossible to form a coherent sentence.

God, oh— Oh, God— My— Yes.

Jordynn had no idea if she spoke aloud, or if the half-formed thoughts simply stayed in her head. She didn't care, either. She moved with him. A remembered rhythm. A perfectly in-synch cadence. Her name, on his lips. His body, filling her.

Seconds became minutes, and the minutes became timeless.

At last, the tempo built to a crescendo, and Dono released an animalistic noise from deep in his chest, and pushed into her a final time. And with a crash, Jordynn came undone, shuddering against him, wave after wave rocking her—and she was complete, for the first time in a decade.

Donovan balanced himself on his elbow for a long minute, admiring the slight part in Jordynn's lips, the flutter of her eyelids and the flush under her freckles. The rise and fall of her chest under the thin bedsheet was even. Comforting. She was, and always had been, the most beautiful woman he'd ever seen.

And she forgives you.

That, more than anything, made his heart swell. It was more than he could have hoped for. More than he could offer himself.

She still doesn't know it all.

Donovan shoved down the little reminder. That was about him, not her. And Jordynn was what mattered.

He traced the line of her bare collarbone. "You awake?"

"Sort of." She opened one eye. "Did you think you were watching me sleep?"

"Maybe." He chuckled. "I think I could watch you for hours."

She lifted the other lid and both blue eyes met his stare. "I'm sure the staring would get old pretty fast."

"Doubtful."

"Creepy, then."

"Maybe that," he conceded, then rolled himself off her and pulled her into a sideways embrace.

He inhaled deeply, drinking in the light scent of sweat and sex and whatever it was that made Jordynn smell perfect. He wished he could hold it in his lungs, hang on to its overwhelming sweetness. He wished, also, that he could hold on to the *rightness* of being together. The afterglow. But he could already feel the pressing need of their situation, rearing its head and demanding to be dealt with.

Like she could read his mind, Jordynn sighed and said, "We need to get back to work, don't we?"

Donovan ran a finger up her arm, elbow to shoulder, then back. "My care aide suggested that I rest."

"Your care aide retracts her earlier assessment."

"Oh, really?"

"In light of your recent demonstration of capability."

He grinned. "Is that what we're calling it now?"

Jordynn's face flushed. "Shut up."

Donovan laughed, then reached over her to grab the red folder from the nightstand. He pulled her in again and opened the file up. He scanned the list of names, properties and values.

"These aren't Haven developments," he said right away.

"No. They all belong to Fryer. See here? This one— Dancer's Cove—I've actually heard of. It was in the news a couple of years ago. It was a brand-new recreational property outside of Portland. Cabins and stuff. I remember it because it burned down. Even with the insurance, a lot of people lost money."

Donovan slid his finger to where she was pointing, then dragged it up. "I recognize this one, too, from a town I was staying in. It was a condo that didn't pass inspection, and the whole thing had to be gutted."

Jordynn sat up, clutching the sheet, her blue eyes wide. "Dono...do you think Haven sabotaged these?"

"All of them?" He pulled the folder to his lap and scanned the list. "There're nineteen properties here."

"I know. But is it really that far-fetched? They murdered someone ten years ago. To me, that's way more unfathomable than one development company trying to take out a competitor."

Donovan leaned back against the headboard thinking about it. She was right. Ivan—and whoever was pulling his strings—had the guts, and the lack of morals, to commit sabotage.

"But I don't think they're really competitors," he murmured.

"Why not?" Jordynn asked.

"Money. Plain and simple." He tapped the sheet. "Look at the prices of these properties. They're worth a tenth of what most of Haven owns. Fryer is small potatoes."

"Except Fryer *did* get the mountainside property."

"Except that."

Jordynn pursed her lips. "What if it's not about the money or the property? What if the mountain is a coincidence and there's something we're not seeing?"

"If that's true, then I guess we should make a concentrated effort to figure out what it is."

"We need the internet."

Donovan gave the room a quick once-over, then nodded toward the phone on the nightstand. "She hasn't even moved on from rotary. I somehow doubt Ella's managed to get a computer in here anywhere."

She sat back, looking deflated. "You're right. What're we going to do?"

"Find somewhere with free computers?"

"Right. Because those are all over the place."

"How about a burner phone with a web browser?"

"Where are we going to get one? It's not even eight in the morning. And it's Sunday. Even the library is closed, and that's probably the one place that *does* still have public computers."

Donovan sighed. "If you're not a part of the solution…"

"I'm thinking!"

"No, I'm thinking. You're shooting down my ideas."

"Because they're bad ideas." Jordynn gave his arm a light shove. "I don't know how you survived without me."

"That's just it, honey. I survived. Nothing more." He reached up and took her hand, then lifted her palm to his mouth and gave it a kiss. "I know I did it to myself, but it was still tough. The first month, I wanted to cry myself to sleep every night. The second month, I kept telling myself it was a bad dream. The third month, I realized it was really real, and I couldn't hold it together. I got on the bus with the intention of coming back *eighteen times*."

"And eighteen times you turned around again."

"Yep. I knew that if I didn't, I would just lose the thing I wanted to come back to so desperately."

She trailed her fingers up and down his hand, and the need for urgency slipped away as he closed his eyes to enjoy the feel of it. Lying with her was like coming home for real. Like those ten years apart were already misting into oblivion.

"Tell me about the night you left," Jordynn said then, her voice tentative.

"It was dark and stormy."

Donovan grinned into her hair as she let out a laugh.

"Such a liar," she said.

"Yeah, well. I'll accept the label. Anything for your amusement." He sighed, wishing he could keep up the lightness, but knowing there was no way to do it. "Maybe it just *seemed* stormy that night. Ivan's men had beat the hell out of me and left me on the side of the road… I was sure that was the end. For me. For us. I knew if I came back into town, I'd have to find a way to explain my injuries. You wouldn't have just let it go. Which is probably why they did it the way they did. So then I came up with this insane idea. I'd fake a car crash. It would explain away most of the physical damaged I'd suffered."

"What changed your mind about doing it?"

He pulled her into a sideways embrace. "I drove out to Hilltop Park. I thought I'd go full speed at a telephone pole or something. Jump out at the last second. Figured if I did it up there, the sound would carry down, and someone would call 911, even if I couldn't manage it myself. But I got to the park, and I just couldn't do it. I was a mess. Blood everywhere. Heart in a million damned pieces. I sat there on the hill, and realized I was in over my head. Way over. And no matter what I did, they weren't going to just disappear."

"Unless *you* did," Jordynn filled in.

"Exactly. And when I decided that, I was finally calm. For the first time in a month, I knew what to do." Donovan lifted a strand of red hair and wrapped it around his finger. "I turned around and I left Hilltop Park. I came up with a new plan, and I drove to our bridge instead, on Greyside Mountain. I knew that old bridge well enough to plan exactly where to push the car off. I stripped down— my clothes were destroyed anyway, and there was more than enough blood on them—and tossed everything into the front seat. Which is when I called you."

"And when I started the fight."

"You might've started it," he said as he released her hair, "but I let it happen. I might even have pushed it a little, thinking it would be easier for you to let me go if you were mad at me."

She pulled away. "Easier? It's eaten me up inside, that the last words I said to you were angry ones. I've spent ten years feeling so guilty. Wishing I could take those words back."

Strangely, Donovan's own guilt didn't rear its head. Sure, it was still there in the back of his mind, tied to the things he still hadn't shared. But the forward momentum—the urge to heal what could be healed—was stronger.

"Do it now," he said.

"What?"

"Take back the words."

Jordynn met his eyes. "Now?"

Donovan nodded. "Yes."

"What good will it do?"

"You won't know unless you try it."

Her gaze dropped to her hands, and when she lifted her face again, there were tears in her eyes. "I take it back, Dono. I didn't mean it when I said you were self-centered and that I was glad you canceled our date. It was mean and untrue. I wish I'd just told you it was fine and I'd see you soon. I thought about the conversation, over and over."

Donovan reached up to wipe away a stray drop. "I never thought twice about what you said. And I never once resented that you were angry with me before I left. And maybe it *was* self-centered, but the thing that mattered most to me was that the last thing I said to you was that I love you."

"That doesn't change that the last thing I said to *you* was to take your excuse and shove it."

"That bit made me laugh, actually. It was so you."

The smallest bit of a smile tipped up one corner of Jordynn's mouth. "Anything for *your* amusement."

He smiled back. "Feel any better?"

"A little," she admitted.

"See? You have to let it out so you can let it go."

He meant it as a joke, but Jordynn's face turned serious again.

"Like you have?" The question was a challenge.

"It's different for me. You said something you didn't mean. I faked my own death and left you and—"

"And I forgave you. For all of it."

He kissed her. "I know."

"So what's it going to take?"

"For me to let it go?"

"Yes."

Donovan closed his eyes for a second, seriously thinking it over. He already felt remarkably light. More at ease than he had in a decade. Forgiving himself, though, was going to take more.

"Resolution," he said softly.

"That'll work?" she asked.

"It sure as hell won't hurt."

She tossed back the sheet and stood up, her glorious curves on display. "Let's go."

Donovan lifted a brow. "Without our clothes?"

Color bloomed in her cheeks, but she just grabbed his pants from the floor and tossed them his way. "Nope. We're going to be trying *not* to attract attention."

He put his hands behind his head and leaned against the headboard. "So now we have a destination in mind?"

"Since we can't get access to a public computer, we need a private one. I'd usually suggest my house or Sasha's, but those are out of the question, so…option C."

"Which is?"

"Work."

"Work?"

"The care home—where I change the diapers *and* the bandages—has computers," she said. "And I have access."

"There's a good chance they're watching the building," he replied.

"Maybe. But I know a secret way in."

He watched her dig through the pile of blankets in search of her clothes. Her hair flung back and forth across her shoulders, and her creamy skin flashed appealingly as she moved.

"Where's my shirt?" she muttered.

Donovan spied it hanging from the edge of the desk.

"I think it's under the bed over here," he lied.

She stepped closer, and as soon as she was in reach, he grabbed her and pulled her to the edge of the bed.

"Hey!" she protested.

"You think the computers will be there for a little while longer?" he teased.

Jordynn's face flushed. "I guess I wouldn't argue if you wanted to stay here for another few minutes."

"A few minutes? Give me a bit of credit."

"I thought I *was* giving you credit."

"Then I guess I should remind you that I'm not an overeager twenty-year-old boy anymore."

She smiled a little too sweetly—almost coyly. "Oh."

"Oh?" Donovan repeated.

"Just…does that mean you're so old that you, you know, *can't*?"

"It means I've been waiting for you for ten very long years. And I don't think I'll ever be so old that I can't."

Her eyes sparkled. "Prove it."

"Oh, I will."

And he dropped down, pressing himself against her and leaving no doubt about the fact that he *could*. That he would. Right that second.

Chapter 15

Jordynn was achy and warm and satisfied. Suffused with a new sense of hope, and a belief that they would succeed. And most of all, she was glad to have had a second chance with Dono. Even if their reunion was still a little too brief for her liking.

Like he could read her thoughts, he turned and shot her a slow wink from his position near Ella's counter, then went back to chatting with the still stern-faced older woman.

Okay. Some *parts weren't brief*, she amended.

Because by the time Jordynn had taken a quick shower—which Dono insisted on joining her for—gotten dressed, then undressed, and dressed again a final time, she'd completely lost track of how many "prove it" minutes had passed. Enough to make her legs continue to have that just-ran-a-mile shake.

And the shake threatened to become a swoon as Dono tapped the counter, said goodbye to Ella, then directed a hundred-watt smile Jordynn's way as he strode toward her. When he reached her, though, he put a hand on her elbow, and it steadied her as they walked out to the parking lot.

"Thanks," she said.

"For?"

"Everything."

"I'm not a hundred percent sure I should say you're welcome for such a vague expression of gratitude."

"It's not vague. It's…inclusive."

"Well, then. You're welcome." He gave her a kiss, opened the passenger-side door for her, then paused. "I'm a little worried that this car is going to attract some unwanted attention."

Jordynn climbed in. "Me, too. Which is why you're going to drive us to Sandstone Lane before we go to the care home."

"Sandstone? In the industrial area?"

"Yes."

"Are you going to tell me why, or just sit there with a smug smile on your face?"

"Smug smile."

"Okay."

Dono closed the door, and Jordynn had to work to keep her lips zipped. She'd come up with the idea at the same moment she'd thought of using the computers at work. She wanted to hold on to the small bit of excitement she had at the thought of giving him a small—hopefully good—surprise. So when he got in beside her and turned the scissors in the ignition, Jordynn reached over, fired up the radio and raised the volume just a little too loud to permit any kind of reasonable expectation of conversation.

And twenty all-but-wordless minutes later, they were

standing together, staring up at an eight-foot fence that bore a sign that read Jake's Storage.

"It's not staffed on Sundays," Jordynn told him.

"Looks like they've got a few security cameras, though," Dono replied, pointing up.

Jordynn shook her head. "None of them work. The guy who runs this place has a grandfather at the care home. Last week, he was complaining that the system has been broken for a month, and apparently can't be fixed without upgrading the whole thing."

"Hmm. So you want to climb over?"

"Nope. I've got it taken care of."

Jordynn grabbed Dono's hand and pulled him toward the numbered panel at the end of the fence. She keyed in her code, ignored his surprised look as the gate slid open, then led him into the yard. She tugged him up the aisle to a rolling metal door.

"There," she said, and released his hand.

He raised an eyebrow. "It's a...storage unit."

She rolled her eyes. "It's *my* storage unit. But the keys are in my purse at home, so you're going to need to work some B and E magic or something."

"Oh, really?"

"It'll be worth it. Trust me."

"Putting aside the fact that you're almost *gleeful* and that's making me worry a bit for your sanity..." Dono shrugged. "Okay."

Jordynn watched him turn and jog back up to the path, then disappear in the direction of the car. Her stomach flipped with nervous excitement. Truthfully, she hadn't opened the storage unit since she put down the first month's deposit. Instead, she paid an extra premium to have the manager check in on its contents a couple of times a year, accepted what he reported, then otherwise ignored it. She hoped now that everything the storage manager had told her was true.

Guess I'll find out in a minute, she thought.

Dono was back, the hot-wiring scissors in his hand. He flashed them Jordynn's way, then bent down. It took him less than ten seconds of fiddling with the lock before it popped off.

"You want me to open it up?" There was a hint of a twinkle in his eye. "Or is that something you need to do yourself?"

Jordynn resisted an urge to stick out her tongue. "You do it. I want to stand back here and watch your face when you see what's inside."

A smile tipped up his lips, and he obediently bent again. Jordynn watched as he rolled up the metal door. As he stepped back and peered into the storage unit, a frown etched itself into his forehead. It disappeared quickly, though, and shock took its place.

His eyes flipped back and forth between the concrete room and Jordynn for several seconds before finally settling on her. "Is that what I think it is?"

"Yes."

She stepped into the eight-by-eight room and brought her hands to the big object at the center. A motorcycle. Well, in name, anyway. Dono had pieced the thing together using bits salvaged from scrapyards and generous mechanics, and Jordynn had watched as the bike went from a hideous pile of unrecognizable metal to the shiny silver-and-black vehicle in front of them now. He'd always told Jordynn he was going to make it street legal, but he'd never actually gotten around to doing it.

Jordynn tapped the bike's seat, then lifted her face and smiled. "Your third love, you always said. Me. Then math. Then this bike."

Dono joined her, his hands running over the handle-bars. "That was a bit of a lie."

"It was?"

"It was always you, then the bike. Then the numbers."

"Why would you lie about that?"

He kissed her lightly, then slung a leg over the bike. "Thought maybe you wouldn't want to be married to a grease monkey."

"Seriously?"

"I was a kid."

"A kid who thought numbers were sexier than motorcycles?"

"A kid who was more worried about providing a stable environment for his future wife and their future kids than he was about being sexy."

Tears pricked at the back of Jordynn's lids and she blinked them back forcibly. "Hey, Dono?"

"Yeah?"

"I'm pretty sure *that* was sexier than a grease monkey *or* an accountant."

"Damn. Sappy is sexy? No wonder I always felt like I fell a little short."

"Sincere is sexy. And I promise you, you never fell short."

He grinned. "Wait. Does this mean we aren't going to take the bike after all?"

"I didn't say the bike *wasn't* sexy," she replied. "Just that your words were sexier."

"Hmm. And what about the math?"

"I refuse to answer on the grounds that it may incriminate me."

Dono chuckled, and his hands snaked out to pull her into an embrace. Jordynn leaned into him. He was warm and safe and smelled delicious. She inhaled deeply, wanting to savor both the feel and scent of him.

Not just those things, she realized as he stroked her back. *Everything.*

Little moments and big moments. A shared past and a shared future. The things she'd long given up on. It seemed utterly unreal that she could have them all again.

"Is this a dream?" she asked softly.

Dono leaned back and lifted her chin, his hazel eyes showing a mix of amusement and concern. "A dream? I thought *I* was the one with the head injury."

"I'm serious. It's what I thought when I first saw you in my yard," she told him, then shrugged. "So I guess I keep waiting to wake up."

He cupped her face with both his hands. "This isn't a dream, honey."

She swallowed nervously. "I'm really scared."

"I know. And to be honest, I am, too. But I'll keep you safe, Jordynn. I won't let Ivan or his men anywhere near you."

Jordynn shook her head. "Not of that. I'm scared that things will go wrong and I'll lose you all over again. That I'll never get to tell you I never stopped loving you, either."

There was a beat, and she knew he was digesting her words.

"Is that true?" he asked, his voice thick.

"It is, Dono." She swallowed again. "I love you. Enough that I'm willing to let go of everything that happened. Which I already told you. But…I don't know if I can go through it again. Wait. Scratch that. I *do* know. I can't lose you a second time. I can't second-guess every move, wondering if you're going to disappear again. I just—"

"You won't have to."

"You say that now, but what if it's a choice between my life and you leaving?"

"I'm not going to let that happen."

"Did you ever think it would happen in the first place?"

"Listen to me," he said, his expression as intense and serious as his tone. "I will *not* let it happen. You're not the only one who can't do it again. We're going to finish this, and when we do, the only thing we'll have to do a second time is plan our life together."

Jordynn stared at him, reading the sincerity in his eyes. Seeing that he really believed what he told her, truly meant every word. And she knew she had to take a leap.

She nodded. "Let's hurry up and get the damned bike running, then."

"Anything you say, honey," Dono said, then climbed off the bike and got to work.

Whoever'd been looking after the bike on Jordynn's behalf had done it right. Tank drained, but a full, sealed gas can on hand. Battery kept in a separate cabinet in the corner of the storage room—clean and charged regularly. A couple of helmets and jackets ready.

Donovan took care of things quickly, reattaching the battery to its connections under the seat, checking the wires and going over each hose to make sure he saw no breaks.

"I seriously can't believe you managed to keep this," he said as he looked the bike over, inch by inch.

"It was the same as your dad and the bridge," she told him. "I *couldn't* let it go. Holding on to it was like holding on to a piece of you."

"A bunch of pieces," he corrected teasingly. "Ugly ones."

"Are you kidding? I loved every bit of that thing."

"You know what *I* loved? Having you ride behind me, screaming for dear life."

"I never screamed for dear life."

He stood up and smiled. "I guess we're about to see which of us remembers correctly. Got the key?"

She grabbed it from the cabinet and held it out. "You think it will run?"

"I know it will."

He climbed onto the bike and went through the steps of bringing it to life, careful not to miss anything. He stuck the key into the ignition. He pulled the choke all the way out, then turned the key to the on position. He checked that the kill switch was off, that the gear shifter was in Neutral, then squeezed the clutch lever. Finally, he pushed down on the start button. The starter turned over, but the engine didn't come to life. Not at all discouraged, Donovan tried again, and this time, he was rewarded. The bike hummed roughly, then smoothed to a light rumble.

"See?" he said. "Good as it ever was."

He cut the engine, then dismounted and moved to the cabinet to retrieve the protective gear from inside. The helmets, leather pants, and jackets were the same ones they'd used years earlier, and Donovan couldn't quite decide whether seeing them made him feel bittersweet or just plain sweet. He pushed for the latter as he handed the smaller set to Jordynn.

"This'll be perfect," he told her. "Even if Ivan and his men *are* watching the care home, they won't be looking for a bike. I put this thing away long before they ever showed up in Ellisberg. And assuming it's been in here for the last ten years…"

"It has."

"Good. We'll just look like another couple, out for a Sunday cruise." He paused. "At least until we're right there and have to get off."

"We won't be bringing the bike in that close."

"We won't?"

"Nope. That secret way in that I mentioned? It's on foot."

"Car to bike to feet. This is getting more complicated by the second."

"Just you wait."

Donovan held out his protective gear. The pants were a no-go—a perfect fit for his younger, scrawnier self, and not at all suitable now. His crisp leather jacket, though, was workable. He'd swam in the damned thing as a kid. He slid his arms into the sleeves.

No swimming now, he thought.

Sucking in a breath to force it closed, he smiled at Jordynn. "I'm all yours."

"Good. Take Sandstone to the old highway, and I'll guide you from there." She planted a kiss on his lips, slid the helmet onto her head, then straddled the bike. "Ready when you are."

And minutes later, as they were whipping across the outskirts of Ellisberg on a roundabout route to the care home, Donovan was damned glad Jordynn had taken the lead. The familiar hum underneath him and Jordynn's warm body pressed to his own were a pretty big distraction. His brain was happy to settle back and follow her signals.

A squeeze on his left arm meant to turn that way. A tug on the right meant to go *that* way. If she hugged his waist a little tighter, she wanted him to drive on. Donovan took that as a sign that he should go faster. Right that second, she was holding on *very* tight.

Behind his face shield, he couldn't help but smile.

For him, this was the second-best thing about riding on the bike. The way it screamed of freedom, but demanded control at the same time. The *first*-best thing, though, was the way it made Jordynn tuck her body close behind his, her arms wrapped around his waist, her face buried in his back. It had been a rush, when they were younger, to drive faster and faster through the back roads, making her squeeze more tightly with every turn. He'd loved making her squeal, while knowing he kept her safe the whole time.

Ten years later, it didn't feel any less exhilarating.

He couldn't believe he'd ever put the bike aside in favor of a book full of checks and balance. Of course, it had seemed worth it. A small sacrifice to make on the road to becoming the kind of man a woman like Jordynn would want to marry.

He'd never have considered the motorcycle to be something she'd hang on to. He was glad she had. Not just because it was a convenient way to get where they were going, either. It felt good to know she'd embraced and valued the part of him he'd always believed wasn't quite good enough for her.

Another reason to love her, he thought as he slowed to round a corner.

The back side of a tidy row of three-story buildings came into view on the horizon. Jordynn squeezed, and Donovan followed the curve of the road to take the next left. The turn swung them around and away from the buildings, then took them into a pocket of high-density residential houses. Jordynn squeezed a few more times, and Donovan obeyed each of the silent commands. And after a few more navigational twists, he found himself facing a long, narrow alleyway.

He slowed even more, then brought the bike to a stop at the corner, and Jordynn spoke into his ear, loud enough to be heard above the purr of the engine.

"Four buildings up," she said. "It's a medical office with an underground lot. Go in, then go all the way to the end. There's a big column. Park beside it."

Donovan nodded his understanding, then pulled the motorcycle forward. He guided it down the ramp, spotted the column in question, then rode toward it and parked. Jordynn was right. It was a good spot. The bike would be out of direct view of the entrance and it was right across from a stairwell, too. Easy to get to, if they needed an alternate escape route.

He waited for Jordynn to climb off, then lifted his helmet and faced her. She pulled her head out of her own helmet and shook her hair free.

"Told you I didn't scream," she said.

"I'm sure I heard at least one yelp," he countered.

"You definitely didn't." She shoved her helmet at him. "C'mon."

Donovan tucked both helmets into the rear storage container on the bike, then followed her to the corner of the parking garage.

"What am I looking for?" he asked.

"There," she said, and pointed straight ahead.

"Is it…a magic portal?"

"Ha, ha. No. A magical grate."

She put a finger on his chin and forced his gaze up a few inches. There it was. A piece of crisscrossed metal, painted white to blend in with the wall, and no more than two and a half feet wide by two and a half feet tall.

"You've got to be kidding," he muttered.

"Nope."

"Have you got a bottle of baby oil hidden somewhere? Because no way am I going to fit through there easily."

She grabbed his hand and pulled him nearer to the wall. "You will."

Donovan eyed the grate dubiously. "Doubtful."

"I know for a *fact* that you will, for the same reason I know where it leads."

"Do I even want to ask?"

"Yes."

"Okay. Fine. *How* are you so sure I'll squeeze through? And where does it go?"

"Six years ago, we had this patient who kept escaping. Poor old guy was turning up all over Ellisberg, but no one knew how the heck he was getting out." Jordynn moved closer to the grate, then pushed on it until it made a popping sound and fell into her hands. "Turned out *this* was his exit point. And he had about fifty pounds—and fifty years—on you. So I'm pretty sure you won't have a problem."

Donovan leaned against the concrete wall and peered into the exposed opening. He couldn't see anything past the first few feet.

"Be easier with a flashlight," he observed. "At least I'd know what I was getting myself into."

"Don't be scared," Jordynn teased, then slipped under his arm. "Ladies first."

Before Donovan could protest, she lifted herself in and slid out of sight. There was the sound of her leather pants skidding across the metal ducting, then her voice carried out from the hole.

"You coming?"

"Not because I want to."

"Don't forget to close the grate."

"Right. Would hate for any rats to get in. Or is it out?"

"Ha, ha."

Donovan positioned himself on the edge, lifted the cover and pulled it up and secured it, then rolled to his back. He took a breath and pushed forward. His shoulders protested against the square edges of the confined space, and he suppressed a groan. He had no idea how a man bigger than him could possibly fit inside, let alone make his way up and out. When he pushed again, though, the passage widened.

"You're going to come to a split," Jordynn called from somewhere up ahead. "Go right or you'll get stuck in an airway."

He obeyed, inching along and ignoring the claustrophobia that threatened to overtake him as the walls tightened again. He was far enough in now that the light from the parking lot was nonexistent.

"Almost there!" Jordynn's voice echoed a little, like she was speaking from within a cavern. "I can see your boots!"

"I don't know how you can see *any*thing," he called back.

"Give it a second."

With a grunt, Donovan gave himself another shove along the slight downward slope. He overshot, though, and when the ducting ended abruptly, he flew out of the end, dropped down about two feet and landed on the damp ground with a thud.

"Could've given me some warning," he said.

"Sorry."

As he stood and inhaled, a thick, unpleasant scent filled his nostrils. He blinked, his eyes working to adjust to the small beam of yellow light illuminating the area.

And even with the ache of his bruised rear end, he recognized the moss-covered room for what it was.

He swept the stone-and-dirt room with his gaze. "This is the old sewer system."

Jordynn nodded. "The guy who kept getting out of the care home was doing it through here. He somehow managed to cut a hole in the wall in the back of his closet. And *that* wall shared one with an unused utility room. And this guy figured out that the room had a removable floor, and under that was an opening and this weird ladder."

"Let me guess," Donovan said. "It turned out to be an old manhole."

"Exactly. How'd you know?"

"I remember my dad telling me how bits and pieces of the system were left all over the city, and that they had to leave in a few access points. I just never realized it was on a scale this big."

"I'm not sure *many* people realized it," Jordynn replied. "When the staff at the care home finally caught on to what the guy was doing, they got curious and followed him all the way through, just to see how he'd managed it."

"By 'they' do you mean 'you'?"

"Maybe."

He grinned and nudged her. "Uh-huh. And what did 'they' find out?"

"That the manhole led under the building, under the road, then under this parking lot." She shrugged. "When all was said and done, the care home fixed the guy's closet and nailed down the floor, and everyone kind of forgot about it."

"The city didn't do anything about the rest of it?"

"They said it would cost the taxpayers a mint to close it off permanently. I guess they have someone who comes down and checks on the structural integrity regularly, but that's about all they care about."

Dono scanned the room again, then held out his hand. "I don't think I've ever been so thankful for fiscal responsibility and magical grates in my life. Let's go."

And less than fifteen minutes later, they were standing in front of a rickety-looking ladder that Jordynn assured him led straight to their destination.

Chapter 16

Jordynn stared up, pursed her lips and said, "I think I'm going to retract my claim that ladies should go first."

"In the name of women's lib, or in the name of you're a big chicken?"

"In the name of only one of us is strong enough to climb the ladder and smash his way through that panel."

"Is that a compliment? Or an insult?"

"You can pick."

"Guess I'll take the former, then."

As she watched him reach for the ladder and start to climb, a sudden rush of worry hit Jordynn. What if she was wrong? What if the *plan* went wrong?

"Dono?"

He paused and turned toward her, one hand on a metal rung. "Yeah, honey?"

At a loss for words, she grabbed ahold of his shirt and pulled him back. She stood on her tiptoes and pressed her lips to his. She tasted his mouth, careful to memorize it all over again. She ran her fingers over his wide shoulders, committing the feel of him to memory, too. And as she pulled away, she could feel tears form in her eyes.

"If we die—"

He cut her off. "We're not going to die."

"But if we *do*," she insisted, "I want you to know I'm glad anyway."

"Glad about what?"

"That you came back. I'd trade my life for this time together."

He touched her cheek. "You're a bit crazy, you know that, right?"

She nodded. "Yes."

"I love you, Jordynn."

"Me, too."

She lifted her face for another kiss, then let him go.

But her anxiety only grew as he tapped lightly on the boards above and the barest sliver of light pushed through.

"I think luck is on our side," he said. "The moisture down here's rusted these bolts pretty good. If you grab me a rock—preferably roundish and palm-size—I might actually be able to work them free without too much noise."

Jordynn scoured the ground until she found one suitable. When she lifted it up, her hands were shaking. And Dono noticed right away.

"You okay?"

She tried to laugh it off. "I'm just really nervous, and I don't know why."

He lifted the rock, and Jordynn watched as he pressed it to one of the bolts and turned. It squeaked once, then came loose in his hand.

He dropped it down to Jordynn and as she caught it,

he asked, "Bad guys threatening our lives isn't a good enough reason to be nervous anymore?"

"No. It is. But I feel like it's something more."

"Hmm." He moved to the next bolt—which came off quickly—then the next. "Is it because we're heading into your work and you're afraid we'll get caught?"

Jordynn reached out to take the pieces from his hand as he finished unscrewing them, and she sighed. "Maybe. I just can't shake the feeling that something's not right."

"Nothing's right. That's why we're doing this."

He worked at the final bolt, dropped it down, then pushed up the manhole cover slowly, lifting the wood on top with it. And Jordynn held her breath, waiting for something bad to happen. Instead, the sliver of light just grew, framing Dono's body into a rough silhouette, the full strength of his upper body on breathtaking display. Then he heaved the cover aside, pulled himself up and disappeared. It immediately filled Jordynn with an even greater sense of foreboding.

"Dono?" she called in a whisper.

His head reappeared above her. "You coming?"

Jordynn took a breath, then grasped the rungs and followed him up the ladder. As she pushed through the manhole into the closed quarters, her toe caught on the edge of the opening. And before she—or Dono—could halt her momentum, she stumbled forward. She smashed into the door, then burst straight through it. And with a yelp she couldn't quite contain, she found herself on the floor, staring up at one of the other care attendants.

"Jordynn!" the girl gasped.

"Hildy."

"What are you doing down there?"

"Um. I fell."

"Out of the closet?"

Jordynn forced herself to keep from turning around, then made herself laugh. "What? No. I was already falling when I got to the closet. I grabbed the door handle and it just flew open."

"Oh." Hildy looked puzzled, but she just shrugged. "Actually, I didn't even know you were working tonight. I ran into Reed a little while ago, and he asked if I'd seen you. He seemed kind of worried. I told him you weren't here."

Jordynn frowned. "Reed? Like, our boss, Reed?"

"What other Reed is there?"

"I just…" She trailed off, confused. "Are you sure it was him? In person?"

"Of course I'm sure. He was with some angry-looking guy."

Jordynn swallowed, willing herself not to panic. "Did Reed look…hurt?"

"Hurt? No. What's going on, Jordynn?"

Deepening worry tickled at Jordynn's brain, making her lips tingle. "The guy he was with…what did he look like?"

"I don't know. Reed's age. But kinda big? Gray hair. Regular clothes. I really didn't look at him too hard."

Was it Ivan?

Jordynn exhaled, wishing her coworker had been a little more observant. But no matter who Reed was with, that fact that he was there at all was a good cause for concern. Did that mean Sasha and the kids were in trouble? She tapped her thigh nervously, wondering if she and Dono should rethink their plan.

"Are you all right?" the other care aide asked.

"I'm fine," Jordynn lied quickly. "Is Reed *still* here?"

"I'm not sure. He sounded like maybe he had somewhere to be, and— Oh! His office was dark when I walked by, so he's probably gone?" Abruptly, the girl's emergency pager went off. She glanced down and offered Jordynn an apologetic look, calling over her shoulder as she hurried away, "Sorry! If I see Reed again, I'll tell him you're here."

Jordynn waited until she was out of sight, then leaned against the wall beside the utility closet, and called softly, "She's gone."

A heartbeat later, Dono was at her side. "Everything okay?"

Jordynn tucked away her worry and nodded. "Let's go."

Dono's brow wrinkled, but she didn't give him a chance to argue. She turned and stepped up the hall, giving him little choice but to follow. She sped through the familiar corridors, careful to keep quiet, and careful to stick to the least-used route, too. She didn't want to run into Hildy again. Or any of the other staff for that matter.

She didn't even let herself breathe properly until they finally reached the office. Quickly, she flicked on the light, then snapped shut the blinds and moved toward the computer. But before she could hit the power switch, one of Dono's hands landed on her arm.

"Hey," he said. "You do realize that I could hear you out there in the hall, right?"

"I know. But it was nothing."

"You always get that worried when your boss is looking for you?"

Jordynn breathed out. "You heard Hildy say Reed was with someone?"

"Yeah."

"That someone didn't sound familiar?"

"She said an old guy with gray hair. Could've been anyone."

"Or it could've been Ivan." Her voice broke a little, and Dono reached for her.

He smoothed back her hair. "Why would your boss be with Ivan?"

"My boss isn't just my boss. He's Sasha's uncle, and he was at the house with her and the kids when you and Ivan showed up. And you know I sent them as far away as I could. But…what if Ivan got to them first?"

"Will it make you feel better if we go looking for him?"

She thought it through quickly, then dismissed the idea. "No. It'd just waste time. Between the medical offices, the long-term-care patients and the ones in the assisted-living quarters…there's almost a hundred rooms in the building. We could search for an hour and not find him. And paging him would draw too much attention."

Dono leaned back. "This could be nothing, too, right? Something as simple as he needed something from his office and brought a friend along. He doesn't know how dangerous the situation is. And he does own this place, right?"

"Yes…" She shook her head, contradicting her affirmation. "But if that's true, then why did he ask for me? He knows I'm not supposed to be here."

"I don't know, honey." Dono nodded toward the phone on the desk. "You want to give him a call? Or Sasha?"

She shook her head again. "I'd still rather leave Sasha in the dark about everything, as much as possible, anyway. And if Ivan *does* have Reed…well, he won't hurt him unless he can use it to get to us. And none of it really changes anything about what we need to do right this second, does it?"

He studied her face for a moment, then reached under

his shirt and pulled out the red folder. "Can I ask you a question?"

She took a breath. "Sure."

"Has the bad feeling you had back there in the tunnel gotten any better?"

"Worse than ever," Jordynn admitted.

He held out the folder. "Then we'd better get this done."

Jordynn stepped over to the computer and switched it on as she sat at the desk. "What do you want to start with?"

"The list of names."

She plugged the first one in, and was immediately rewarded. A picture and a link popped up. She clicked, then read aloud from the new page.

"Reggie L. White, CEO of Fryer Developments, inherited the company from his father-in-law."

Dono bent down behind her, resting his chin on her shoulder as he scanned the rest of the bio. "Nothing new there."

"He doubled the net worth, though." Jordynn tapped the screen. "Look at these numbers from thirty years ago versus the ones from today."

"But Fryer still doesn't touch Haven as far as dollar bills are concerned. Go to the next one?"

She glanced at the open file, then typed in the name. "Harold Stepford, COO of Fryer Developments."

"Appointed shortly after White took over. Nothing new there, either."

"Next?"

"Uh-huh."

Jordynn moved down the line. "Janine Elwood. CFO. Appointed nine years ago when the former CFO, Lance Ranger, abandoned his position."

"Abandoned?"

"That's what it says."

"How long before Elwood took over did Ranger abandon his position?"

Jordynn looked back at the screen, and the hair on the back of her neck stood up. "One year earlier."

"One year earlier," Dono repeated, then he leaned across to angle the keyboard his way and clicked on the former CFO's name.

Lance Ranger.

The article that popped up at the top made Jordynn's throat tighten.

Ranger was a single man, with no extended family to speak of. It had taken the police weeks to notice his disappearance. And when they did, their search left them puzzled. The CFO had a nice apartment in Portland, and he'd left it as if he was going to come back any second. Computer on. TV set up to record his favorite shows. Housekeeping service still in place. Not a single thing amiss in his life.

"So why did he walk away?" Jordynn wondered aloud.

"He didn't."

Dono's voice was low, and the grimmest she'd ever heard it. When she tilted her head to look at his face, she saw that his expression was the same as his tone. He was thin-lipped and pale. And his eyes were fixed on the computer. Trained directly on the photo of Lance Ranger.

"That's him," he said. "The man I saw Ivan shoot, ten years ago."

Donovan breathed in and out, trying to steady his mind. He wasn't having much success. Seeing the man's face…putting a name to it… Donovan wasn't prepared for it. Anger and sadness mixed, and the combination momentarily floored him.

"Dono?" Jordynn's soft voice brought him out of the haze. "Are you sure that's him?"

"I'm sure, honey. I'll never forget him. Or the look on his face when he took that bullet." He ran his fingers over his hair, trying unsuccessfully to shake out the buzz of the bad memory. "But at least we know who he is."

"And it confirms that the rivalry between Haven and Fryer is real."

"But we still don't know why." Donovan hit the back button on the keyboard, then scrolled through the list of articles attached to Lance Ranger's name.

"That one," Jordynn said, pointing.

He clicked and scanned the text. "It looks like the police dropped the case after Fryer Developments revealed that Ranger had been skimming funds and officially stated that they weren't pressing charges. The police decided he'd simply skipped town and chose not to pursue."

"But look at the date on the article. It's almost a full year after he disappeared. Why would Fryer wait so long to release that info? Why not go to the police right away?"

"Maybe they needed more proof. Just like us. Because if your theory about the sabotaged properties is right— and I'm guessing it is—then Haven's been chasing Fryer for years. Over something personal, probably."

"Then that's what we need to look for—a personal connection."

"I'm sure it's here. And once we have it…"

She smiled. "We can go to the police ourselves."

"Exactly." Donovan lifted his gaze as an alternative occurred to him. "Unless it's not true."

"What do you mean?"

"Maybe Ranger *wasn't* skimming at all. And maybe the reason Fryer didn't contact the police is because whatever was going on was something they preferred the police *not* to know."

"You think so?"

"When did Fryer win the bid on Greyside Mountain?"

"I'm not certain."

"Could it have been nine years ago?"

"Possibly," she said. "Your dad kept things pretty tied up, but I'm a hundred percent sure Fryer had already purchased it before he really started throwing up the red tape."

Donovan reached around her to get to the computer again. He opened up a second browser window, then typed in, Fryer Developments, Greyside Mountain, date of acquisition.

A list of suggested articles popped up, and Donovan selected the one at the top. He scanned through it quickly.

"Nine years ago," he confirmed. "They put in a *very* high bid on the property. Twice what the Haven Corporation had previously offered. Probably took out the competition without even blinking."

He could hear puzzlement in Jordynn's reply. "Where did they get that kind of money? And why did it happen right after Ranger died?"

"I dunno. But it can't be a coincidence."

"Do you think that someone at Fryer figured out what happened to Ranger and they needed a plausible reason for his disappearance, then used the story about the missing money as a cover-up?"

Donovan tapped his thumbs against the keyboard, tossing the idea around in his mind. Something about the explanation didn't quite ring true for him.

"Could be," he said. "But let's see what else the internet has to say about Lance Ranger."

He typed in the man's name and title, then scrolled through the links. There were a few about his disappearance, a few about the end of the police investigation and not much else. He scrolled further.

"Wait," Jordynn said suddenly. "What's that one there?"

"Looks like someone scanned a bunch of newsprint articles and uploaded them to some kind of archive. It's a Michigan paper, though."

"Open it anyway."

Donovan clicked and read aloud. "'Developer on the rise. Young Enterprises.'"

"Young Enterprises."

"Is that company name familiar to you?"

"I don't think so."

He gave the screen another look. "Well. On top of it being over two thousand miles from here, this happened almost thirty years ago. I was a baby, and you weren't even born yet."

"Can you zoom in on the picture?"

"Sure."

He hovered over the article, then increased the size and read the blurry caption at the bottom of the photo. "'Young Enterprises, founders and family meet with mayor.'"

There were three men in the picture. Beside them, a little boy—maybe three or four years old—held up a balloon, which was embossed with the company's initials.

"Anyone you know?" he asked.

"Maybe. I don't know. Maybe not? The quality's pretty bad." Jordynn squinted at the screen for another second before frowning at him. "I wonder why this article came up in the Lance Ranger search. The people in this picture are in their thirties. Ranger died twenty years later, and he was barely thirty *then*."

It only took Donovan a second to figure it out. "He's the kid."

Her eyes went from him to the screen and back again. "You're right. He has to be."

Jordynn slid her arm underneath his to pull the keyboard back toward her. He watched as she plugged Young Enterprises into the search engine.

"So many names," she muttered as she waited for the results to load. "Fryer… Haven… Young…aha! Look. Wait. Does that say Pleasant Falls, Michigan?"

Donovan bent to see. "Yep."

Jordynn drew in a sharp breath. "That's weird."

"What?"

"Pleasant Falls is the town where my parents lived. Where my dad died." Her face was a little pale, and she pulled away from the computer. "What does the rest of the article say?"

He skimmed over the first part. "Young Enterprises were involved in an embezzlement scandal. It's kind of vague, but it sounds like one of the partners stole money from the other and the company fell apart as a result."

"No names?"

He read through the rest, lifted his hand to give his ear a worried tug, then met her eyes and spoke cautiously. "Just one."

"Just one?" she repeated. "Who is it?"

"The one who was left behind after the money was gone."

"C'mon, Dono. Who?"

"Reed Walker."

If he'd thought her face was white a second ago, it was positively ashen now. "Reed?"

"Yes."

She licked her lower lip nervously. "So thirty years ago, this other guy ripped Reed off in an embezzlement scandal. And twenty years later, a second embezzlement scheme comes up. Only this time it's here?"

"And so is Reed. He's the only common denominator that I can see," Donovan said, then changed his mind and added, "Well. The only common denominator aside from the kid, who we think is Lance Ranger."

"That newspaper caption said family. What if Ranger is the other partner's son?"

"Logical conclusion."

"Okay. So maybe Reed's just a coincidence. Ranger and his dad each scammed a development company. But what does the Haven Corporation have to do with any of it, and how did Ranger wind up dead? I feel like we're zigzagging around, looking for a way to get from *A* to *Z*, but missing the twenty-four letters in between." She let out a frustrated groan, then shook her head. "Maybe we should go looking for Reed after all."

"Maybe we should."

Donovan started to push back from the computer, but as he did, a shadow crossed in front of the drawn office blinds. He leaped out of his seat.

"Behind me," he barked. "Quickly."

It was all he had time to say before the door flew open, and Ivan's familiar form blocked their way out. The other man held a weapon in his hand, and he had a dark smile on his face.

"Mr. Grady, you are a serious thorn in my side," he said.

"Likewise."

Ivan glanced toward the computer. "Find anything interesting?"

"Nothing *you* don't already know."

Ivan smiled, then motioned with the gun. "Turn it off. Then get up and come with me."

"And if I say no?"

"Putting aside the direct threat to your life and to Ms. Flannigan's…there's an awful lot of innocent people around."

"Exactly. Potential loose ends. And I know how you hate those. You think you could kill us, then take care of all of them without attracting any unwanted police attention?"

The older man's smile didn't slip. "I'd call your bluff, but I don't have to. I brought a bit of insurance."

He stepped sideways, just far enough that Donovan could see into the hall. Two more thugs stood outside. Each of them held the arm an older gentleman, who hung limply between the two of them, his head down and his feet loose.

Behind Donovan, Jordynn gasped. "Reed!"

Crap.

The unconscious man was her boss.

Ivan covered the door again, his smile now growing even wider. "Shut down the computer, hand over the file and follow us outside. And don't make a single damned noise, or it'll end very badly."

Furious at himself for leaving them vulnerable, Donovan lifted the red folder and held it out. Ivan's gun didn't waver as he took the paperwork.

"Now the computer," he ordered. "Clear the browser, too, sweetheart."

Donovan clenched his jaw to keep from releasing a tirade. They were so damned close. And now…

All wasted.

He shook his head to himself as Jordynn followed orders, clicking through the history and making sure no evidence of their search remained. Ivan picked up on his consternation immediately.

"You could've made things a hell of a lot easier for yourself if you'd just stayed dead," the older man said.

Donovan studied Ivan's face, sensing more than a bit of dishonesty in the statement. "That's not quite true, is it?"

"Maybe not this time around. But if you'd just done it for real the first time…" Ivan's smile became a smirk— one he directed at Jordynn. "I'm guessing your boyfriend didn't tell you about our offer."

Donovan steeled himself. He knew what was coming.

"I don't care what offer you made," Jordynn said, her voice firmly defiant. "You're a liar, a killer and a thief. Your word would've meant nothing."

"Think what you like about me," Ivan replied. "But Mr. Grady could've saved you a monster of a headache if he'd been able to follow instructions. You'd be safe in your house and your boss would be with his family."

"*Less* than nothing," Jordynn said back.

Ivan swung toward Donovan. "You can tell her while we walk. Move."

He closed his eyes. He'd known that he'd have to disclose the final details eventually. He just hadn't thought it would be like this, under duress.

Chapter 17

Jordynn didn't know where to focus her attention as they moved through the hall. So instead of looking at any of them, she kept her ears open and her eyes down. But except for the light thump of their shoes on the linoleum—and the accompanying drag of Reed's feet behind them—the corridor remained silent.

She was concerned about her boss, and she wished she could wake him. She wanted to know why he'd come back. Or if he'd left at all. She wanted to know how he'd figured out that she'd be at the care home. And—of course—to make sure he was okay and to ask where Sasha and the kids were, too.

But Ivan and his fellow thugs were more than a little distracting. Especially the older armed man behind them. She could feel his gun, trained on their backs. She could hear his breaths as he ushered them along. And she remembered what he'd said about not leaving any more loose ends. Jordynn was terrified that someone would see them and *become* one of those loose ends.

They reached the service wing, quickly, though, and Jordynn breathed a little easier. At least it was an area with little to no traffic coming through on the weekend.

She allowed herself a glance at Dono, who walked beside her. His presence—even like this—was comforting. He walked a little stiffly, though, and in spite of her own dismissal of Ivan's credibility, she could tell that his claim disturbed Dono.

It piqued her curiosity.

What could be so bad? He'd faked his own death. Let her suffer. And though she now understood why, she was hard-pressed to think of something worse than that. In fact, the *only* thing that came to mind that would've hurt her more badly was if he'd died for real.

Oh.

Her gaze flew toward him. "They wanted you to—"

He cut her off. "Yes."

Her heart squeezed. "You couldn't have—"

He interrupted a second time. "I could have, Jordynn. I could've stayed inside the car when it rolled over the edge. I could've let myself die for real. It was what they suggested, actually, and the reason I thought of faking the car crash in the first place."

"Dono… No."

"We gave him the choice," Ivan said. "And he made the wrong one."

Now Jordynn's heart didn't just squeeze; it threatened to collapse. "That's not a choice."

"Keep telling yourself that, sweetheart," Ivan replied. "But if you really think about it…what difference would it have made to you? You'd have gone through the same thing. Every moment of the past decade would've been identical. The only change would be what's happened over the last two days."

Dono met her eyes, and the pressure in Jordynn's chest grew. She could see the heartache there, and the self-doubt, as well. She could too easily picture the moments that led up to what he thought of as a *decision*. She imagined him, sitting alone at Hilltop Park, beaten and broken, his life as he knew it already over. Searching for a way out. And grabbing on to the only one he could find. The one that would satisfy Ivan and his crew, but also keep her safe.

"I'm sorry," he said softly. "Again."

"Don't be sorry that you're alive."

"I'm not. I'm just sorry that I didn't tell you the whole truth until now."

They'd reached a heavy, unarmed exit that would lead them into the overflow parking lot at the back of the facility. As the two thugs in front of them shuffled Reed so that they could open it, Dono took her hand, squeezed it once, then let it go.

"And now you know," Ivan stated, his voice smug.

Even though the two thugs had already gone through the door, and Dono was now holding it open for her, Jordynn spun back.

"I know *what*?" she said. "That the man I wanted to spend my life with didn't have a death wish? That he was smart enough to *out*smart you and your plan?"

Ivan appeared unmoved by her anger. "How about the fact that he valued his life more than your own, so he took the easy way out?"

She stared at him, shook her head and spoke slowly— like she would to a small child. "You think it was easy for him to let me believe he was dead? Easy for him to know how badly I was hurting? If you really believe that,

I feel sorry for you. Because it means you've never loved someone enough to know that it was the hardest damn thing he could possibly do."

Ivan smirked. "You're a hell of a pair, aren't you?"

"I like to think we are." Dono was answering Ivan, but his gaze was fixed on Jordynn, and now it held no doubt at all. "A damned good team, actually."

He released his hold on the door, and it swung shut with a bang.

Instinctively, Jordynn stepped back.

And then—with the smallest of nods—Dono lashed out at Ivan with a perfectly placed roundhouse kick.

Jordynn jumped back even farther, moving out of the way as one booted foot slammed into Ivan's calves. The sudden move knocked the older man halfway to the ground, and his hands automatically came out to break his fall. The reactionary movement loosened his grip on the gun and sent it skidding across the floor. The sound of metal on tile echoed through the hall, and for a second, everyone froze, eyes following the weapon as it skidded to a stop. Then the two men on the other side started to bang, and everyone started moving again at once.

Jordynn went for the gun.

Ivan reached for Jordynn's ankles.

And Dono went after Ivan.

Together, the three of them toppled to the ground, falling like dominoes, one on top of the other, Jordynn on the bottom.

As they landed, Jordynn kicked out with her free foot. Her attempt went wild, hitting nothing but air. Ivan yanked on her other leg. She tried to wriggle out of his grip, but he held fast, grunting as Dono squeezed his hips. Jordynn drew back her foot again, and this time she hit her mark. Her foot slammed hard into his shoulder. He grunted and released her. For a blissful moment, she was free. She scrambled across the floor. Behind her, she could hear the continued struggle between the two men. But her eyes were on the prize. Which is probably why she didn't realize Ivan had kicked himself free, too. And the pain-filled yell that came from Dono alerted her a second too late.

She whipped back just in time to see that he'd landed against the far wall. He had a nasty gash above his eyebrow, and it was already oozing.

"Dono!"

"The gun," he groaned.

But Jordynn's hesitation—or Dono's words—were enough to remind Ivan, too. The older man lunged forward. Jordynn pushed to her knees and tried to block his path, but he just barreled into her, knocking her sideways and flattening her to the cold tile. As she fell, her fingers smacked into the weapon. It sent the gun up the floor a few more inches. Out of reach.

Dammit.

She tried to push, tried to shift to free herself. Ivan was too heavy. And he was starting to climb over her, too, his knees digging into her calves. Her eyes watered as the thug made it all the way up her back, then shoved her down even harder. He moved past her, his hands stretched out for the gun.

And then Dono was there. He dived past Jordynn, managing to tackle Ivan. But the other man had his fingers closed around the weapon.

Jordynn grabbed the wall, pulled herself up and took a shaky step toward them both. But the sound of feet, echoing from far off, made her freeze. It had to be Ivan's men. Had they abandoned Reed? She'd momentarily forgotten that he'd been pulled into the mix. The pounding boots grew slightly louder. How long did they have?

She took another step in Dono's direction. He had the upper hand now, crushing Ivan's wrist while pushing his elbow to the man's throat.

"Go, Jordynn," he urged. "Hurry!"

"I'm not leaving you here."

The gun fell from the other man's hand, and Dono flipped him over, pushed him down and met her gaze. "Pass me the gun."

Jordynn stepped around Ivan to reach the weapon, then held it out.

Dono took it with a grateful nod. "Can you get out of here safely?"

"Probably, but—"

"Then go."

"Donovan—"

"Please, Jordynn. I can't protect you and hold down Ivan and kneecap two other men at the same time." As if to emphasize his point, Ivan bucked, and Dono's muscles strained enough to make him grunt. "Go and help your boss. Get him out of here, and take that red file to the cops. I think we have enough to get them to take us seriously."

"You'll find me?"

"You know I will."

Before she could argue herself out of doing it, she bent to pick up the folder, then turned and pushed her way through the heavy door. For a second, she was startled to find the top of the stairs empty. Where was Reed? She quickly reasoned that they wouldn't leave him out in the open. The rear parking lot didn't face the main street, but that didn't mean no one could see it. So…where *would* they put him? After quick consideration, she shook her head and decided she didn't have time to find out. What she needed to do was find a phone and call the police.

She scanned the parking lot, wondering if she could safely turn around and get back into the care home somehow, or if she should try instead to find another open business.

But she didn't get a chance to decide. A gun clicked beside her head, and someone spoke in her ear.

"Fight me, and I'll shoot. Scream, and I'll shoot. Do a single thing that I don't ask you to do directly and...?" The voice trailed off expectantly.

"You'll shoot," Jordynn filled in.

"Exactly. I'm putting my hand onto your back and I'm lowering the gun to your waist. I want you to take my elbow, then head toward the gray vehicle with a smile on your face."

She took two small steps, then realized she recognized the luxury SUV he'd pointed to.

"That's Reed's car," she said aloud, momentarily forgetting the instructions the stranger had just given her. "Is he okay?"

The low chuckle that came in reply slammed into her like an icy bucket of water, and she at last realized that her underlying anxiety had a source: betrayal.

Donovan poised himself above Ivan, gun at the ready. It was safe to assume that the men were coming around the corner, and even though guns weren't his preferred means of incapacitating someone, he was prepared to do it.

At least he was until the person attached to the booted thump rounded the corner.

He blinked, too startled to even think about squeezing the trigger. "Reed?"

The gray-haired man blinked back. "Donovan Grady."

Donovan took a quick, surprised inventory. Jordynn's boss didn't look injured in the slightest. In fact, he was damned sure *he* looked worse than Reed did. The man stood tall, his gaze as gray and steely as his hair.

Donovan's eyes drifted down to the other man's hand. "Why do you have—"

"A gun?" Reed filled in, cocking the pistol in question. "In my own facility?"

Beneath Donovan's knee, Ivan laughed. And too late, he realized what was happening. He lifted his weapon.

"Before you fire," said Reed, "you might want to walk over to that room there and have a look out the window. Feel free to take Ivan with you as collateral."

Slowly, Donovan stood, yanking Ivan with him. He was already sure of what he'd find, but a morbid need for confirmation made him look. He shuffled to the door that Reed had pointed at, then nudged it open. He pulled Ivan across the dim room to the narrow, wire-lined window. Sure enough, his fears were confirmed. Across the parking lot stood both men who'd been dragging Reed through the halls. One had his jacket open, the flash of a weapon glinting in the afternoon sun. The other held on to something far worse.

Jordynn.

Like he'd been waiting for Donovan to appear, the first man closed his jacket, gave a little salute, then opened one of the SUV's sliding doors and nodded at the second man. And the second man grabbed Jordynn's shoulder and shoved her roughly into the vehicle.

Donovan's teeth gnashed together in anger, and he spun toward Reed. The man was watching him impassively from the doorway.

"They have strict instructions," Jordynn's boss said. "If I'm not down there in five minutes, they'll kill her."

"A lot can happen in five minutes," Donovan growled back, his hand flexing on the weapon he still held.

"You're right. Men can live or die. They can witness something that changes the course of their lives forever. They can make a decision they regret for ten years."

"You son of a—"

"Easy, Donovan. Let's save the name-calling for the *really* bad bits. Give Ivan your gun."

Donovan held tight to the weapon. "She trusted you. She thought you were *helping* her."

"I was," the other man said, his voice a shrug. "I've been watching over her for ten years. Making sure the fallout of losing you didn't take too bad a toll. Giving her a job and a fatherly shoulder. I'm not the one who abandoned her. Or the one who endangered her, again and again. That's all on you. All on the choice you made. Less than four minutes left of those five I gave you, by the way."

"You expect me to believe you're really going to let her live?" Donovan replied.

"I won't make her suffer."

"Not good enough."

Reed sighed. "You want to keep playing Russian roulette with her life? Fine by me. Three minutes."

Donovan's eyes strayed to the window. He could just barely see the flash of red in the backseat of the silver car. His gaze went back to Reed, who was looking at his watch. He had no doubt that the man was planning on killing Jordynn. Planning on killing both of them.

"Two and a half minutes." The statement was a dark, velvet-covered threat.

If there's a chance, however slim, to save her...

Donovan turned the gun in his hand, and—resisting an urge to clock one, or both, of them over the head with it instead—held it out.

"Good choice," said Reed as Ivan snatched the weapon.

"Take me to her," Donovan snapped.

"Glad to."

As they made their way from the hall to the door to the exterior of the building, Donovan's body tensed with heavy, uncomfortable emotion. Regret. Fury. Frustration. He felt them all. He couldn't stand the fact that he was on the verge of letting Jordynn down. Again. By the time they actually reached the vehicle, his muscles had the shaky, used-up feeling he got at the end of a boxing beat-down.

He scanned the parking lot in search of an out. A way to escape that wouldn't endanger Jordynn's life, or his own. He saw none.

Ivan slid open the side door. "Get in."

Donovan paused to meet Jordynn's eyes, careful to keep his expression neutral. He didn't need her worrying that he hadn't yet come up with a plan. She looked terrified anyway.

"Honey—"

Ivan cut him off with a shove. "No chatting."

Donovan flashed him a look. "You're lucky I've got some serious self-restraint."

"Pretty sure *you're* the lucky one in this case," the other man countered, then gave him another push. "A lack of self-restraint would only get you killed faster."

Donovan bit down to keep from lashing out. He didn't feel lucky at all. And the hopelessness of their situation grew even more as the arrangement in the vehicle became clear. Reed and one of the thugs were in the front. Ivan and the other were in the back. He and Jordynn were sandwiched between them in the middle row, guns aimed at them from all sides.

Hell.

As the SUV purred to life, and they pulled out of the lot, Jordynn reached over to take his hand. She looked at him like she wanted to say something, but Reed turned the music up to a volume that made it impossible to talk. Which was his intention, of course.

They rode through the streets without speaking, the happy pop tunes on the oldies station completely at odds with the tension in the vehicle. It only took a few minutes of flashing scenery for Donovan to figure out where they were headed.

"Greyside," he murmured to himself, a new spike of concern filling his mind.

Sure enough, they soon reached the turnoff. He couldn't think of a single good reason for the upward trek. Jordynn's grip on his hand tightened, and he knew he wasn't alone in his worry. The SUV climbed the mountainside smoothly, the familiar trees and rocky terrain passing by in a blur. At last they reached their apparent destination—the same bridge where Donovan had disposed of his car ten years earlier, the same spot they'd fled from earlier.

Reed pointed at the big Fryer Development sign, and the driver coaxed the SUV off the road and over the bumpy ground. He pulled the vehicle in behind, safely under the cover of the surrounding trees, then put it in Park. At last, Reed cut the music.

"What now?" Donovan asked, hearing the unease in his own voice.

"Now we take care of business," Jordynn's boss replied.

They unloaded, and Reed gave calm orders to Ivan and the other two men.

"Flank these two at all times," he said. "No more mistakes. Show me your guns."

Each of the men opened his jacket to expose their metal weaponry. One lifted a pant leg to showcase a knife.

Reed nodded his approval. "Now show them to Mr. Grady and Ms. Gallagher."

"Hell of a production," Donovan said as the men turned their way and repeated their actions.

"I want to be clear on where we stand."

"There are four of you and two of us." Donovan's voice was dry. "You have guns and we have none. I think we're clear."

"Good. Let's get moving."

Guided by the gunmen, they moved past the sign, then pushed farther into the woods. With each step, Jordynn's hand grew more viselike. Donovan wished he could reassure her, but the deeper they got, the more dread filled him. He had a bad feeling that he knew exactly where they were headed, and it dredged up a part of the past he'd just as soon leave buried.

The trees were thicker now, and they had to move in single file to get through, and the going was slower than Donovan remembered.

Maybe because you're not running for your life this time.

He couldn't block out the memory. The dark, all around him. The slap of branches against every inch of exposed skin. The snag of underbrush on his jeans, slowing him down. All of it happening with a furious, unknown man—armed and definitely not afraid to kill—

chasing him down, while Jordynn marched down the hill, totally unaware of the danger.

Donovan's gut churned and squeezed. Young or not, he hadn't been a timid man ten years ago. Even less so now. But watching someone get gunned down in cold blood had changed him. In the weeks that followed, he'd tried to erase it from his mind. He'd failed. Only time and distance had dimmed it. Now, being here again, headed over the same path—with their lives directly on the line—it brought it all back.

The worst had been the final moment. The one where he'd tripped, and the shooter—Ivan—had caught up. Donovan had thought it was over. Some twist of fate had intervened. A noise up the path had redirected Ivan's attention, and off he'd gone. It'd given Donovan just enough time to recover and move along to safety.

Temporary safety.

Finally Jordynn cleared her throat softly, pulling him back to the present. He glanced around to give her a quick look. She had her face aimed at the ground and her hands up to protect the rest of her body. The two men following behind had dropped back just enough to give the illusion that she was walking along of her own free will.

She spoke then, and her voice came out with an apologetic quaver, so quiet that no one farther away than he was would hear. "I'm sorry. I had no idea it was him."

Donovan seized on her fear to push aside his own, speaking softly over his shoulder. "I never suspected someone local, either."

"But you weren't here. You weren't exposed to him every single day." Her breath caught momentarily. "But if you had been, maybe you would've seen something."

"No. I would only have seen what Reed wanted me to see, just like you. He's smart enough to cover his tracks.

His name wasn't anywhere on those documents. It sure as hell didn't come up on any of the searches I did. The man was hidden because that's the way he wanted it."

"He was in every part of my life, Dono. My education, my career."

He hazarded another look back, just in time to see her shiver.

"This whole time…" she added before trailing off.

"I know." The trail widened, and Donovan scooped up her hand again.

They were almost at the clearing now. He could smell the pungent scent of the nearby bog, feel the slight shift in the air that went along with the fumes being given off. They were walking faster, too, even though Donovan would rather have slowed, stopped and turned around completely.

"I'm sure you'll recognize this place," Ivan said from the front of the line, sounding pleased as he came to a halt.

"Hard to forget a murder site," Donovan replied.

He stepped up beside the other man, then took a slow breath, trying to give himself a second to adjust. Everything looked the same. With one exception. Someone had driven in single large piece of heavy equipment and left it at the edge of the clearing.

"Do you know what that is?" asked Reed.

"Can't say I do," Donovan said back.

The man, who really did look more like someone's grandfather than a criminal mastermind, moved closer to the machine. "It's for drainage. Belongs to Fryer Development."

Donovan's eyes found and held the edge of the clearing. The source of the scent and undoubtedly the target of the drainage equipment.

"I pulled some strings," Reed told him, "and had the project halted while they assess the environmental impact of clearing this space out. I know it won't last. The bog is barely half a mile wide, and Fryer bought this side of Greyside with no limitations on development. It was a key point of the deal, actually. Can you guess why that is?"

Donovan frowned, his brain working to figure it out. And it only took a second.

Chapter 18

As a slow, smug smile stretched across her boss's face, Jordynn's heart lodged in her throat, and no matter how she tried to clear it out, it insisted on staying there. And the next sentence out of Dono's mouth confirmed the why of it.

"The body," he said.

Jordynn's gaze found the murky, peaty bog.

"You had him dumped there," she said.

Reed turned his smile her way. "Ivan thought it was the smart thing to do. And he was right, at the time. Impossible to drag a body out of there without draining the whole damned thing. And of course, the Haven Corporation was lined up to buy this little piece of real estate, so that would leave me in the clear."

"Leave *you* in the clear?" Jordynn frowned, her puzzlement temporarily pushing aside her horror.

It was Dono who answered. "I think he *is* Haven, honey."

"Gold star. Though technically, it's a publicly owned co-op. And these co-ops are owned by some other companies. Or something. Truth be told, I don't really understand anything except that none of it can be traced back to me. Apparently, it'd take a year just to get the ties to *start* to unravel. Lucky for me, I just pull the strings at the top." Reed's smile widened. "Still. Don't really want a body lying around, making people ask questions and feel a need to *want* to start unraveling."

Jordynn couldn't fight a shiver. "But Fryer bought Greyside *after* Lance Ranger died."

"Yep. Sure as hell didn't see that one coming. Ranger and I had history. He knew all along it was me behind Haven. Sneaky kid stuck a clever clause into his will. Posthumously managed to pave the way for solving his own murder."

"But why did he want to buy Greyside in the first place?" Jordynn asked.

"Because *I* did. Ranger hated me."

"Can you blame him?" Dono interrupted. "You and your company had been sabotaging *their* developments."

Reed's eyes tightened, just a little. "Figured that out, did you?"

"Jordynn did," Dono said, and her boss turned her way and gave her a nod.

"Astute girl. Yes. Haven had been undermining Fryer's projects. But with damned good reason."

"What do you mean?" Jordynn wanted to know.

Ivan cut in then. "Why the hell does it matter?"

She tossed a glare at the big thug. "Because Reed's been my *family* for a decade. He's my best friend's uncle. Practically a grandparent to her kids. I think I deserve an explanation."

Reed's expression softened, and he looked almost like the man she'd thought she could count on for the past decade. Except for the gun in his hand and the confession that he'd orchestrated a murder, of course.

"It's fine. There's no reason not to explain," Reed said with a sigh. "Thirty or so years ago, I unexpectedly inherited a business from a distant cousin. Turned out to be a midsize development company. I didn't know much about real estate, or building, or anything that had to do with running a corporation at all, actually. So I took on a partner. A man named Eli Lu. A financial guru who I trusted to run the show. We were doing well. Buying large, cheap pieces of land. Some we subdivided, then sold at a huge profit. Some we subdivided, then built on ourselves, then sold at an even bigger profit. But ten years in, I figured out a few things. Not only was Lu siphoning funds off the top, but his builder had been cutting corners. Knowingly. Intentionally. Three people died as a result of their negligence. A little girl lost her leg. All because of Lu and the bottom line. What kind of man—what kind of father—deals in business that way?"

He paused then, as if to make sure Jordynn had caught it.

"So Lance was his son like we thought," she said. "But he was a little boy when all of that happened."

"That's true. But as they say…the apple doesn't fall far from the tree. Let me ask you something, Jordynn. Do you know who died as a result of those cut corners?" he asked, his eyes burning.

"How could I know?"

"Because one of them was someone close to you."

Her breathing turned shallow. "You're lying."

But a memory was surfacing. A connection being made. And she couldn't stop it.

"It's impossible," she stated.

"It's not impossible. Just the opposite. And in this case, I'm the most honest man you know. Your dad—he was an electrician. Died in a workplace accident."

Dono put a hand on her back. "You don't have to listen to him, honey."

But she knew that she *did* have to, because what he was telling her tied directly to her own past.

"Young Enterprises," she stated. "In Pleasant Falls, Michigan."

"That's the one," Reed said. "We hired contractors to work on our projects. One of them was your father."

The world spun, and Dono was the only thing keeping her upright. She clung to his arm, knowing any second Reed was going to pull them apart. Reed's company was responsible for her father's death.

"Why didn't you just go to the police?" Her voice quavered.

"And tell them what?" her boss asked. "That my own company was directly responsible for the death of three men? That a little girl would never ride a bike because of me? There was no way for me to untie myself from the responsibility. Like I said, Lu was a guru. A genius at creating the perfect scapegoat, then disappearing."

Donovan cut in again. "So you did what? Decided you were already culpable, so you might as well just embrace it?"

Reed laughed, short and just shy of bitter. "Hardly. I set out to make things right. I compensated the families of the people who died. I shut down the company and I started Haven instead. I was careful to keep my name out of it. I wasn't going to let myself get caught like that again. Then I hired people to find Lu. Aggressive men, who wouldn't just give up. I was so determined to find him and make him pay that I turned a blind eye to what they were doing to get me what I wanted. When they were done...Lu was dead, and a lot of people wanted *me* dead. Got myself in enough trouble that I needed even more help. So I hired Ivan and his trained specialists on a full-time basis."

Jordynn shivered and bit her lip. "There's still time to undo it, Reed."

Her boss shook his head slowly. "There really isn't. I've made too many mistakes already."

"So don't make another one now."

"I won't."

Jordynn wanted to feel relief, but something about his face told her to hold back. "That's...good?"

"Good for me," Reed said. "In the past, I've let the wrong people live for the wrong reasons. I've done it for sympathy. Or because I thought someone was good. Or trustworthy. I made the mistake with Lu's son. I gave him the benefit of the doubt, and I believed everything he said about wanting to distance himself from his father's past. I even gave him seed money so he could buy in as a partner with Fryer Development when the company was first starting up. Then I watched as he turned the company sour from the inside out. Fryer quickly became as corrupt as Young Enterprises. And Ranger was skimming off their profits, too."

"So you started sabotaging them," Dono said. "Stopping them from doing what Ranger's father did with Young Enterprises. If they can't buy the properties, they can't start any more cut-corner projects."

Reed nodded. "Simplified and far nobler than my true intentions, but yes."

"Then Ranger found out what you were doing, and he retaliated," Dono added.

"He did. Probably figured it out sooner, even, than he let on. And the truth is, I offered to back down. Sasha had just got married and her husband was on the road a lot. They were already talking about kids. But Ranger couldn't accept that I'd just stay in Ellisberg out of familial obligation. He couldn't wrap his head around the idea that I was buying and developing here so I could stay close to Sasha. He became fixated on this place. Kept turning up at the construction sites, asking questions."

"That must've been so stressful for you," Dono snapped.

Jordynn shot him a look, pleading with him silently to not make things worse. He narrowed his eyes, but pushed his lips together and nodded.

"What happened next?" Jordynn asked. "Why did you…do what you did?"

Her boss blinked. "Why did I have Ivan kill Lance Ranger?"

Hearing him admit it—so coolly, so casually—made her throat tighten. "Yes."

"It wasn't my decision, at first. I tried to buy him off. I made the mistake of underestimating how badly he wanted revenge. He came at me full force. Brought in documents that implicated me in the negligent deaths, years earlier. Would've made his dad proud, I'm sure. So I didn't have a choice."

Jordynn's heart thumped nervously. "But you do have one now. We *can* be trusted. And you know me. You *know* I'm a good person, Reed. You've been taking care of me for years."

He tipped his head to the side. "And yet, here you are. With the one man who can put me behind bars."

Tears formed in hers, then spilled over. "Let him go. Please. Everyone thinks he's dead anyway. I'm not going to tell anyone what I know, and if you just—"

He cut her off. "You can't tell me anything I don't know. Or suggest anything to me I haven't already considered. I've spent more than three decades doing this. I'm a sixty-year-old man, Jordynn. I want to live my golden years in peace, and the two of you are the last thing left that can connect me to a crime that started a lifetime ago."

"But you didn't even commit the original crime." Jordynn knew she was begging now, and she didn't care.

"Not that one. But others since," Reed said.

"What about Sasha and the kids?"

"What about them?"

"She's my best friend. Her kids call me Auntie Jo."

"They'll get over it."

With that statement, spoken in what seemed like an impossibly indifferent tone, her boss turned his attention to his group of hired lackeys. He moved closer, speaking too low for Jordynn to hear. But seconds later, Ivan was on her, a rope in his hands and a smile on his face. And it made her tears come that much harder.

Every fiber of Donovan's being was coiled in anger. Tamped down and ready to burst. The sight of the murderer's hands on Jordynn's body was enough to make him want to let go of his carefully maintained control. Her muffled sobs made it even worse.

But he was sure acting on his fury would end badly.

Four armed men. The life of the woman he loved. Not a wager he wanted to make.

He did his best to give Jordynn a reassuring look, but it was a struggle.

What Donovan really needed was more time. Some breathing room to think of a way out of this.

But what can I use to get it?

Jordynn's conversation with her boss had already bought them a few minutes. Maybe he could build on that.

Donovan studied Reed's face as he gave more muted instructions to the other men, searching for a solution. Jordynn had likely asked her questions based on the hope of doing just that. Donovan knew better than to think that would happen. He recognized both the resigned look of a person who believed his fate was predetermined, and a man who seemed to have outgrown any sense of moral responsibility. He'd seen the former on the faces of many of the victims who came to Carlos's gym for help. He'd seen evidence of the latter in the actions of the people chasing those same victims.

People like that had spiraled down too far to come back.

So, no. There was no way Reed was backing out of his chosen course of action. He'd simply answered Jordynn's questions because he liked the sound of his own voice.

The man was smart. And knew it.

That doesn't mean he can't be stalled.

Donovan cleared his throat. "How did you do it, Reed?"

"Do what?" the other man replied.

"Get Lance Ranger out here to this spot."

Ivan had finished tying Jordynn's hands together, and he grunted a dismissive interruption. "Again, it doesn't matter."

"It matters to me," Donovan argued. "If I'm going to die because of him, I want to know it all."

"Might as well tell him, Ivan," Reed said. "Kill some time while we set everything up."

Ivan sighed, then gestured to the pair of thugs. They moved toward Donovan as he explained.

"Luring the man out here was easy," he said. "All I needed to do was figure out what motivated him. Just like I figured out what motivated you."

Thug one shoved Donovan against a tree at the edge of the clearing.

"Sit," he ordered.

Donovan gritted his teeth, but complied. He didn't need to start a fight he couldn't win.

Thug two dragged his hands behind his back and fastened them together. "Stay."

He ignored the man's grin, and addressed Ivan instead. "What was it? The motivation?"

The older man smiled. "With you?"

Donovan didn't take the bait. "I'm aware of how you got me here. I want to know what you did with Ranger."

The killer's smiled drooped. "He only wanted one thing. Control over Reed. So I offered it to him. I told him that in exchange for handing over any and all physical evidence that put Reed in the crosshairs for Young Enterprises' misdeeds, he'd get a controlling share of the Haven Corporation."

"He believed you? Just like that?"

"Men like him are egotistical. They think they're above getting caught."

Donovan nodded, his eyes drifting automatically to Reed. "I get it."

Jordynn's boss laughed. "Not me. I knew all along I *could* get caught. I've just lived the last thirty years making sure it didn't happen."

"Ranger was the last hole that needed to be plugged, before you came along," Ivan added.

For a second, Donovan closed his eyes and let regret wash over him. It all seemed so senseless. There was one thing Ivan and Reed *hadn't* explained, though.

He opened his eyes again. "Why did Lance make buying Greyside Mountain a part of his will?"

Reed lifted a brow. "Ranger believed that there were a few other…secrets…buried up here."

Donovan's guts twisted with anger and disgust. "You used this bog as your own personal dumping ground."

The other man shook his head. "I didn't. Ivan and his men are smart enough that they spread out their conquests. But like I said, the man was fixated, and I have to admit…his will blindsided me. At that point, I thought we were in the clear as far as Fryer was concerned. Never even checked if our bid for Greyside was contested. Found out too late to do anything about it. Tried to buy it back from them, but Ranger's instructions were clear, and they refused to circumvent his wishes. The project is going to net them more profit than they could dream of."

"And that's why *they* didn't go to the police," Donovan said. "And you didn't have to worry about it for almost a decade, because my dad tied up the site in red tape."

Reed nodded. "It was kind of perfect, really. The police—other than Sergeant Grady himself, of course—weren't interested in looking around up here. And even Sergeant Grady was only focused on one thing—the bridge. Kept things in limbo until he died."

"Then I showed up at the funeral."

"And here we are now. You've given me the perfect setup, actually."

Reed's words lit up Donovan's mind with a flash of understanding.

"I'm your fall guy."

Jordynn's boss nodded. "When Fryer gets the go-ahead

to drain this little bog, they'll find Lance Ranger's body. But before that, they'll find yours. And hers."

From across the clearing, Jordynn let out a muffled whimper. She had her lips pressed together and her chin held high, but her fear was evident in the shake of her body and the continuing tears on her cheeks.

"They'll find a file—covered in your fingerprints— that connects her father's death to Young Enterprises. Without my name on it, of course," Reed said, his voice full of conviction. "And it might not make sense to the police at first, but it won't take long for them to connect the dots. Lance Ranger's father killed Jordynn's. You took revenge when you found out, ten years ago. You found out about the development going through, and you knew you were in trouble. So you came back and confessed it all, hoping Jordynn would understand and maybe flee with you. Instead, she threatened to turn you in, so you had to kill her, too. Then you took your own life."

He turned away then, his attention focused on lining up the thugs into the perfect position. They couldn't seem to agree on what would make the murder look "most natural."

And Donovan still hadn't come up with a plan. The only option seemed to be a desperate, chaotic escape attempt.

Yeah. And that'll only work if I can get free.

Which seemed unlikely.

He lifted his arms behind the narrow tree and wiggled his wrists under the rope. It was fastened far too tightly to stand any chance of loosening quickly enough. Frustrated, he dropped his hands down. They smacked against something sharp, and whatever it was, it tore into

Donovan's skin. Carefully—making sure not to attract any attention to himself—he felt along the edges of the object. It was cool. Made of metal, and boxlike in shape.

*No. Not box*like. *It* is *a box.*

With a strange, surreal feeling running through his veins, Donovan ran his hands over it again. More slowly. He didn't know how he was so sure of what it was, but he had no doubts. Even before his fingers found the etched lettering along the side.

DG and JF, forever.

The simple inscription he'd carved in himself, ten years earlier when they'd used the box as a place to hold their memories.

His palm made another stunned pass over the time capsule, and he quickly figured out that what he'd hit the first time was one of its corners. And that edge was broken down. A little sharp. Chipped, probably from when he'd been forced to drop it, then further degraded by the elements.

And useful.

Donovan lifted his wrists a second time, then slammed them down with precision. The rope snapped. So quickly that he stayed still, momentarily too stunned at his success to react. He sat still, his mind frozen for several seconds before he gave himself a mental kick and told himself to act.

He lifted his eyes, assessing the scene in front of him. Priority one was getting Jordynn free. Reed and the two nameless thugs were closest to her, while Ivan stood nearest to Donovan. Thankfully, the man's attention was on the other three.

Slowly, Donovan inched upward, the metal object

grasped in his hands. He got to a crouch, and still no one turned his way. He had a rough plan worked out now. All he needed was for it to work.

Chapter 19

From the edge of her vision, Jordynn saw Dono inch up to a crouch. At first she thought her tears must be blurring her sight. But no. When she blinked, he continued to rise, and was already three-quarters of the way up the skinny tree.

She looked away quickly, not daring to let her eyes linger on him. But her mind raced with worry. What was he doing? He couldn't possibly think he stood a chance of coming out on top in any kind of fight. Not while he was tied to a tree. Their situation was desperate, but she couldn't imagine him taking such an unnecessary risk.

She hazarded another quick look.

And then she saw one of his hands slide out from behind his back.

He's free, she realized, hope lifting her heart.

She started to drag her gaze away quickly, but couldn't, because it landed on the smallish, metallic object in his hands. And she could barely contain a gasp of surprise. She'd recognize that box anywhere. It had once held all their future hopes.

And maybe it was about to again.

Because Dono was moving now, the time capsule a weapon. His hands swung it forward with enough force that he let out a grunt that carried over the clearing. He hit Ivan's knees, and the older man fell forward hard enough to smash his face into the dirt. His weapon discharged a wild shot, and all three other men rushed forward, Jordynn temporarily forgotten. It was four against one.

He needed her help.

Jordynn brought the knotted roped at her wrists to her mouth. She didn't care how unceremonious or unattractive it looked; she'd literally work like a dog to get free so she could do whatever needed to be done.

But when she looked up, Dono was already in action again.

As the first thug reached him, he sprung to his feet, then used the metal box again, slamming it into the other man's head. It sent him reeling. Then—with a tuck and a spin—Dono drove the time capsule up to the second man's jaw. He flew backward, too, then landed on the ground and stayed there, unmoving. The first man pushed up from the dirt and made it two steps before Dono rounded on him again. Another smack, and the thug went down twitching.

The knot on Jordynn's hands refused to spring free. It refused to even loosen. And she watched in horror as Ivan recovered. As she continued frantically trying to get out, he pulled himself up to a tree and was fumbling for something at his side.

His gun. "Dono!" His name ripped from her throat in

a shriek, but Jordynn's shrill warning didn't come quite quick enough.

A bang tore through the air, then another and another. And a fourth. The shots came in quick succession, echoing through the clearing. A scream built up in Jordynn's throat, but faster than it could make its way out, Dono lifted up the metal box. The bullets hit it—*smash-smash, smash-smash*—and the impact knocked him over.

He hit the ground and groaned, but didn't move again. He just held the time capsule tightly against his chest, the flattened bullets right over his heart.

Ivan stepped closer. Then closer again. He was right on Dono, poised above him.

Jordynn hurtled forward, intent on knocking him down again, her tied feet be damned. But before she could take a single hobbled step, Dono was back in action. He leaped up, and in a fluid motion smashed the box into Ivan's thigh, then into the hand that held the gun. The man crumpled. The weapon dropped straight into Dono's lap. And for a brief joyous moment, Jordynn was elated.

Then there was a click in her ear, and hope fell away.

"Don't move," said Reed in his soft, familiar voice.

Jordynn lifted her eyes to find the barrel of a gun pointed directly at her forehead.

And Reed added, over his shoulder, "I assure you, Mr. Grady, if you fire that one bullet you have left, I will, too. Point-blank. Whether I mean to or not."

Donovan went still. He had a gun in his hand. His finger was less than a quarter of an inch from the trigger. He'd knocked two men into unconsciousness and turned a third into a rag doll. Yet here he was. Wavering. Because the fourth man—the one who'd been pulling the strings since the beginning—held the woman he loved at gunpoint.

"Let her go." The command came out as a thick growl.

"You know I can't do that, Donovan," replied the grandfatherly man.

"She doesn't need to be a part of the way this ends."

Jordynn's boss shifted sideways so that his weapon was just above her ear. "You also know that's not true."

Donovan forced his eyes to stay on the man's face rather than the gun. "We can negotiate this. Maybe make a straight trade."

"You for her?" Reed replied. "Interesting. But no."

"I'm not putting down the gun," Donovan said firmly. "Not unless you let her go."

The other man sighed. "Tell me what you think is going to happen if I do that. That she's simply going to turn and walk away? She knows everything that you know. She has a close, personal relationship with my only niece and her children. Even if she walks away this second, it won't be forever. She won't be able to run, like you did. My men would hunt her down in a day."

Then Jordynn spoke up, too. "He's just going to kill us anyway, Dono."

Donovan's teeth ground together. That much he *did* know was true. If he lowered his weapon, the other man might just shoot Jordynn straightaway. Or he might turn and fire at Donovan himself. He'd certainly proved both his creativity and ruthlessness already. And if he fired, he took the chance of Reed's finger squeezing before the shot hit him. Or of the man simply using Jordynn as a shield.

Then an idea occurred to him. A risky one. But it might be his only chance.

Slowly—deliberately—he shifted his aim from Reed to Jordynn.

The other man's eyes widened with surprise. His gun dropped. Just enough.

Jordynn's eyes met Donovan's, full of trust. Then closed.

And Donovan put his finger on the trigger.

Jordynn breathed in. The pistol clicked.

Jordynn breathed out. The pistol cracked.

Jordynn breathed in. And beneath her, the ground exploded.

Heat whipped across her ankles as the bullet severed the rope that held her. Little tendrils of the synthetic fibers melted and seared against her skin. She didn't have time to think about the pain. She didn't have time to think at all. Reed was already lifting his gun again, this time aimed at Dono, who was running forward, straight into the line of fire.

The self-defense tips.

Jordynn moved quickly, putting Donovan's lessons into practice.

She lashed out with one of her newly free feet, slamming it straight between Reed's legs. He groaned and stumbled, then spun toward her.

Then she brought up her hand—palm open—and drove it into his chin. He stumbled again, this time backward. And straight into Dono, who was ready. He slammed against her boss's shoulders with his hands, and Reed went down. He pushed again, and her boss flattened to the ground. He gave the older man one of his signature one-punch knockouts and looked up at Jordynn.

"Still in one piece?" he asked, his voice gentle.

"Yes. Well. Except for that the fact you didn't let me finish my girl fight techniques," she joked weakly.

Dono offered her a grim smile. "Actually, I kind of thought we could try something I should've done a long time ago."

"What's that?"

"We could call the police."

Jordynn exhaled. "Okay. Option B is it."

Working together in silence, they pulled collected every pieces of rope they could find. They tied the four men up individually, then lashed them together. By the time they were done, Jordynn was shaking, and when Dono pulled her in close, all she could do was sink into him.

"Is it over?" she asked, her voice as wobbly as her body.

"I think so, honey." He clicked on the phone he'd pilfered from Ivan's pocket. "You ready to get this part over with, too?"

She nodded. "Definitely."

He tipped up her face and gave her a tender kiss, then pulled away and smiled at her. "Good. Because once the bad guys are locked up, and we've taken a long nap… I'm will be *so* ready to give our second chance a running start."

She couldn't help but laugh. "The last few days weren't a fast enough start for you?"

He lifted an eyebrow. "Well, I thought maybe telling you we should take things slow and steady lacked a certain…punch."

She tipped her face up for another kiss. "Slow and steady actually sounds nice right about now."

Dono cupped her cheek. "Good. Because I've got ten years to make up for, and with the exception of getting us off this mountain, I'd hate to rush a single second more."

Epilogue

Eight weeks later

The chime of the doorbell lifted Jordynn's attention from the legal forms she'd been staring at for the past hour. She let out a thankful sigh. Dono had asked her to go over the details—who knew there was so much paperwork involved in reclaiming the life of someone who'd come back from the dead?—but truthfully she'd be happy to sign whatever was needed so long as it brought them closer to that goal.

The two months that had passed felt like a very long time. The world around them certainly hadn't slowed down.

Those eight weeks had been long enough for Reed to plead guilty and be sentenced to life in prison without parole. It had been long enough for his assets to be dissolved, and for Sasha to start some much-needed counseling. It had given them time to issue enough official statements to the press that most journalists had already moved on to the next big thing. And enough time for a few other things, too.

Jordynn ran her hands over her stomach affectionately. She hadn't told Dono yet. She was waiting for the doctor's appointment later in the week. But she was sure, just the same.

The doorbell rang again, making her jump a second time.

"Baby brain already," she murmured, then called, "Coming!"

She hurried from the kitchen to the front door, where she automatically paused to glance through the newly installed peephole. Another small change. A new precaution. But her tension eased a little every day, and when Dono was home, she really did feel as safe as she ever had. And more settled than she'd been in ten years.

And it was him on the front step now, a bunch of grocery bags in one hand and a cardboard box in the other. Before she could lean back and get the door open, he lifted his foot and rang the bell a third time. With his boot.

Jordynn swung the door wide, a teasing chastisement on the tip of her tongue. It died on her lips, though, when she saw what it was that he had inside the box.

Even though he was pretty damned sure his arm was about to break off completely, he couldn't help but laugh at the excitement in Jordynn's eyes.

"You gonna help me or what?" he teased.

She was quick to grab the cardboard box first. "You went by the police station?"

"They called me on my cell while I was at the store. I couldn't wait."

He redistributed the grocery bags and followed her into the house. He barely had time to set them down on the countertop before she dragged out the badly warped metal container. He felt a twinge of nerves. He hoped she wouldn't be too disappointed once she actually saw inside.

"It's locked." She sounded let down already.

Donovan shrugged. "Yeah. Well, the cops probably didn't want it to look like rifled-through evidence. But you do have the key, right?"

"Yes. Wait here," she said excitedly, then rushed out.

Donovan heard the thump of her feet as she ran up the stairs, followed by the creak of the bedroom door upstairs, and then the clatter of what could only be the key dropping to the floor. He fought another chuckle.

He ran his hands over the bullet-size holes in the top of the time capsule. He still thought it was remarkable that he'd found it at all, and he could hardly believe that it had saved his life.

"It's pretty incredible, isn't it?"

At the sound of Jordynn's awed voice, he swiveled his head and found her standing in the doorway, her eyes fixed on the box.

"Miraculous," he agreed. "I almost feel guilty opening it."

"Oh."

He caught her disappointed look, and he grabbed her hand to put her close, then draped his arms around her. "Not guilty enough to actually stop you from doing it."

"Oh, thank God."

She wriggled away, then stuck the key into the lock and twisted. Donovan knew she'd be expecting him to be looking at the items she was supposed to be pulling out, but instead, he was watching her face. Cataloging her emotions. Disappointment. Confusion. Then guarded delight, as she lifted out the tiny black velvet box.

"I'm sorry, honey. The other things were ruined. Between the bullets and the police and the moisture that was in there already…" He trailed off, then nodded toward the box. "But I thought maybe we could make *new* memories, starting with that."

She flipped it open and stared down at the shimmery topaz. Her birthstone.

She lifted her eyes, and they were as bright as the rock. "What happened to slow and steady? And not rushing a single minute?"

Donovan popped out the ring, then slid it onto her finger. "Is that what I said? Maybe you misunderstood."

"Oh, I don't think so."

"Are you sure? Because I'm sure I said I was in a giant rush to marry you and that I didn't want to *waste* a single second."

She shot him a narrowed-eyed glare that lasted about a heartbeat before her eyes went back to admiring the ring.

"So?" prodded Donovan.

"What?"

"Will you?"

"Oh! Yes." She jumped into his arms, but pulled away quickly and leaned back to meet his gaze. "But…"

"But what?"

"There's probably one little thing I should tell you about first…"

* * * * *

If you loved this suspenseful story, don't miss Melinda Di Lorenzo's next exciting book, coming in June 2017!

And don't forget her previous book WORTH THE RISK available now from Harlequin Romantic Suspense!

ROMANTIC suspense

*Undercover FBI agent Josh Howard is supposed to be
investigating Leonor Colton's involvement in her mother's
jailbreak, but a hitman may force him to reveal his identity
to save her life!*

Read on for a sneak preview of
COLTON UNDERCOVER, the next book in the
***THE COLTONS OF SHADOW CREEK** continuity*
by USA TODAY *bestselling author Marie Ferrarella.*

"Back at the club, when we were dancing, you told me that I
was too perfect." *If you only knew,* he couldn't help thinking.
"But I'm not. I'm not perfect at all."

So far she hadn't seen anything to contradict her
impression. "Let me guess, you use the wrong fork when
you eat salad."

"I'm serious," Josh told her, pulling his vehicle into the
parking lot.

"Okay, I'll bite. How are you not perfect?" Leonor asked,
turning to look at him as she got out.

"Sometimes," Josh said as they walked into the B and B,
"I find that my courage fails me."

She strongly doubted that, but maybe they weren't talking
about the same thing, Leonor thought.

"You're going to have to give me more of an explanation
than that," she told him.

Making their way through the lobby, they went straight
to the elevator.

The car was waiting for them, opening its doors the
second he pressed the up button.

He'd already said too much and he knew that the more he talked, the greater the likelihood that he would say something to give himself away. But knowing he had to say something, he kept it vague.

"Let's just say that I don't always follow through and do what I really want to do," Josh said vaguely.

That didn't sound like much of a flaw to her, Leonor thought.

After getting off the elevator, they walked to her suite. She used her key and opened her door, then turned toward him.

Her heart was hammering so hard in her throat, she found it difficult to talk.

"And just what is it that you really want to do—but don't?" she asked him in a voice that had mysteriously gone down to just above a whisper.

As it was, her voice sounded very close to husky—and he found it hopelessly seductive.

Standing just inside her suite, Leonor waited for him to answer while her heart continued to imitate the rhythm of a spontaneous drumroll that only grew louder by the moment.

Josh weighed his options for a moment. Damned if he did and damned if he didn't, he couldn't help thinking. And then he answered her.

"Kiss you," he told Leonor, saying the words softly, his breath caressing her face.

She felt her stomach muscles quickening.

"Maybe you should go ahead and do that," she told him. "I promise I won't stop you."

Don't miss
COLTON'S UNDERCOVER by Marie Ferrarella,
available April 2017 wherever
Harlequin® Romantic Suspense books
and ebooks are sold.

www.Harlequin.com

HRSEXP0317

THE WORLD IS BETTER WITH

Romance

Harlequin has everything from contemporary, passionate and heartwarming to suspenseful and inspirational stories.

Whatever your mood, we have a romance just for you!

Connect with us to find your next great read, special offers and more.

f /HarlequinBooks

y @HarlequinBooks

www.HarlequinBlog.com

www.Harlequin.com/Newsletters

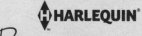

H HARLEQUIN®

A *Romance* FOR EVERY MOOD™

www.Harlequin.com